The Horseman Who Came from the Sea

Jeff Turner

PAGE PUBLISHING
Conneaut Lake, PA

First originally published by Page Publishing 2023

Cover Photo by Zack Turner & Benjamin Turner
Watch Hill, Rhode Island

Graphic Design by Julianna Wasniewski Cameron

ISBN 979-8-89157-581-3 (pbk)
ISBN 979-8-89157-597-4 (digital)

Printed in the United States of America

"I have seen things so beautiful they have brought tears to my eyes. Yet none of them can match the gracefulness and beauty of a horse running free."

Author Unknown

For Nan

Also by Jeff Turner

The Way Back (2013)

The Hero of Willow Creek (2015)

Lost Boys of the River Camp (2017)

The Choices He Made (2019)

A Rescued Soul (2021)

One

It was a clear, sunny morning as Henry Cameron drove slowly along the narrow sand-swept road in Bridgeport, Connecticut. Traffic was light, making it fairly easy to find a parking space not too far from a boardwalk stretching along the shoreline. He removed his barn jacket along with a knitted watch cap and tossed them both in the back seat, figuring he'd be plenty warm enough with just a flannel shirt. It was balmy weather, unusual for November, and he breathed in deeply, filling his lungs with fresh sea air.

The boardwalk wasn't too crowded and offered a splendid view of the water. In the distance he could see several oil tankers making their way to open waters and a large ferry heading for port. Henry stretched his back after his long drive, rubbed the back of his neck, and took a few moments to get his bearings. He hoped this hadn't been a wasted trip.

It didn't take long to spot what he was looking for, a guy sitting by himself on a bench at the far end of the boardwalk. Henry headed his way.

As he got closer, Henry could see that every so often the fellow would reach into a paper sack containing what appeared to be bread crusts. He tossed a few at a time to a small band of waiting gulls that squawked and scrambled until they got their reward. Henry stopped a short distance away from the bench, not wanting to disturb or interrupt. Instead, he just stood there and watched.

The guy was dressed in heavy clothing, peculiar attire for such a warm day. He wore a long olive greatcoat, a scarf wrapped around his neck, gloves, and a fedora pulled down low, the brim covering most of his brow. He wore a pair of dark, circular, wireframe sunglasses.

Henry moved toward the bench and as he did, the guy apparently sensed the approach and hiked the collar of his coat and slouched, looking as though he was trying to shrink inside of it. This didn't deter Henry, who casually sat down on the left side of the bench. Several people walked by on the boardwalk, none stopping.

They sat in silence for a few minutes before Henry remarked, "Beautiful day."

The guy didn't respond, choosing instead to look out at the water.

Another few moments of silence.

Henry would have none of it and pressed on. "Hard to believe it can be this warm in November, right?"

This time the guy straightened and took a swig of whiskey from a pint that he removed from his coat pocket. He winced as he swallowed, capped the bottle, then looked Henry's way. "How'd you find me?" he asked.

Henry flashed a smile. "Last time we spoke, you said your likely hangout after the war would be feeding the seagulls at the shoreline with the old geezers. When I drove by, I knew immediately the guy sitting on the bench was you."

The man nodded his head a few times in amusement and returned the smile. He extended his hand. "How're you, Henry?"

"I'm good, Mickey. It's been a while." They gripped hands and held on for an extra moment or two. Mickey's grip was strong.

Mickey was Mickey Parker, a bunkmate of Henry's a few years ago when the two enrolled at Camp Dewey, a civilian-backed Junior Naval Reserve installation located in Uncasville, Connecticut. The camp hugged the banks of the Thames River and sought to prepare teenagers for service in the navy or merchant marine. Youngsters were taught the lore and lure of the sea along with a heavy dose of military training.

At the time, both Henry and Mickey had ambitions to join the navy.

Mickey threw a bread crust toward the waiting gulls. "So, why're you here, Henry?"

"For starters, because I've missed you, but I also came for other reasons."

Mickey pondered this while watching two kids throw a football back and forth on the sandy beach. He lowered his head a bit and mumbled, "I didn't think I'd ever see you again," his voice trailing off.

Henry swallowed hard, knowing inside he should have come sooner.

After a second or two, he said, "Do me a favor, Mickey. Take the sunglasses off, will you?"

"Why?"

"Because I want to be able to look at you. While you're at it, ditch the hat and the scarf. For cripes' sake, it's hotter than blue blazes today and you're sitting over there sweating bullets."

Mickey took the sunglasses off. "Satisfied now?" he asked, his eyes narrowed.

Henry nodded and moved closer, resting his hand on his friend's shoulder. "I know what happened to you over there." Mickey was injured during the war when an enemy artillery shell exploded near his position, causing the loss of his left hand and forearm. He also suffered facial burns requiring medical treatment.

"Now the gloves."

Mickey let out a long sigh then pulled the righthand glove off by gripping one of the fingertips between his teeth and pulling it off. "The lefthand glove stays put," he said.

Henry studied him for a minute or two. "You've healed nicely, I must say."

"Think so? You're not saying that just to make me feel better?"

"Nope, I mean it. Your facial burns are less visible and your skin is much smoother. Your skin grafts are working and your scars are barely noticeable. You've had several surgeries, right? No rejection of the skin grafting?"

Mickey started laughing. "No rejection, but the surgeries were a pain in the ass. That's because they used skin from my ass to replace my damaged facial skin." He rolled his eyes and sighed. "But I have to apply special creams and ointments every day to help the healing process. Such a pain in the ass." He broke out in a laugh.

"Seems like a small price to pay. Even your hair and eyebrows have grown back. When I last saw you, your hair was singed and growing back in tufts. It looks good now."

Mickey nodded and smiled. It was easy to see he was pleased.

Henry touched Mickey's left arm and raised a brow. "You have no feeling in your residual limb?" he asked.

"It took a while for my surgical procedure mainly because there have been so many amputation surgeries over there. My fitting for a prosthesis took forever. He rapped on his artificial prosthesis. This one is made of solid wood, but I'm told they now make them with some kind of aluminum, something called duralumin, I think. The prosthesis is made from that stuff and it is less heavy and more flexible."

"Do you always cover your residual limb?"

Mickey replied, "I do. Sometimes I put my arm in a sling or pin my shirtsleeve. Sometimes I think my hand and forearm are still attached. I can feel different sensations, especially pain. That's the worst. Sometimes it throbs, it really hurts that much."

"What do your doctors think about this?"

"They said it's fairly common among amputees and they even have a name for it, Phantom Pain Syndrome. They tell me this is the pain the soldiers go through, and for many it may take a few years."

"A few years? What are you supposed to do in the meantime?"

Mickey scoffed. "I'll show you what I do." He reached into his coat pocket and retrieved the pint bottle of whiskey. He took one gulp, smacked his lips, then swigged once more. He offered the bottle to Henry, who declined.

He couldn't blame Mickey for turning to spirits to quell the pain.

They both leaned back on the bench and for a while neither spoke. It was peaceful by the water, the gentle shoreline waves calming. They both leaned back and lounged in the pleasant warmth of the sun.

Henry finally said, "You know Mickey, you don't need to cover yourself up with all the stuff you're wearing. Like I said, you've healed nicely. No one is going to gawk at you."

Mickey shrugged. "I know, I know. It's just that I don't get out that much and I'm still very self-conscious, especially with my arm.

When I first got home, there was finger-pointing and whispering. Of course, my face was pretty messed up back then, too."

"You've got to stop being so self-conscious." Henry waited a beat before continuing. "Mickey, your injuries do not define who you are as a person. Remember that. You went to war and fought for your country. You're strong and you're a patriot. Your character and courage rise far above any scars you brought home from overseas."

Mickey sighed, then nodded. He fiddled with his gloved prosthesis for a few minutes, apparently thinking matters through. Finally, he turned Henry's way and said, "You said you came to Bridgeport for several reasons. What else are you here for?"

Henry leaned forward, resting his elbows on his knees. "I'm afraid I've got some bad news to share with you." He paused. "Lieutenant Cooper died," he said, his voice dropping off.

Mickey raised his eyebrows and sputtered, "Died? When? How?"

"He caught the Spanish Flu a few months ago, probably when he took me to see my mother in Boston a while ago. He never recovered. He just couldn't fight it off."

"Were you with him when he died?"

"I was, right until the end."

Mickey lowered his head. "That must have been hard. Jeez, I'm really sorry, Henry. I know the two of you were close."

Henry nodded and agreed. "He was like the father I never had. We were close. While you were away, he got himself appointed as my legal guardian." He let a moment pass, then continued. "I thought he'd be around forever. It still hurts to realize he's gone."

Mickey's eyes widened. "He became your legal guardian? Are you serious?"

"I'm serious. The lieutenant had no family and he knew I didn't either. So, he took me under his wing, taught me everything I know. And get this. When he passed away, I was shocked to learn that he left his entire inheritance to me. I'm talking all of his bank holdings, stocks, the entire farm, as well as the fifty acres it occupies."

Mickey let out a soft whistle. "Wow, that's really incredible Henry."

"It's also worrisome and intimidating. Lots and lots of responsibility."

Henry stood and took a few steps so that he was facing Mickey. "That's another reason why I'm here, Mickey."

"What might that be?"

"I want you to come back to Vermont with me. I want you to work on the farm. Lord knows, I need all the help I can get. I need honest people, folks I can trust and count on."

"You want me to go work on a farm? Henry, in case you haven't noticed, I'm a cripple."

"You're not a cripple, there's lots you can do to help out. I'm being serious, Mickey."

"Give me one good reason why."

Henry said, "Okay, I'll give you two. One, I could really use your help up there. I could use a friend." He was silent for a minute. "Second, I want you out of Bridgeport so that you can open a new chapter in your life, get a fresh start. Look around. There's nothing here for you, Mickey. You need to move on. You're not being pitied by me, you're being given an opportunity, a fresh start."

Henry folded his arms.

Mickey just sat there, a portrait of apprehension and trepidation. His eyes darted back and forth and he began to nervously wiggle his feet. His face clouded with uneasiness. Finally, he spoke. "What about pay and a place to stay? I'm living like a poor man down here. Hell, I'm still living with my mother eating stale peanut butter and jelly sandwiches."

Henry smiled. "We can change that. The salary's good, no one on board up there has complained about it. If you don't like it, we can negotiate. Room and board are included with the job. I'll even give you an advance to buy some practical work clothes."

Mickey scratched his chin, and he thought some more. "When does the job start?"

"Today, right now. I drove down from Vermont to get you and I'll be damned if I'm going to drive back home in that car alone."

Mickey stood up. "You came all the way down here just to get me?"

Henry nodded. "Come hell or high water, I was going to take you hostage."

They both grinned.

"So, we got a deal cookin' here or not?" asked Henry.

Mickey thought about it some more then nodded his head. "Okay, we've got a deal. Let's head north."

They maintained eye contact and shook on it, the new farm owner and the wounded war veteran, two old pals banding together, looking to pick up where their friendship had left off.

Two

It didn't take them long to hit the road. They stopped at Mickey's house just long enough for him to change, pack a suitcase, and say goodbye to his mother. He put the suitcase in the back seat along with the greatcoat he wore earlier. He'd donned a baggy, army-issued knitted sweater, one that had unraveled in several spots and sported more than a few stains. His pants were too short and partially torn on the left leg. He wore his fedora and the glove remained on his left hand.

Henry watched him and flinched at his appearance. He was dressed like a poor, disheveled street person, a forgotten and disabled war veteran, a victim of alcohol who had aged far beyond his years. Henry looked at him with a mixture of sadness and unhappiness.

Henry knew he had to rescue this poor soul, breathe life back into his being, and take away the tragic hurt that had crippled him. He felt a protective surge directed toward his best friend.

While Mickey arranged his possessions in the back seat, Henry continued to study him. His skin grafts were indeed successful, although the surgical areas reddened with his exertion. He had a furrowed brow and dark rings under his eyes, the latter likely caused by his excessive drinking, maybe lack of sleep. His once boyish looks were gone, replaced with the scars of war, cruel reminders of the torment he experienced in the nether world of French trenches.

Once underway, they had to stop at a filling station for gas before heading for the hills of northern Vermont. Mickey took the opportunity to relieve himself before the journey. Henry watched him as he got out of the car and made his way to the restrooms. He walked slowly, almost stiffly. Perhaps his sense of balance was off. His head and neck seemed to angle forward when he walked. Henry wondered if nerve damage had occurred when the artillery shell had exploded.

When Mickey returned to the car, Henry remarked, "You seemed a bit unstable when you walked away. I was watching you."

"Unstable how?"

"You walked slowly, cautiously, almost as if you were afraid of falling."

"Nothing wrong with being cautious, right?"

"You're right. But I wondered if you suffered nerve damage when you were injured."

"Nope."

"The doctors never examined your back or your hips?"

Mickey shook his head. "It was a field hospital, Henry. They were more concerned with my missing hand and forearm, not to mention the blood I was losing."

Henry nodded and didn't say anything. He searched for more to say but couldn't find the words.

Mickey playfully punched him in the arm. "Henry, stop worrying about me. I'm good, I'm okay. Just a little stiff is all, a few aches and pains. Once I get moving, I'm fine. Really."

"Okay, just checking," Henry said, showing a small smile.

Meanwhile, Mickey pulled a fresh pint of whiskey from his back pocket, broke the seal, and sent a gulp or two down the chute. He offered the pint to Henry who held up his hand and again politely refused. "Got to keep my eyes on the road, mate."

The mood changed as soon as Bridgeport was left behind. They chattered away nonstop. They laughed, shared stories, reminisced about days gone by, told jokes, traded barbs. Good conversation. No mention of war, no mention of injuries. Henry wasn't about to delve into any part of it again, at least not now.

In due time, the conversation drifted to Mickey's new job. "I don't mind telling you," Mickey said, "I'm more than a little nervous about this job you're offering."

"Why's that?" replied Henry.

"For starters, I have no left hand and no forearm. Come on Henry, I'm a gimp, I'm damaged goods. What can I possibly do to help you out on the farm? How can I keep up with the others?"

"I don't want to hear you talking like that again, Mickey. I mean it. You're not a gimp or a cripple. You can do lots of things. You don't need two arms to hold a paintbrush, steer a tractor, drive a car, shoot a pistol, do some bookkeeping, pick apples, or a hundred other things. We're going to get you up and moving. I'll work alongside you at first to help with the chores, show you how to get the hang of things."

Mickey sat there listening, trying to absorb it all.

Henry added, "You're also going to learn how to ride a horse."

Mickey did a doubletake. "Wait a minute, I'm going to do what?"

"You heard me. We're going to get you on a horse."

Mickey turned in his seat. "Henry, I've never been on a horse."

"Neither had I when I first started working on the farm. The lieutenant taught me how to ride, little lessons at a time until my confidence grew. The more I rode, the more I realized that he'd given me a gift. I want to do the same for you. I'll get your ass up in that saddle."

Mickey slowly shook his head. "Come on, a one-handed horseman? Are you serious?"

"We'll take baby steps. All the horses are very gentle and patient. You'll get to know them and they'll get to know you. I've already picked one out for you and made a small platform to help you mount until you get the hang of saddling on your own. You'll have a special stall, too."

Mickey appeared moved. "You're serious about this aren't you?"

"I am."

"Why? What's the big deal anyway?"

"You need to restore your strength and heal. Horses can be part of the mending. When I was going through my rough time and taking my lumps, the lieutenant showed me how important horses can be in my recovery. They're incredibly loyal and dependable. They taught me how to be a better human being, a more decent person. Somehow when I'm in the saddle, I see a different, better version of myself."

Mickey grew silent, thinking about what was just said. He eventually nodded his head. "Okay, I'll give it a try, but you've got to be patient with me. I got pretty banged up over there as you know and I need to rebuild myself from the bottom up."

"Of course. When you're ready we'll take a little at a time. There's no need to rush anything." Henry coughed into his hand. "I should add that your life on the farm will be like that. Low key, relaxed, laid-back."

"Everyone gets along?"

Henry nodded. "We're successful because we work as a team, everyone pulls together."

"You sure I'll fit in?"

"Absolutely, you'll love all of them. You already know Hudson Delaney, who rode with the lieutenant during his cavalry days."

"He was the guy working with the lieutenant when we attended the junior naval reserve camp, right?"

"That's correct."

"Good man. I liked him."

Henry agreed. "He's the farm's foreman. In addition to being a fine horseman, he procures horses for the farm. He also oversees the cultivation of our cornfield and apple orchard and oversees everything. Hudson maintains all farm vehicles and repairs firearms."

"That's a lot of responsibility, don't you think?"

"I agree." Henry hesitated, then glanced at Mickey. "That's why I brought you onboard. You'll work with Hudson when he needs you, and you'll work with me when I need you. We'll make a good team."

"Who handles the horses?" asked Henry.

"The lieutenant used to, but of course he's gone. In the coming month or two we're set to hire a new horse trainer. I'll be working with the horses as well."

"How many horses do you have?"

"At the present time we have five, but we'd like to double that."

Mickey nodded, trying hard to take everything in.

"Then we have Julia and Carl Dawson, our caretakers. Julia handles housekeeping chores and cooks while Carl is a jack of all trades, a regular handyman. Julia balances the books and orders supplies and such, but she's going to need help with all kinds of paperwork. This is another important area you can help us plug."

"Do all of you stay on the farm?"

Henry nodded and grinned. "We're one big family. We live in a two-story farmhouse that has six bedrooms, three bathrooms, two fireplaces, a big living room and a huge kitchen and dining area. Our caretakers stay in a stone cottage, a short walk from the farmhouse. We've also renovated three cabins that sit not too far from the farmhouse. Hudson, our foreman, lives in one of them. You'll get the grand tour of everything once we get there."

———

They drove a while longer and the fuel was getting low. They needed to find a filling station and eventually found one not too far from a diner. After topping the tank, they decided to get a quick bite to eat before continuing their journey.

The diner was small and offered counter service as well as a few tables. They chose a table in a corner and ordered ham sandwiches, apple pie, and coffee. The place was fairly busy and seemed to be the local hotspot for food and drink. Conversations among customers were steady, creating a buzz of chatter. When their food was served, they found the sandwiches and pie delicious plus the coffee had been freshly brewed.

At one point, Henry leaned toward Mickey. "I've got a question I've been meaning to ask you, something I need to get off my chest."

"Fire away, boss."

"When the American Expeditionary Force decided to join up with the allied forces overseas and go to war, I know a group of midshipmen, including myself, banded together and decided to enlist."

"Right, we were all underage but heard that some recruitment centers were easier than others for the underaged to use forged birth certificates. We decided to meet up in Bridgeport then travel to New Haven and sign up."

"I remember that five or six of us planned on jumping ship under the cover of darkness."

"That was the plan, yes."

"What happened when I didn't show?"

Mickey inhaled sharply, then let it out. "We were all taken by surprise. We waited for you as long as we could. We couldn't call the cadet camp so we tried calling you at your home in Boston. No one answered the phone. You'd disappeared without telling anyone."

Henry's voice was tight. "Was the group angry?"

"Angry is soft pedaling it. The group was furious. The general feeling was that you were a coward, a traitor. We regarded you as one of our leaders and you turned tail and ran away."

"What then?"

"We waited a few hours then took off. We did our thing in New Haven without any problems. Everyone passed the physical examination. We eventually went through basic training at Camp Devens in Massachusetts then got shipped to France for more training."

"How'd that go?"

"At first, we were upbeat. We regarded everything as some kind of great adventure, you know, firing the guns, wearing the uniforms, saving the free world from anarchy and chaos." But then a shadow fell across his face. "We were bold and brave; that is, until we were sent to the front lines, which quickly became a nightmare. The trenches smelled like a sewer and were full of mud and muck. The stench of death was everywhere. Bloodied corpses had to be removed almost every hour. The food was always cold and drinking water was scarce. Sleeping was near impossible. It was a living, stinking hell."

While Mickey talked, Henry had a flashback to when he chose not to join his friends and enlist. An undercurrent of guilt and shame still lingered inside of him. Initially, he agreed to the plan and was supposed to be with them over there. He wondered if Mickey blamed him for leaving his side.

Mickey continued. "One rainy night the Germans battered us with steady and deadly artillery strikes. We huddled in our trench absolutely terrified, the explosions getting closer and closer. We knew that after such intense shelling the enemy would launch a frontal attack first thing in the morning. Our ammunition was running low, reinforcements never showed. Everyone was on edge, sleep was impossible. Many of our guys trembled, some cried, others begged to go home and had to be restrained to remain on the line."

Mickey paused, looking as if he was trying to remember something. His eyes wandered and he got a little misty-eyed.

Henry felt another flicker of guilt.

Mickey picked up where he left off. "I can remember saying to the boys to be brave, that this was what they'd signed up for, being trapped in stinking trenches was part of the deal and our choice." He had a faint smile while looking Henry straight in the eye. "That's when your name came up."

Henry raised his eyebrows. "My name?"

"Yeah, your name. Someone said they were wrong to condemn you and we had no right to criticize your decision. You weren't a coward or a quitter. Instead, you were the only one who was smart enough not to enlist, that you'd made the right choice. Others in the trench agreed and voiced how foolish they'd been racing overseas as boys to fight and die in a grown-up war."

Mickey leaned forward, reached for and clasped Henry's hand. "You did the right thing, Henry, don't let anyone tell you anything different." He lowered his head and chewed his lip, hugging himself. He spoke softly. "I just wish I'd stayed home with you."

Three

They made good time on the road, traveling through Massachusetts and New Hampshire before crossing over into Vermont. When they approached Compton, Henry slowed down and looked for a parking space. He found one in-between a grocery store and post office. A hardware store stood nearby.

Mickey was confused. "Why are we stopping here?" he asked. "Something wrong with the car?"

"Nope, everything's good. We're going clothes shopping to get you some new duds," Henry replied. "We're only about fifteen miles from the farm and this town has a good clothing store. We buy all our clothes here and I know they carry what you're going to need. Plus, there's a young lady who works here that I need to talk with. I hope she's here."

"What's her name?"

"Maeve." Henry spelled it out for him. "Scottish name. The lieutenant couldn't figure out the correct pronunciation of her name at first and called her, '*Ma-vah*.'" They had a few laughs over that. "Anyway, the name Maeve rhymes with knave."

The two strolled along the sidewalk until they reached their destination, an overhead sign identifying the store as *Heritage Clothiers.* When Henry opened the door for Mickey, a bell above the door tinkled their arrival, announcing their presence. Inside, a few customers were milling around the women's clothing aisles while a few were trying on footwear at the back of the store.

Henry spotted Maeve immediately, standing at the front counter next to the cashier. She was talking to an elderly woman, apparently a customer. He watched the interaction closely, paying particular attention to Maeve. She was as he remembered, petite, green eyes, auburn hair. Her hair framed her high cheekbones and tapering chin. Her eyes were bright and sparkling. She was beautiful.

Henry guided Mickey to the front counter with him and waited patiently for Maeve to finish with her customer. When she did, she saw Henry for the first time. She looked at him, her face expressionless. "Well, hello there," she said, her voice void of inflection. She looked at him for a moment, then looked down.

"Hello Maeve," he said, taking a step closer. "It's been a while."

"Yes, it certainly has," she said, lifting her eyes and looking at him warily. "I didn't know if I'd ever see you again." Now she wore a stony expression and maintained a cold disposition, one that had lost its usual charm and friendliness.

Henry stood there and wavered a bit, trying to comprehend what it was that had unearthed Maeve's tone. He told himself that this wasn't the time or place to figure out what was bothering her; instead, he chose to stay silent until they had some time alone.

Maeve's voice cut through the silence. In a dull monotone she asked, "How can I help the two of you?" She was all business.

Henry turned toward Mickey. "Maeve, I want you to meet my friend Mickey Parker. Mickey is a soldier who just returned from the war. He needs to be outfitted with some new clothes. He'll be working with me at the farm."

Maeve moved toward Mickey and offered her hand. "It's a pleasure to meet you, Mickey. I'm Maeve Adair."

Mickey nodded, keeping his left hand in his pants pocket, shaking hands with his right. "My pleasure, Maeve."

She smiled at him.

Henry pulled a shopping list from his pocket, one that he'd written earlier that listed all the clothing Mickey needed, at least for the time being. He handed it to Maeve.

Maeve looked over the list and nodded. "We have all of these items in stock."

Henry looked at Mickey, who was surveying the store and its merchandise. He suggested that Mickey walk over to the men's department to see what styles he liked, especially footwear. Mickey sensed the tension and left, leaving Henry and Maeve alone.

As he walked away, Henry turned to Maeve. "He's going to need some help. Can you send one of your male clerks over there to help him out?"

"Yes, I can. But why?"

"He's likely going to have some trouble trying on new clothes. He lost his left arm in battle and wears a prosthesis. He also experienced some pretty bad skin burning."

Maeve nodded and immediately summoned a clerk to assist Mickey. She handed Henry's list of needed clothing to the clerk and explained the situation. He, in turn, made his way to the men's department.

Henry looked at Maeve. "Thank you," he said.

Maeve looked at him and nodded.

Henry cleared his throat. "I think we need to talk. Have I done something wrong?"

It took a moment or two before she responded. She inhaled deeply and let it out slowly. Finally, she said, "Yes, you've done something wrong." Her expression hardened. "For starters, where on earth have you been? The last time I saw you was months ago. We were supposed to get together, or don't you remember?" She stood there, arms folded across her chest, simmering.

"I'm sorry, I truly am, but I've had some tough sledding since we last talked. I should have stopped by and spoken to you, explained why I haven't been around."

"Well, why didn't you? I mean, you could've at least asked the lieutenant to fill me in."

Henry just stood there, his voice silenced by a lump in his throat.

"Henry? Did you hear what I just said?" she said with a huff.

Henry nodded. "I heard you." He looked at her with sadness and felt his composure deserting him. "The lieutenant has died, Maeve."

She wavered trying to grasp what she just heard. Her hands flew to her mouth. "No," she said, "that isn't possible. Tell me that isn't true."

"I wish I could, but he's gone."

Tears began to shimmer in Maeve's eyes. She turned to the cashier and said, "I'll be gone for a little while in the office. You're in charge until I get back."

The cashier nodded.

Maeve turned to Henry. "Will you come with me so that we can talk in private?"

Henry agreed and she led him to a fairly large office. She switched on the light and pulled two chairs close together facing each other. She gestured for him to take a seat.

She closed the office door before she sat down. "When did this happen? How did he die?" Her mind shuttled back and forth between anxiety and heartbreak. "I ask because he was one of my favorite customers, and the two of you always brought cheer whenever you stopped by." She dabbed at her eyes with a handkerchief and sniffled. "Please fill me in."

"It happened not too long after we last saw you."

"How? What went wrong?"

Henry straightened in his chair. "Do you want the short or long version?"

"If you don't mind, I'd like to hear anything that you're willing to share."

He swallowed hard and said in a wistful voice, "As you know, my mother lived in Boston. I left home and was living at the lieutenant's horse farm when I learned she'd contracted the Spanish flu. A nurse called the farm and shared that my mother's condition had worsened and death was near. The lieutenant drove me to Boston so that I could see my mother before she passed." He leaned forward in his chair and wrung his hands. "We managed to see her, which was a relief. She died a week later after we'd returned home to Vermont."

Maeve asked, "Both you and the lieutenant saw her?"

"Yes, he never left my side."

"Were you close with your mother?"

"No, not really."

She nodded. "None the less, I'm sorry for your loss, Henry," she said. She was silent for a moment. "Then what happened?"

"While we were in Boston, we went to her apartment so that I could gather some of my personal belongings." Henry decided not to include the lieutenant's violent altercation with his uncle, Bill Cameron, nor did he mention the time he spent with Lily Corwin, his old girlfriend, and her parents.

"When we went back to the farm, the lieutenant seemed fine. We did our regular chores, worked the horses, all that stuff. But after a few weeks he started slowing down, quitting work earlier. He coughed a lot, not dry but wet coughs. He didn't eat as much, even when his favorite foods were served. He started losing weight. It was hard to watch."

Henry had growing despair in his voice and he struggled to keep his voice steady.

Maeve wore a mask of silent sadness on her face. As she listened, she lightly tapped the tips of her fingers together. Tears shimmered in her eyes.

Henry continued. "Then came the fatigue, body aches, difficulty breathing, and fever. He was taken to a doctor and was diagnosed with the Spanish flu. The hospitals were overflowing so he decided to try recovering at home. He got worse and he spent his remaining days in his own bed."

Henry took a deep breath and slowly exhaled. "We provided him with care and comfort until the very end. He wanted my companionship, even if meant my just sitting in a chair a safe distance away."

Maeve slowly shook her head. "That must've been hard to witness."

"It was, like I said. The toughest part was seeing him get weaker day after day and knowing there was no cure for the demons he was fighting."

Henry slumped back in his chair.

Maeve watched him, once again using her handkerchief to dab at the tears in her eyes. When she was finished, she stood and outstretched her arms. "Henry, come here."

Henry did so and she put her arms around him to lend comfort. Henry felt her chest heaving a bit and she started crying. In time, she stopped and pulled away but still clasped one of Henry's hands. "I'm so sorry for you. You've had so much loss in your life. I didn't know. Please forgive my cold welcome when you arrived. That was so wrong of me, so selfish. I just didn't know about any of this happening."

Henry was quick to respond. "Of course, I forgive you, Maeve. You've done nothing wrong. You had no way of knowing about my mother or the lieutenant." He gently squeezed her hand and stepped back.

They gathered themselves and decided that they needed to check on Mickey's clothing purchases. As she reached the door, she stopped and turned to face Henry. "The horse farm," she remarked, "what about the lieutenant's horse farm? Does this mean you'll be moving away somewhere?"

A faint smile crossed Henry's face. He shook his head and said, "Oh no, I'm not going anywhere. This will be my permanent home. Before the lieutenant passed away, he bequeathed the entire farm to me, including the horses." He thought for a few seconds. "Everything he owned, really."

Maeve couldn't contain herself. She broke into a wide grin and she held her hands against her face, her green eyes sparkling. Then, without any hesitation she went up to Henry and kissed him on the cheek, pulling away quickly and opening the office door. Henry followed, too stunned to manage anything else.

They found Mickey in the men's clothing aisle sitting alone in a chair while trying on insulated boots. Henry had specified the slip-on kind, which would enable Mickey to pull them on with one hand. Next to him was a stack of clothing piled high and wide. It consisted of a winter coat, knit cap, flannel shirts, dungarees, scarf, gloves, long underwear, belt, socks, as well as toiletries such as a razor, shaving cream, soap, shampoo, toothpaste and countless other items.

Mickey looked up at Henry. "I can't believe you're doing all this for me," he said.

Henry just nodded and grinned. "The price of friendship is steep, *hombre*."

"I hope I'm worth it."

"I'm betting you are." He hesitated for a second. "Hey, why don't you select something you can wear now since Julia, Carl, and Hudson will be waiting for us." Of course, Henry wanted him to shed his worn and tattered clothing before they arrived.

"Good idea." He did just that and headed for the dressing room.

Henry looked over at Maeve. "You know those people, right? Julia, Carl, and Hudson?"

She smiled. "Of course, I do. They've been in the store many times."

"They're my family, now. They're all I have."

While they waited for Mickey, Maeve and the clerk put everything into bags and boxes.

Henry said, "When you do up a bill, put it under the farm's account but in my name. I'll take care of everything the next time I'm in town."

With a quick glance at him and a hint of a smile, she nodded.

Henry picked up on it at once, and returned the smile.

When Mickey returned, he looked stylish and natty in his new clothes. He no longer wore a hat or extra clothing to cover his perceived disfigurement, although he was still sensitive about his battle scars. All three of them carried the purchases outside to the car, then made a second trip to retrieve a few final packages. When they were done loading, Mickey turned around and extended his hand to Maeve. "It was nice meeting you, Maeve Adair. Thanks for everything."

She rolled her eyes at Mickey's formality then surprised him by brushing his hand aside and giving him a hug. "You come back soon and see me." She pointed her chin towards Henry. "When you do, bring that wagon boss over there with you."

"I'll do that," he promised.

Meanwhile, Henry stood looking at the exterior of the clothing store building. He looked at Maeve and said, "I never realized your store had two floors."

"It doesn't. The second floor is just an apartment. Its entrance is in the back."

"Looks dark and empty."

"It is, the last tenant just moved out last week."

"You got someone moving in?"

"Not yet, but we have someone coming this week to look the place over."

They turned to face each other.

"You okay, mister?" she asked.

Henry nodded.

"I want to apologize again for my behavior and want to also thank you for sharing what's happened in your life. I share your pain, Henry, and I'm here to help you get through this."

She reached for Henry's hand and slipped a note into his palm. On it she'd written her telephone number and home address. "Here's where you can find me."

"Thank you," he said. He reached for her and the two embraced and held on to each other for an extra minute.

When they separated, Henry turned and caught Mickey staring. "What are you looking at, Parker?"

"Nothing, chief," he replied as he climbed into the car, red-faced. Maeve stood there at the curb giggling.

Henry started the engine and looked sideways at Mickey. "It's been a long day. What do you say we head for home and get you settled in your new nest?"

Mickey smiled wearily. "That suits me just fine. We're running out of daylight and we're just sitting here flapping our gums. Let's get cracking."

And with that, they pointed the car north.

Four

T he skies had darkened by the time the two travelers finally reached their destination. Henry left the car parked outside the farmhouse to make unloading easier and announced his presence when he opened the door, Mickey in tow. Not seeing anyone around, he hollered, "Anybody home?"

Julia came around the corner from the kitchen drying her hands on a dish towel. "We're in here, just finishing up with dinner. I'm glad you're here. I'll set a place setting for both of you. We didn't know what time you'd be arriving so we went ahead and started eating. Please come join us."

Julia stood smiling, wiping the corners of her mouth with a napkin. She wore a wraparound knit sweater over a flannel shirt tucked in her dungarees. Julia had a rosy complexion and wore her hair up in a bun. Her smile accentuated deep dimples in her cheeks, giving her a youthful and attractive appearance. She looked to be in her sixties and spry for her age.

She and Henry shared a warm hug before she turned to Mickey. "You must be the famous Mickey Parker," she exclaimed. "Welcome. I feel like I know you already." She smiled and grasped his outstretched hand. She never gave his prosthesis more than a glance.

"Thank you for having me, Mrs. Dawson," he replied.

She grimaced and placed her hands on her hips. "We'll get along much better if you drop the Mrs. Dawson baloney and just call me Julia."

Henry nudged him in the side and said, "I forgot to tell you about that."

Mickey mumbled with his head. down, "Sorry, Julia. It won't happen again."

When Julia led them into the kitchen, Hudson and Carl rose from their chairs. Julia introduced her husband, Carl, and Mickey already knew Hudson from an earlier visit. Mickey politely shook hands with Carl but Hudson swatted his hand away and grasped Mickey around the chest and gave him a big bear hug. "Welcome aboard, mate," he grunted, holding him tight. When Hudson released him the two grinned at each other. "It's damn good to see you again, Mickey. I'm happy you're here," Hudson said.

"I'm just as glad to be here, sir," replied Mickey.

Hudson admonished him with a wag of his finger. "It's just Hudson, Mickey. We're both out of the army now." He rolled his eyes. "Thank the good Lord for that, right?"

Mickey agreed with a smile.

"Let me take a good look at you," Hudson said, squinting to examine both sides of Mickey's face, then ran his fingers through Mickey's hair. "You've healed nicely, son, and I'm not just saying that." He patted Mickey's cheek. "You can think of your good looks now as a badge of courage and healthy mending."

They both laughed playfully.

Off to the side, Julia pulled two chairs out from the table. "You boys come sit," she said. "I have beef stew with vegetables, baked potatoes, a freshly baked loaf of bread, and for dessert, bread pudding. Now come sit before everything gets cold."

Henry interrupted and said, "Julia, we first have to unload Mickey's belongings from the car and get him squared away in his bedroom."

"Nonsense," she said in a huff, turning toward her husband. "Carl, go empty the car and bring everything up to the big bedroom. That will be Mickey's room now."

Carl nodded and got his coat from the closet. Carl was on the short side but husky. He had short hair and brown eyes, along with prominent ears and a large nose. He always looked like he was smiling, even when he was eating or reading. He and Julia looked to be about the same age.

Carl started for the door, but suddenly stopped and turned around. "While I'm up there do you want me to leave out sheets and blankets for Mikey?"

Julia replied, "No need, I've already done up the room."

Carl started turning toward the door but stopped again when Julia said, "And Carl, our guest's name is Mickey, not Mikey."

Carl stopped for a few seconds, gave a half-shrug, then disappeared out the door.

Julia shot Mickey a wry smile.

Henry and Mickey didn't waste any time digging in, Julia and Hudson joining in with steaming mugs of coffee. The stew was excellent and the freshly baked bread was still warm from the oven. They slathered the bread with butter and did the same with the baked potatoes, savoring every bite. They polished off the bread pudding with a flourish, then pushed their dishes away from the edge of the table and slumped back in their chairs.

"Delicious meal," said Henry.

"Excellent," echoed Mickey. "Thank you, Julia," he said as he stood and began stacking the dirty plates and gathering the silverware.

Julia immediately rose. "There's no need for that," she said to Mickey. "You have plenty to do upstairs unpacking your stuff and getting the bedroom to your liking. I'm sure Henry will lend a hand and show you around."

Hudson added, "You fellas come back down when you're squared away. We've got some catching up to do."

Mickey's bedroom was the largest of the six that occupied the spacious second floor of the farmhouse. The room had been freshly painted and was furnished with a double bed, bureau, closet, and an end table stationed next to the bed. An area rug covered a portion of the wide floor boards and a coat rack stood in one corner. A window was located on the far wall, replete with window shade and curtains. The bedroom smelled clean and fresh.

"Perfect," Mickey proclaimed, "much bigger than I expected and just about the nicest bedroom I've ever seen." After he said that, he scrunched face. "What am I saying? This is the nicest." He was thrilled with his new digs.

"Across the hallway is one of the bathrooms and another is at the other end of it," said Henry. He looked around at the room smiled. "This was my bedroom when the lieutenant was still alive, and it was his when he was a kid growing up. You'll really like it up here. Nice and quiet." He walked over to the window with his hands in his pockets. "When you wake up tomorrow and look out the window, you'll be able to see the cornfields, the horse stable and our wooded property."

"Does Hudson sleep in a bedroom up here?"

"No, at least not for now. He's chosen to bunk in one of the cabins not too far from the farmhouse. When it gets colder and the snow starts falling, he'll likely move in up here. He usually locates at the far end of the hall, so you'll still have plenty of privacy."

"How about Julia and Carl? Do they sleep up here?"

Henry shook his head. "Nope, they live in the stone caretaker's cottage. I'll show you the cottage and the cabins tomorrow so you can get a feel for the place."

Carl had put all of Mickey's purchases neatly on the bed, an impressive pile of men's clothing. Mickey and Henry sorted everything and placed the new belongings in appropriate locations. When they were done, Mickey looked everything over. "I've never done this before, never really had the clothes to hang." He shook his head and laughed sarcastically.

"Well, you're set for a while with these new duds. They turned to leave but Henry stopped. He looked at Mickey and said, "Since we've squared away your belongings, why don't you scrub up in your new bathroom. I'll wait here and when you're done, we'll go downstairs and see Hudson."

Mickey grabbed his toilet kit from the top of the bureau. "Good idea," he said with a smile, "I'm on it, boss."

When they went downstairs, they found Hudson sitting in one of the living room's easy chairs reading a magazine, feet propped up on a hassock. A pair of small reading glasses was perched on the end of his nose.

"Julia and Carl left for the night?" asked Henry.

"Yep, a short while ago," he said while removing his glasses. "They shouted goodbye but I guess you didn't hear them."

Hudson stood and went into the kitchen, returning with a tray holding a bottle of vodka and one of rum, as well as three glasses. He set everything down on a table nearby where the two had chosen to sit. "Help yourself gents, you've had a long day. I'd say it's time to wet your whistle."

When the glasses were filled, Hudson raised his and said, "A toast to our new hired hand, Mickey Parker. Welcome aboard, mate." They hoisted their glasses, clinked them together, and sent the fire water down the hatch.

―――――――――

The three of them sat down. After a few moments of grimacing and face twisting from the booze, all of them got comfortable. Hudson looked at Henry and asked, "How'd the Dodge run for you? Any trouble?"

"Ran like a charm, no problems at all."

Hudson took another sip. "I'll get it in the garage tomorrow and look things over, change the oil, check the brakes, and what not, then wash the exterior."

Henry nodded. "While you're at it, will you pull the flatbed out? I'm going to give Mickey a tour of the property. I'll drive him around the old dirt road encircling the farm. It's best that I use the flatbed until Mickey gets his land-legs back."

Henry was referring to one's sense of balance, slowly regained after a time at sea. For Mickey, it meant a recovery from his numerous stops along the English Channel culminating with his long trans-Atlantic journey back to America.

Hudson agreed. "Good thinking on your part. I'll park the flatbed out by the farmhouse first thing in the morning."

Mickey studied Hudson as he was talking. He looked good. Mickey estimated Hudson to be in his mid-fifties. He still wore his blond hair in a floppy, shaggy style, giving him somewhat of a disheveled appearance, and still laid claim to a wide, mischievous grin. He'd lost weight since Mickey last saw him, a look which suited him well. The former calvary sergeant appeared both robust and healthy, quite handsome in fact.

Hudson poured another drink for everyone.

When he sat back down, he looked at Mickey. "You have an artificial arm." A statement, not a question.

Without hesitation, Mickey replied. "Yes sir, got it not too long ago. I wear it all the time except when I'm sleeping or taking a bath."

"Any chance of our seeing it?"

Mickey nodded. He stood and removed his shirt, putting the prosthesis on full display. He walked over to Hudson and then to Henry, giving each a closer look. Hudson tapped the artificial arm with his fingertips a few times. Mickey removed the glove and displayed the artificial hand and fingers.

"I'm impressed," said Hudson. who touched each of the fingers then helped Mickey put the glove back on.

"I was telling Henry this one is made of wood but now they're making them out of lightweight metal." He touched the top of the prosthesis. "This end is hollowed out and has a suction-based attachment that enables the prosthesis to fit over my upper arm. It stays in place by the suction, along with a leather strap. The suction can be improved by a sleeve that helps with the fit and gives me skin protection."

Hudson said, "Your recovery has been remarkable."

Mickey replied, "I got off easy. You should've seen the sights at our field hospital. I saw soldiers who had both legs ripped off, and those with both arms missing. I saw one guy with neither arms or legs." He lowered his head and his breathing slowed. "But the worst to see were those soldiers in need of facial reconstructions, those without teeth, chins, noses, jaws, cheekbones or eyes."

The living room was blanketed in silence.

Henry cleared his throat and looked at Mickey. "What do you say we change the subject and talk about the farm and you." He glanced at Hudson while he spoke. "You know that Hudson is our foreman and he oversees the total operation of the place. He makes sure we're running smoothly. You'll be getting job assignments from him, as will everyone else. I should add that we're close to hiring a horse trainer and she'll be coming on board soon. I've met her and know you'll like her."

"A female horse trainer?" croaked Mickey.

"Yes, a female horse trainer. Get used to it, mate. She knows more about horses than the three of us combined, and I've seen her in action. She was the lieutenant's choice to work with our horses, and my choice, too."

"What's her name?" asked Mickey.

"Her name is Abigail Emory, and she joins us with glowing recommendations."

Hudson chimed in. "Mickey, we need to make clear our expectations about you and your role here." He let out a breath. "We're going to start you off slow, give you time to rest and get a feel for the place. Henry will drive you around the property tomorrow, and after that we want you to just poke around the buildings and ask questions about anything you don't understand. When you do start working, you'll be taking baby steps. We'll have you doing simple repairs and chores, like gathering eggs, feeding the chickens, hauling light firewood, clearing brush, that sort of stuff. Julia will not only need help with canning and stocking the root cellar, but also assisting her with bookkeeping and ordering supplies. Of course, Carl will need assistance with whatever projects he undertakes, so you might be asked to be his gopher person." He scratched his beard then ran a hand through his tousled hair. "Again, nothing really strenuous Mickey, for now all low-key. Sound okay to you?"

"Sounds perfect. I can do all the things you mentioned."

Hudson wasn't done. "I need to make clear that Julia and Carl are the linchpins that drive this farm day-to-day. We can't function without them, whether it be Julia preparing our daily meals or Carl fixing a leaking faucet in the middle of the night. They are vital and we need them. The farm can't operate without them."

"Are we clear on this?" he asked Mickey.

"We're clear on this," came the reply.

At that, Hudson stood and said, "Then let's seal the deal with a final nightcap." He picked up the bottle of rum and poured. "Rum is what the lieutenant Cooper drank in the end. Let's honor him with a toast. Mickey, he would've loved knowing that you are now part of the crew." He raised his glass and said, "Let's always keep Tom Cooper at the forefront and make him proud of how we're striving to fulfill his vision. Wherever he is, you can bet that he's watching."

Five

The next morning, the flatbed truck was sitting outside the back door, just as Hudson promised. He'd left the rig running given its long summer and fall hibernation. The flatbed was an imposing vehicle with its large tapered hood, widely spaced wheels, big headlamps, and rear carrying bed. It was called the Mack Bulldog, likely the most famous Mack truck on the road. It looked both ominous and menacing.

Henry pulled himself up into the driver's seat and got himself comfortable while Mickey climbed aboard. In between them was a box containing a large thermos no doubt filled with coffee along with fruit and a sack filled with a generous assortment of molasses and oatmeal cookies. Julia's doing, of course. They were both dressed in warm outerwear given the open-air cab and early morning cold temperatures.

They started off slow, driving along a serviceable but rutted dirt road. They passed the two-story stone cottage located not too far from the farmhouse and stopped the flatbed in front of the farm's three cabins. Henry kept the engine running, set the emergency brake, and the two walked over for a closer look. Henry unlocked the front door and Mickey looked inside, discovering that each had a living room, a single bedroom, a small kitchen, bathroom, and woodstove. The cabins were originally designed for seasonal workers in need, such as those working the apple orchards or corn fields.

"Nice and clean," Mickey observed.

"Carl and I repainted them all and reroofed each of them last summer.

Mickey looked around. "All three are like this?"

"Identical. Of course, you know that Hudson is living in one for now."

He nodded.

"All insulated and winterized?"

"Yep. You know, you could move into one of these if you wanted to. Give you some more privacy."

Mickey shrugged. "I like where I am now, but I'll think on it."

They hauled themselves back into the flatbed's cab and drove over to the large maintenance building. When they walked in, they found Hudson at a workbench making repairs on a broken truck headlamp. He turned around when he heard their footsteps. "Ah, the two midshipmen are up early I see." He flashed a wide grin.

Henry snapped off a salute. "Wanted to show the new guy our vehicles and your workshop."

Mickey stood there, hands on his hips, admiring the row of vehicles lined up against the side wall.

Hudson wiped his hands on an oil-stained rag, then stuck it in his back pocket.

Hudson nodded and replied, "Of course, you're currently riding this morning in our 1916 Mack Bulldog flatbed truck. We use it just about anywhere on the farm because it has great power and traction. It's used for everything from towing, snow plowing, hauling crops and supplies, you name it. It rides rough, but it's practical and dependable."

Hudson walked over to the Dodge Touring Car. "You guys drove the Dodge back and forth to Bridgeport. As you know, the car is a four-seater and four-door rig. It has a convertible top, as well as removable side panels for winter weather." Hudson nudged

Henry in the ribs. "We call it the family car now, or our goin' to church car." They both laughed.

Finally, Hudson walked over to the last two vehicles, the boys trailing. "What you see here are Avery Bulldogs. These are the vehicles used for planting and harvesting and can do just about anything, from tilling the soil to harvesting, cutting silage, and threshing."

Mickey was in awe of their size and stared wide-eyed at them.

Hudson clapped his hand on Mickey's shoulder. "Get used to all of them, son. I'll teach you all about these four this winter and we'll take each out for practice runs when weather permits." He reached into his back pocket for a handkerchief and blew his nose. "You'll be ready when springtime rolls around."

Mickey was puzzled. "Wait, I'll be ready? Ready for what?"

Hudson glanced at Henry, who gave him a slight nod to continue.

"You'll be ready to be our main driver for all of these vehicles. We'll be hiring one more driver come planting season."

Mickey did a double-take, not believing what he just heard. "Did you just say I'm going to be a driver?" He shook his head with a mixture of denial and disbelief. He threw up his hands in exasperation. "Are you guys serious? I've never even driven a car, let alone these monsters."

"You'll learn," Hudson said patiently.

Mickey held up his artificial arm. "With this?"

"Anyone can drive these vehicles with one hand, it just takes practice. You'll drive slowly and on a field, not a road. You're right-handed, correct?"

"I am."

"Good. Virtually all of your instruments are on the right side, and those that aren't I'll relocate to that side. Everything will be within reach. I'll teach you a little at a time until you're comfortable." He had more to say and wanted to find the right words. "I'll make this simple. We need two drivers, Mickey. Henry and I will be focused on our own work assignments so we've got to lean on you to get the fields plowed and ready for planting, as well as other chores requiring wheeled vehicles. If we didn't think you could handle it, we wouldn't be asking."

Henry walked over to Mickey and deliberately stopped and stood in front of him. "Mickey," he said, "you can do this. Once you get the hang of it, you'll never think of your prosthesis as something holding you back. I really want you to look at what the rest of your body can do instead of letting your amputation dictate what you can't do."

Hudson interjected. "My understanding is that Henry is going to give you a tour of the stable and our horses later this morning. I ask that you be open-minded when you see them, too. In the beginning you'll likely have hesitation about even approaching them. In time, though, you'll develop your skills and become a horseman." He nodded. "You should know that many riders who've mastered the skills of this trade have done it one-handed and with other disabilities. Stick with us and we'll show you how you can achieve the same mastery."

It became quiet in the garage. Mickey took everything in, processing it all. Finally, he nodded, tentatively at first and then with more assertion. "All right," he said, "I'll try my best to do this." He looked at both Henry and Hudson. "I'll need your help and plenty of it. But be patient with me. I'll show you that I'm no quitter."

Hudson replied, "That's good enough for me." He turned and walked back to his workbench. As he brushed past Henry he said softly, "Kid's got gumption, I'll give him that."

They got back into the flatbed and continued to follow the dirt road. They came to the acreage designated as the cornfield. It stretched as far as the eye could see, a farmer's paradise waiting to be tilled, plowed, seeded and cultivated. "This will be your territory. It needs your tractor and equipment," Henry said to Mickey. "The lieutenant wanted sweet corn to prosper in these fields like it did when he was young, so that's what we're going to do. You'll be the one to make his vision a reality."

They continued their tour, driving past the corn fields and eventually coming to the farm's apple orchards. Henry engaged the emergency brake and the two got out and climbed a sloped hillside, a good vantage point to survey the orchard.

Mickey couldn't believe his eyes. He shielded his eyes from the sun and took in hundreds of apple trees stretching far into the distance and ending at a tree line. The orchard was as wide as it was deep.

"This is enormous," Mickey explained. What kind of apples grow here?"

"Mostly McIntosh and Cortland. This is an enterprise in itself, one that's separate from the sweet corn and the horses."

"All the trees look pretty barren now. When do they start producing?"

"The apples are ripe enough to pick from late August through late October."

"Who does the picking?" His brows knitted. "It can't be just us. Please tell me it can't be just us."

"Of course, it's not just us. We have an independent orchard manager who harvests our apples each year. He has a crew that gathers the crop in addition to overseeing such things as pruning, and applying bacterial and insecticidal sprays. More importantly, once the apples are picked the orchard manager markets them through his farm stores and also ships them to supermarkets and restaurants.

"Impressive operation."

"It is," replied Henry, "but we're in the process of looking at cost efficiency and where we want to go with the orchard, including putting its total management under our control instead of relying on an outsider." Henry looked over at Mickey, his mind racing on potential changes he'd turned over in his mind. He knew he had to slow his thinking down and take on one project at a time. "At any rate," he said, "that's a topic for another day."

They continued their journey, Henry pointing out along the way a plot of blue spruce trees, a spring-fed pond, the lieutenant's shooting range, and horseback riding trails cutting through dense forests. When they reached a level stretch of road, Henry stopped the flatbed.

"So, what do you think so far?" Henry asked.

"I've never seen so much land, so many different parts of your territory. But from what I can see, every part seems separate but connected."

"It was made that way, Mickey, far before our time." Henry reached for the thermos and the cookies prepared by Julia.

They sat for a while, munching on molasses and oatmeal cookies, and washing them down with coffee from the thermos. It was a quiet time for both.

At one point they saw a deer rustling in the woods and then emerging, full view. Henry slipped out of the cab. The deer stared at him before stomping a foot and then snorting before turning tail and running off.

Henry thought nothing of it and positioned himself back in the cab. When he got comfortable, he looked over at Mickey and just smiled, as if to say, 'I'm in charge of this part of the farm and the wildlife's in charge of the woods.'

Mickey felt safe alongside Henry's presence. "Do you hunt up here?" he asked.

"Nope, at least not yet anyway." He looked sideways at Mickey. "Is that something you want to do?"

"I don't know, I've never killed any wildlife," Mickey replied sheepishly. "That probably sounds strange coming from a soldier trained to kill humans on a battlefield."

"Well, we can think about hunting wildlife as time goes by. As I recall, you were a crack shot at the junior midshipman's camp, a real sharpshooter."

Mickey snorted. "You, my friend, were the marksman. Even the lieutenant said so."

The two straightened in the cab and moved on, this time finishing around the far end of the property loop. They then made their way to the farm's corrals and horse stables.

When they got to the main entrance of the stable, Henry parked, turned the flatbed off, and the two walked in.

Henry's appearance caused quite a stir. The horses thumped and snorted, sensing his presence. He shouted at them, by name, announcing his presence. After a few moments, the horses settled down. Henry looked at Mickey and they both smiled.

For Mickey, the smell of the barn was something he'd never experienced before, and it took him a little while to adjust, the sights and smells overwhelming him. Although he was okay inhaling the manure and such items as the sweaty leather, fresh pine shavings, liniment, hay, and tack, he winced when he detected the ammonia smell coming from urine in the horses' stalls. It took him a few minutes to adjust before he joined Henry, who was busy visiting each stall and lavishing attention on each horse.

"I'm going to let them loose so that they can go outside and get some fresh air," he announced. "You might want to watch and take some mental notes." He opened the barn side door and went back to each stall, attached a lead rope to each harness, and led each horse to the ramped doorway. He talked to each of them as he stopped at the doorway, removed the tack, and watched each horse make haste for the fresh air and space the corral provided. One by one, they whinnied, neighed, and nickered, their way of greeting each other and enjoying the freedom of moving without restraint.

Henry and Mickey joined each other outside, leaning against the corral fence, each positioning a foot on top of the lowest railing. "They're something, aren't they?" asked Henry.

"They're beautiful animals, no doubt."

"I know entering a barn for the first time can be a bit overwhelming, especially the manure, but it can actually become kind of pleasant when you get used to it. There will come a time when horses smell wonderful to you, even when they are sweaty and dirty. For me, all of this has created a belongingness to a peaceful and happy place. My time here is full of caring for these remarkable horses, and I wouldn't want it any other way."

He turned to Mickey. "I want you to be just as content around them as I am. But whether you do or not, is up to you. The opportunities are here, and if you stay with us, you'll see how the happenings on this farm can open up a new chapter in your life." He stopped talking, wondering if he'd come on too strong or too pushy.

Mickey turned to face his friend. "I'm on board, Henry, and I'm staying here with you for the long run. That's something you can count on. I'll get used to everything here, including the horses. That's a promise."

Six

Mickey and Henry stayed outside for a while, leaning against the corral and watching the small herd interact. A fairly stiff wind had started to blow and the tall trees on the northeast corner of the property swayed and groaned. Thin clouds skirted across the pewter sky.

"Do you keep them outside for very long?" asked Mickey.

"Weather permitting, most of the day. They need the exercise, free space, and contact with each other. Water and hay are outside in a paddock if they want it. Hudson and I saddle them up as often as we can and take them to the wooded trails."

Mickey watched them mingle in the corral. "Do they all get along?"

"Why don't you tell me. What have you seen so far?"

"Well, after you released them one at a time they took off on their own, galloping back and forth, but then they looked for the herd and joined it."

"Think it's a friendly herd?"

"I think they all get along, if that's what you're asking."

Henry nodded.

Mickey rubbed his chin. "But I should add that some seem closer to others than the rest."

"How so?"

"When you released them from the barn and after they stretched their legs, it looked like some neighed and wanted to attract the attention of a friend." Mickey got quiet, perhaps mulling things over before he continued. "This is guesswork on my part but it seemed like the buddies moved closer to each other and appeared to be nuzzling, sometimes bumping their pals."

"For someone who hasn't been around horses, you've got a keen eye."

"I saw a lot of horses in France, Henry." He let out a deep breath. "But in my final days over there, the horses were brutalized in such a way that I still get nightmares."

Mickey mentally drifted off to another place and time, prompting Henry to give his friend some space. They stood watching the horses for several minutes, neither saying a word.

Finally, Henry spoke. "We're going to get you up on one of the horses you're watching."

Mickey held up his left arm and snorted loudly, his attitude mixed with the element of disbelief. "Even with this prosthesis?"

Henry was calm in his response. "Absolutely, even with your prosthesis."

"And just how are you going to do that?"

"For starters, we're going to give you a calm and reliable horse, one that will become a true partner, one loyal to you. Over time, the two of you will strengthen the bond you share."

With that, Henry stuck two fingers in his mouth and let loose a loud, shrill whistle not once but twice, a signal heard by all the horses, but intended for one in particular. A dusty gray gelding jerked its head up immediately toward the sound, located the source, and came running toward Henry. The horse was as sleek as it was handsome, and as it got closer, began to nicker and whinny. It ignored Mickey, but cozied up to Henry, even nudging him in the upper shoulder. Henry liked the nuzzle and held on, enjoying the embrace.

Eventually, Henry pulled away from the horse and announced, "Mickey, this is Monte. He'll be your horse." Mickey slowly took a step forward, Henry closely watching the interaction. Mickey paused at one point then continued to approach Monte. Henry had given him a few hints about making friends with horses. He approached the horse slightly to the side, primarily to avoid the blind spot right in front of Monte.

"Let him hear your voice but speak softly," advised Henry.

Mickey did as he was told, and introduced himself quietly, along with other subdued exchanges.

Monte watched every move Mickey took. Mickey did the same.

As he got closer, Monte let his ears relax and they flopped toward the side. He was at ease, neither aggressive or defensive. Mickey stopped when he was about an arm's length away from him. He raised his good hand towards Monte, flat and outstretched, and the horse sniffed it, then licked his hand. This was a good sign, so was Monte's decision to run his muzzle up against Mickey's arm.

Henry liked what he was seeing. "I'm impressed. He likes you, Mickey. He doesn't do that with everyone. Move closer and let him pick up your scent."

Mickey followed the instruction and also stroked Monte's neck. As he did so, Mickey looked back at Henry.

Henry grinned. "Good," he remarked, "you're doing good."

Monte had made his new acquaintance, and for now, he'd had enough. He began backing up, then turned his body away and galloped back to join the herd. More than one horse nickered, welcoming him back.

"There you go, Mickey," Henry remarked. "You've passed muster."

Mickey watched the horse return and blend in with the herd. He fell quiet and carefully measured his words. "What just happened was good, but when the time comes, you expect me to just climb aboard that horse and take full control?"

Henry replied, "Yep, that's the plan, *amigo*, but only when you're ready, of course. You'll have lots of lessons along the way."

"I'm going to need a heap of help. I'm a far cry from a rider who can control a horse. For starters, I don't even know how I'm going to get myself up in the saddle." He laughed. "Hell's bells," he scoffed, "for that matter I don't even know how I'm going to stay on or even how I'm going to get off. If I had to make left and right turns, I'm a goner."

Henry laughed out loud. "We'll talk about this," he said but then stopped in his tracks. "Wait a minute, now is as good a time to give you a few things to think about. Let's walk over to the stable."

———————

They walked slowly, chatting along the way. Henry said, "Monte was once my horse, a mount given to me by the lieutenant to train. Monte was a tough horse to bring into the fold. He needed personal attention for everything, from feeding to riding."

Mickey looked sideways at Henry. "Why?" he asked. "What made it so hard?"

"Monte was involved in a horse trailer crash. His parents died in a fire that followed, but Monte somehow broke free from the crash site and ran away like the wind. He was eventually found and to make a long story short, was never the same. He looked for his parents over and over. He became ornery and difficult to control. Had a big chip on his shoulder and was skittish when anyone approached. I was appointed his guardian keeper and my job was to calm him down and get him to trust again. My goodness, I spent hundreds of hours with that horse, walking with him as we explored the trails. I took him everywhere to help him recapture his social skills. Much of our time was spent mingling with our other horses. In due time, he became the most obedient and trustworthy of them all."

"So, what was your secret?'

"There really wasn't one. I suppose being gentle and nonthreatening were important cornerstones for building trust. Monte learned that he was safe here, and that our care provided him with protection and safety. In time, he learned to form attachments with others, and to trust his handlers." Henry let loose a heavy breath. "This took a good amount of time and patience."

"You'd never know he had those kinds of problems."

"Not now. He's the most easy-going horse on the farm. A pleasure to ride. He's responsive to commands and alert, a horse that's gentle and mindful of his rider at all times." Henry paused. "This all makes Monte a natural for you."

They got to the stable and found Carl mucking the stalls.

"Morning, Carl," said Henry, Mickey also nodding Carl's way.

"Mornin'," a grunt acknowledgement from Carl, who leaned over to shovel a heap of horse manure over his shoulder and depositing it in a large, waiting wheelbarrow, a load eventually heading its way to a compost pile out back.

That was the most they got out of Carl.

"So, what's with that guy? Why does he wear that old fedora and tool belt around his waist? Why is he so quiet?"

"Don't worry about Carl. The fedora and the tool belt were gifts and he keeps them close. He had a head injury during the early years of his marriage with Julia. At times he's a bit off kilter, but we all accept the person, and not the injury. He's no threat to anybody, and he works like a horse without complaint. You'll get to know him and love him."

———

They walked to the back of the barn. In the middle stood an elevated 4x4, anchored at each end with wooden supports. A bunk-size mattress had been placed over the beam and a Western saddle was draped and buckled over both. Bolts had been driven into the 4x4 to secure the mattress to keep it from moving.

"I set this up last week so that you could see the steps involved in mounting a saddled horse," said Henry.

"With just one arm."

Henry nodded. "That's right cowboy, with just one arm."

Mickey walked over to the saddle.

Henry said "The height of the saddle is set so that you're looking at the approximate height your mount will be."

Mickey inspected the length of the stirrups and the saddle horn, wondering how he was going to step into a stirrup and use the saddle horn to hoist himself up onto the saddle. All this with one arm.

Henry walked around Mickey to the left side of the saddle. "Come over here so that you can see how you're going to get yourself up and on the saddle." Henry put his left foot in the stirrup and clenched the saddle horn with his left hand. Putting all of his weight on his left foot, he stepped up to a standing position, then swung his right leg wide and over the saddle. He sat down in the saddle gently then put his right foot in the other stirrup. He made sure that the ball of each foot was on the stirrup, not his toe or heel.

"Impressive," said Mickey, as he watched Henry swing his leg forward and dismount by sliding from the saddle to the ground.

"You with me so far?"

Mickey nodded.

"Okay then, let's go to the right side of the saddle and try doing the same thing." Henry slipped his right foot in the stirrup, grasped the saddle horn with his right hand, and swung his left leg up and around the saddle before sitting.

He sat there for a while before dismounting and looking at Mickey. "What did I do differently?"

Mickey looked at him and smiled. "You used your right foot and hand; in fact, your whole right side determined your mount." He was silent for a few moments, then said, "If I'm not mistaken, you just did the opposite of what you did on the other side."

Henry grinned. "You catch on fast, Parker. I did this on purpose to get you thinking. This is the side where you're going to learn how to mount your horse. You need to practice the sequence I just showed you, over and over. Your right hand and the right side of your body need to be strengthened so that you can mount your horse. Many repetitions are needed to get the sequence down pat. You need to develop strength in your right arm." This will be your winter workout, Mickey."

Mickey said, "I'll need your help getting started."

"You'll always have that," Henry emphasized. "That's a given, plus there will always be somebody holding Monte steady while you mount. He's pretty steadfast when a rider climbs on board, but we'll need to give him time to adjust to you." He looked around the barn. "We've also built a small platform for you to mount Monte if you need one. It's kind of like a step-stool." Henry found it in a corner and pointed it out so Mickey could see.

"Thank you, Henry, you've thought of everything." He stroked his chin for a moment, thinking. "Okay, let's say I've managed to get myself up in the saddle, and I'm looking for the reins. I suppose there's two that I hold, one for each side. What if one or both slip from my grasp? Once I'm in the saddle, how am I supposed to lean over and fetch one or both without falling out of the saddle?"

"Good question. You won't have that happening. You'll be taught early on how to use what are called Romal reins instead of split reins. With Romal reins, the two reins are attached to the horse's bit and are joined together. Everything is connected. They won't fall on the ground and you won't have to retrieve them or anything else by dismounting. Romal reins allow for minimal movement of your good hand and it will be your right hand that will create more precise, gentle cues to Monte. Romal reins also prod you to use your legs for commands, which will be ideal for you."

Henry put his hands on his hips. "All of that is down the road, Mickey, so relax. We don't want to get too far ahead of ourselves today, so I'll stop here. I don't want to confuse you."

Mickey held up his hand. "Okay, I understand, but I have two questions before you stop."

"Shoot," said Henry.

"Okay, first question. Is Monte familiar with the use of Romal reins and the difference between split reins?"

"Absolutely, he's been trained with both." Henry grinned. "His training was conducted by me."

Mickey nodded.

It got quiet for a minute or two.

"What's your other question?" asked Henry.

Mickey said, "Hudson claimed that many impaired men and women have mastered horseback riding, some with only one good hand, many with other kinds of amputations. Was he trying to make me feel good, or is this possible?"

"Hudson has not been dishonest. Many impaired riders have demonstrated proficiency with one hand as well as other kinds of amputations. We do this by likely utilizing Romal reins, teaching impaired riders to convey verbal commands to their mounts, and having them use variations in leg pressure to control the speed of the mount." He paused and found Mickey's eyes. "You'll learn more of this down the line."

At that point, Hudson made an abrupt appearance and walked in the barn. "Henry, Julia tells me you've got a phone call over at the house. Says it's important."

Henry patted Mickey on the back and turned to leave. "We've covered good ground here, but there's much left for you to see and do."

As Henry walked past Hudson he said, "No idea who's calling?"

Hudson met Henry's eyes and replied, "Nope, such weighty details are way above my pay grade, boss." His laughter was subdued and playful.

Before he left, Henry leaned in close to Hudson. "Keep him busy," Henry said. "Show him your workshop, point things out to him. Let him walk around and get familiar with the place."

Hudson obliged.

Henry walked outside. Out of the corner of his eye, he spotted Monte, who had wandered back from the other horses and returned to the fencing near the barn. Nosy, as usual, prying and meddling, the resident snoop of the yard who spied on everyone. Henry walked over to where Monte stood and stroked his head and ears. He stuck his nose against Monte's mane and kept it there for a long minute, taking in his scent. After a while, Henry spoke softly in the horse's ear, "You've got your work cut out for you with that new kid in the barn, mister. He's gonna need a lot of work and a ton of your patience." He stroked then patted Monte's neck a few times. "Get your rest now, *mi caballo*, you're going to need it."

Seven

Henry beat a hasty retreat to the farmhouse, flung the screen door open with great gusto, the door flying open and contributing to a well-worn crease on the outside of the farmhouse. He announced his presence and found Julia in the hallway chatting nonchalantly on the phone with the unidentified caller. Julia looked up when Henry arrived, and after excusing herself, handed the phone to him. "For you, Mr. Cameron," she said to him, a wink included.

"Hello out there, whoever you are," said Henry into the phone. "This is Henry Cameron. What can I do for you?"

Henry still hadn't mastered the telephone and the best way to engage a caller, but for the time being, simple worked.

"Henry," the caller said, "this is Abigail Emory. My hope is that you remember me."

Henry remembered her immediately, a fusion of memories of Arabian diving horses, Niantic's Golden Spur; a romantic interlude involving she and lieutenant Cooper; and an earlier visit to the Vermont farm by Abigail only to discover the lieutenant had passed away.

All of these memories were separate but distinct, and all merged together. "Of course I remember you, Abigail. How are you?"

"I'm fine, Henry. I was just speaking to Julia about organizing my life and would very much like to visit you and look at employment possibilities. Would it be possible to drive to Vermont and see what's going on up there?"

Henry had to think about this, an early test of his ownership responsibilities. He found himself stumbling for an answer and didn't know exactly what to say. The best he could do was muffle the phone and quietly ask Julia. He got her attention and said, "Is it okay if Abigail comes to visit for a few days to look things over?"

Julia smiled. "Absolutely, provided she stays for Thanksgiving. In fact, why don't you encourage her to stay longer?"

He relayed the message, and Abigail was thrilled. She couldn't have asked for a better arrangement and thanked Henry and Julia profusely.

Henry said, "Maybe we can get a little horseback riding in, depending on the weather up here. So far, it's been mild, but winter is lurking, we can all feel it."

"This is all good news," Abigail replied. "I need to tie-up a few loose ends down here, but barring any mishaps I'll see you up there in a few days, okay?"

Henry agreed and wished her a safe journey. He hung up the phone and walked in the kitchen, where he found Julia.

"Thank you for helping me on that, Julia."

"No problem. I'm sure she'll be a delightful guest, plus this will give Abigail an opportunity to meet all of us."

"We have a room available for her, right?"

"There's plenty of room, you know that. I'll tidy up one of the upstairs bedrooms for her and make sure she receives ample towels and bedding."

Henry stood there, shifting his weight from one foot to the other. He hesitated, "But what if she'd like to stay longer? She's already been offered the job by the lieutenant, including room and board, so she just might want to stay here and move in. We okay with that?"

"We're good, don't you worry. We've got four vacant and furnished bedrooms, plus two cabins. It sounds like she wants to look the place over before making a decision. Smart woman. Who knows, maybe she'll turn the offer down and keep looking somewhere else. We'll take good care of her either way. Now don't go fretting about that. We got Mickey on board safely and we'll do the same for Abigail if this is where she wants to live."

"Perfect," he nodded and began turning away.

Julia touched his shoulder. "Henry, you might want to give some thought to drawing up a contract for Abigail."

"Why?"

"Well, for one thing it will make her employment official. Do up a list of duties and responsibilities, as well as your expectations, and when you finish, I'll type it and include all the needed details."

"Do you think we should let Hudson take a look at the contract too, yes?"

She agreed.

Two days later, Abigail arrived. She pulled up without fanfare in the driveway next to the farmhouse behind the wheel of a 1916

Oldsmobile flatbed. The flatbed was covered by a large canvas tarpaulin, held in place by copper metal fasteners.

She pulled up and stopped short of the farmhouse. She got out and stretched, arms high above her head. She wore a quilted overcoat and a flannel shirt. Her hair was pulled back in a ponytail.

Henry emerged out of the farmhouse and warmly embraced her. They hugged and held on to each other for an extra minute or two.

"You made it," Henry said. "On your own and without mishap."

Abigail smiled, still holding on to his arms. She looked at Henry and just shook her head, fixing her eyes on his. She blinked a few times to clear her vision. "I know I've said this to you before, but I swear you could've been the lieutenant's son. The likeness is incredible, more so now than the last time I saw you." She could feel her heart skipping a beat.

On two other occasions in Niantic, Connecticut, the three had met and Abigail was taken back by Henry and lieutenant Cooper, the physical resemblance between the two striking. She couldn't believe they weren't father and son. Her heart was still heavy with the loss of lieutenant Cooper, and seeing Henry magnified the loss.

Henry said, "Everyone comments on the likeness and now I've grown to accept this as a compliment."

They both nodded, and she hugged him again.

As far as Henry was concerned, seeing Abigail was an elixir, and knowing that she'd arrived safely was a blessing. Her physical features were just as he remembered: chestnut hair, piercing brown eyes, and a smooth, rosy complexion. She was buoyant upon her arrival, her mood light and happy. She'd experienced a long drive and was visibly relieved that she'd finally arrived. Given the assistance of Henry, a few suitcases from the front seat were carried to a bedroom prepared for her. The readiness of the bedroom, along with the friendliness and helpfulness shown by Henry made Abigail feel embraced and secure.

"What about your belongings under the tarp in your truck?" asked Henry. "Should we unload those items, too?"

"Not yet," Abigail said in a clipped tone. "Leave them under the tarp for now. I'll decide on them later."

Henry nodded and moved away from the truck.

The first night, they dined on a meal of spaghetti and meatballs, a favorite recipe of Julia's. She also made a large salad and baked several loaves of garlic bread topped with butter. The meal from the master chef didn't disappoint; rather, compliments abounded around the dinner table. Once dinner was finished, everyone pitched in to clear the table and scrape the plates clean. A separate crew consisting of Hudson and Henry washed and dried the dishes. With so many hands on deck, it didn't take long to have the large kitchen back in tip-top shape.

They moved to the living room to stretch their legs and relax. Carl scurried about bringing in firewood to create a roaring fire, and Hudson prepared a trayful of wine glasses for a fireside toast. Of course, the focal point for the evening was Abigail's arrival, and to that end, Hudson proposed a toast to her presence and safe arrival to Vermont.

All toasted, all drank, all smiled.

They sat down and relaxed in each other's company, but it wasn't long before attention focused on Abigail. She willingly answered all questions about herself and her background, feeling immediately at ease with the informality of it all. "I was an only child raised in several parts of the country, starting in Arizona, then moving to northern parts of the country. My father died early and my mother never really recovered from the loss. We arrived in New York, where my mother's sister lived, hoping to find a better life, but found nothing but poverty and violence lurking in every corner. My mother became sickly and suffered from depression." Abigail bowed her head. "She was eventually institutionalized but never got better. She died at a young age." She looked around the room. "I can honestly say I really didn't know my father and mother.

Abigail went on. "Meanwhile, I got over my losses and knew I needed money to make ends meet. I looked everywhere for any kind of job. I didn't have any job skills but was willing to do anything. I was still living with my aunt and wanted to contribute to the household. By pure luck, I met J. W. Gorman, an entrepreneur offering Arabian diving horses amidst a carnival setting. He was looking for someone to tend to his Arabian horses. He told me to get some experience." She looked around the table and smiled. "I've always loved horses, in fact when we lived in Arizona, I worked in a stable when I was a young teenager. I worked after school and did a little bit of everything, from mucking the stalls to exercising the horses. I learned to saddle and ride on a gentle Morgan horse owned by an old rancher. It was a good experience. He taught me so much about horses."

———————

Abigail stared into the fireplace flames. "I got the job with Mr. Gorman and finally had a steady income. I liked what I was doing and made a lot of friends. But Gorman's act was a road show, so it required a lot of traveling. I had to leave, it seemed, soon after making good friends but then having to say goodbye. I still miss them and stay in touch with some."

Hudson asked, "So you stayed on with the show?"

She sighed. "I did, but the traveling really got to me. When I was young, traveling long distances was never a problem. In fact, it was an adventure." She thought about this, then slowly shook her head. "But over the years working Gorman's show, I got worn down going from city to city, town to town. I never had the chance to find a home, you know, establish roots, somewhere, anywhere. I didn't know it at the time, but a chance meeting with the lieutenant and Henry at the Golden Spur in Connecticut provided me with an opportunity."

The logs crackled in the fireplace, shooting sparks up the chimney.

"I can remember meeting with the lieutenant and Henry and learning about this horse farm being developed. He needed a horse trainer and asked me if I might be interested in the Vermont position. We agreed to talk further once my season was over with the diving horses."

Abigail filled in some other aspects of her life, weaving into her narrative the fate of Gorman's road show. The novelty of the diving horses began to dry up in America. As time wore on, Abigail began to see smaller crowds and the cancellation of many bookings because of a general lack of public interest. Money became tight after the war. Heated criticism by animal rights activists shut down many performances, critics maintaining that such shows were frightening for the horses and could easily lead to injuries and even death.

"So, you left the Gorman enterprise?" asked Hudson.

"I did, I packed my bags and bid farewell. I'd had enough."

"What was your next stop?" asked Henry.

"I worked at several horse farms, all good, but all were seasonal positions. I tended to the horses in the fall but got my walking papers shortly thereafter. With no anchor in place, I moved on from one ranch to another, a couple of frigid winters in-between. The pay was good and I knew that I was skilled at what I could offer, but no one offered me a full-time commitment or a vision for the future."

Henry uttered, "Until you met us."

"Exactly," she said, a sigh of relief accompanying her words.

She looked at Henry and smiled.

"First and foremost, I was looking for a horse farm that offered permanent training and caring for the horses. I wanted to work full-time and be on call for any problems needing my attention. I wanted to work with people who cared about each other and worked as a team." She looked around at the faces of those in the room. "I wanted to find a horse farm that I could call my home, a lodging that could offer me the chance to become a part of a family." She smiled to herself. "I guess you could say that right now in my life I really need to be needed."

She took a deep breath, and let it out slowly. "So here I am in Vermont on a farm that so far looks pretty inviting. With your okay, I'd like to stay for a few days and see what makes this place tick. In so doing, it will give all of you the chance to see what makes me tick." She raised her eyebrows and smiled. "How's that sit with you?"

Henry replied, "That sits just fine. We'll start tomorrow morning. What would you like to do first?"

Without any hesitation she replied, "Saddle up."

Eight

The next morning the two of them walked to the barn and the horses. It was a bit on the chilly side, but the sun was already breaking through some low flying clouds. Along the way, Henry reached deep into his leather saddlebag and produced a pair of gloves, a long rag wool scarf, and a beige watch cap.

He handed these items to her. "These are for you," he said. "You'll need them, it's chilly up here in Vermont, and the thermometer will drop." He pointed up to the sky. "Pretty soon that white stuff will start falling and it's going to get much colder. The next time we're in town, we'll get you outfitted with some warmer outerwear."

Abigail accepted Henry's gesture with a smile.

They gabbed until they reached the barn, then opened the wide doors. They were greeted by a chorus of nickering and whinnies, quite the welcome for them. The horses twisted their heads as much as they could to get a glance of the visitor.

Henry and Abigail walked in. It was the first opportunity Abigail had the chance to see the inside of the barn and the stables. It was impressive, the scent of fresh lumber and carpentry shavings everywhere. Abigail could see that each horse had its own stall, five total, all completely clean and the occupants fed. An additional five stalls had been constructed on the opposite barn wall, all empty and waiting for new arrivals.

Abigail liked what she saw. She stood with her hands on her hips and surveyed everything, her eyes moving slowly left and right. The barn was perfect for expansion and the lieutenant had already gotten things well underway before he passed. Abigail thought of him, remembered his handsome face as well as his compassion for horses.

Henry turned to her. "Ready for a review of the troops?"

"That I am," she replied, smiling. "Show me the way."

They walked inside the wide barn, their eyes adjusting from the outside light to the barn's darkened surroundings. They were accosted by barn odors, both pleasant and unpleasant, hay, grain, saddle soap, and leather mixed with the rich loamy fragrance of the horses themselves. The mixture of the barn smells didn't bother Henry or Abigail.

Henry and Abigail walked back and forth, inspecting the stalls as well as the inside structure of the barn itself. Henry said, "We own five horses with plans to purchase five more." He pointed toward five newly constructed stalls along the opposite wall. "We've got all quarter horses for now but we're looking to add a few more, maybe some Morgans."

Abigail said, "Two great breeds, I like working with both."

Henry changed subjects. "Let me introduce our crew," he announced. They approached the five stalls. Henry said, "Here are the three horses that were here when I came aboard," he said, pointing to the first three stalls: "Norman, Rufus, and Monte."

He took a few steps back and introduced Abigail to Lola and Morning Star. "These two make up our string of horses," he said. "They are our newcomers, and so far they haven't disappointed." Henry paused and leaned against a railing. "Good mounts, all of them. Trained personally by the lieutenant, each passing his inspection. Alert and dependable, all three."

"Behaviors of each?" asked Abigail.

Henry thought for a moment, then replied, "Norman is a seven-year-old, a very gentle Sorel. A delight to ride. He's been Julia's mount since I've been here. Rufus is our most reliable mount and our strongest horse. He's always on alert to protect the herd, and tells us when things aren't right."

Moving on, Henry said, "Rufus is our leader, and he knows it. He likes to watch over the others and keep them close. His response to commands is extraordinary"

Henry paused once again, this time as he focused his eyes elsewhere, this time on Monte.

"Finally," he said, "we have Monte, my old mount. He's friendly, obedient and dependable, plus he's another one always on alert. I hate passing him on to another rider, but he's the perfect steed for Mickey. He'll be gentle and easy for Mickey to handle."

They ambled over to the last two stalls to see the two newcomers, Morning Star and Lola. Both had been hand-picked by Hudson a year ago and brought home to Vermont."

"Have they both been broken?" asked Abigail.

"They were when Hudson bought and transported them, but I'm not entirely sure they remembered all of their lessons. When they arrived, the lieutenant began training them both before he got sick. Among his last words spoken to me were that they both needed more work."

Abigail nodded and kept walking to the back of the barn, coming upon Mickey's makeshift saddle and mattress. "What's this?" she asked.

"It's something I made for Mickey. Come closer and take a look."

Henry had already explained Mickey's amputation, as well as his desire to get Mickey up in a saddle. He described how his rig would help Mickey learn to mount a horse from the right side, and how the necessary movements would take practice and patience.

"Mickey's right-handed, correct?" Abigail asked.

"Correct."

"So, you want him to mount from the right side?"

"That's my goal, yes," Henry replied.

She went over and ran her hand along the length of the saddle.

"Why is getting him up on a horse so important to you?" she asked.

Henry had to think about that one for a minute or two. He replied, "Because I'd like him to experience what I did when I first rode. I want him to experience the partnership he can establish with a horse, the freedom he can experience as a rider, that special companionship unavailable from others."

Abigail nodded, then stood there thinking. "So, you've built this so Mickey can increase his coordination and his confidence in mounting from the right side."

"That's my goal, and I've got a backup plan for him, too." He pointed to the stepped platform he'd constructed, located right next to Monte's stall. "Maybe this can be an alternative way for him to step up and get into the saddle."

Abigail appeared nonplussed with the platform. "That's good, just don't let him use it as an easy way out."

"Meaning what?"

"Mickey's young and regaining his strength, he's not infirmed or fragile. He needs to find his mettle and master the mounting sequence you first described. Mickey will likely need someone in the beginning to steady Monte while he mounts and dismounts, otherwise he should be okay. If I were you, I'd use the platform only as a last resort."

They kept talking as they continued inspecting the barn.

Abigail said, "I understand that Mickey's loss of his left-hand is traumatic, but he's got to learn to overcome it. I like your reasons for getting him up on a horse. It will take effort on his part, but the rewards will overshadow his sweat. If you wish, I will work with him to master this challenge."

She tilted her head and looked at Henry.

Henry looked backed at her. He wondered if this was meant to be a clue that she was going to stay.

They walked a little more. "So where did you pick up the two-sided way to mount a horse?"

Henry grinned. "Where else? The lieutenant. When he taught me how to mount and dismount a horse, he always preached that there are two sides to a horse. At first, I thought he was joking but then he told me how cavalry troopers needed to learn how to mount a horse from both sides. He shared several times how he was pinned down by the enemy in Arizona, and out of necessity had to mount his horse on the right side instead of the left side to escape."

When he recalled the lieutenant's stories, Henry grinned and floated back to those days he remembered. "I can remember him saying, 'Do you think renegades were going to wait for me to mount on the left side? You take whatever side your mount offers, and you'd better be able to climb on board no matter which side is available, and then you need to high-tail it out of there as fast as you can.'

Henry laughed again, then continued. "From that point on, we practiced mounting on both sides of the horse."

Abigail was intrigued with all this. "Was it hard? I mean, hard because you'd been trained mounting a horse exclusively from the left side?"

"Yes, it was very hard, and my body ached from muscles I'd rarely used. But the lieutenant was persistent in his teachings. When I failed, he was the first to correct my mistakes, and I listened. Then he got me back up in the saddle to try again."

Abigail cut in, changing the subject. "So, do you truly believe Mickey can do all this?"

Henry responded, "Absolutely. That guy has got the heart of a lion."

Abigail was impressed, but also persistent in pushing the well-being of both rider and horse. "So, once you get him up on a saddle, do you think he can take command of his mount? What about the reins? Can he master those?"

Henry responded, "I think he'll be okay with the reins. Instead of split reins we've outfitted his tack with Romal reins. This will eliminate the problem of him dropping the reins and having to stop and retrieve them."

Abigail nodded. "Good, very good." She thought out loud for a minute. Have you given any thought to teaching neck-reining with one hand?"

Henry shook his head.

"Well, you might want to think about that. He can gather the reins in one hand at the horse's neck, then pull on the reins in the direction he wants Monte to turn, nudging the horse with the opposite leg. From what I've seen, it works."

Henry was impressed. He had much to think about.

———————

Abigail was itching to ride. "So, what do you say we hit one of the trails this morning with your two new horses and we'll see what they've got."

"You mean Lola and Morning Star?"

She smiled. "Of course, I'll saddle Lola and you take Morning Star." She hesitated. She said, "I get the feeling that with the lieutenant gone, Morning Star has become your mount of choice." With that, she went about her business with skill and command. Henry took heed and saddled Morning Star.

Before climbing on Lola, Abigail spent a good amount of time stroking and nuzzling her, talking slowly and quietly. She wanted to say hello before she mounted. When Abigail did mount, Lola pranced a bit at first but then settled down gradually as Abigail talked to her soothingly and gently stroked her neck.

Riding side-by-side, Abigail and Henry rode past the farmhouse from afar, and he pointed out the cabins as well as the cornfields. Henry then took point and led Abigail along several trails weaving in and out of the forests. Abigail wanted to see the limits of the acreage and the two of them kept pushing forward. There was much to see. They took their time and traveled for several hours scoping out the property.

They came to a wide stretch of plain between two forest trails, and pulled up. The expanse before them was inviting. It was about fifty yards wide and over one hundred yards deep.

Abigail said, "What do you say we find out what these two horses bring to the table." A statement, not a question.

Henry arched his eyebrows, not sure what she meant.

Abigail responded. "What I mean is, let's open the throttle and let them run."

They let them gallop and when they pulled up at the far end of the clearing, they took a breather and the two horsemen let their horses refresh themselves from a fresh water stream babbling nearby. They dismounted and Henry tied the horses to a stand of spindly weeping willows, nearby the stream. Both Henry and Abigail stretched and sat together on a blanket as they surveyed the flat ground.

Abigail said, "For a young guy, you're a very good rider. I've been around skilled horsemen my whole life, and they've got nothing on you. You're gentle with your horses and take good care of them. The attachment I see is both strong and reciprocal."

Henry mumbled a thank you and smiled shyly. He'd brought along a canteen of water and he passed it back and forth with Abigail.

After a while, Abigail asked, "So tell me, Henry Cameron, what's your story?"

"My story?"

"Yes, your life story. How did a Boston boy end up here in the hills of Vermont?"

Henry hemmed and hawed before finding the words. "After my naval cadet training ended, I realized I had nowhere to go. I'd lost both my mother and father, and didn't have any siblings. My friends had enlisted and gone off to war. I was truly alone. I traveled up here and was welcomed with open arms."

"And the riding skills?" she asked.

"All taught by the lieutenant."

"How many years up in the saddle?"

"Just a few."

Abigail shook her head slowly. "Amazing skill level after only a few years. So, start from the beginning and tell me about yourself."

Henry paused, not sure where she wanted him to go with this. "Well, like I said, I'm a single child. I came from a navy family and traveled at home and abroad based on my father's assignments. He served in the Merchant Marine and piloted an oil tanker, so his boat to and from the United States was always on assignment. At home, our family vacations were short-lived and always on the water. We owned a boat for a while, and that was fun. I liked the water and wanted to join the navy."

"Did your parents encourage you to turn to the sea?"

"They did. My father signed me up for a summer camp run by the Junior Naval Reserve in Uncasville, Connecticut. His brother Bill was in charge of the cadets."

"So, I'm guessing your uncle was a big deal in camp?"

"He was." Henry paused. "At least he tried to be."

"What was it like following orders from your uncle?

"Not good," Henry replied, dropping his eyes to the ground. "I'll just say the two of us were never really close." Henry watched his tone carefully. He wanted to tell her what happened, but knew this wasn't the time.

"Were you close to your parents?" Abigail asked.

"No, not really. My father was away from home most of the time and my mother was always busy with her job." He hesitated. "I never had much contact with either one of them. My mother's sister was the person really in charge of my upbringing."

"Do you and your aunt stay in touch?"

"No, she died a while ago."

Abigail nodded. "But then you found the lieutenant up here."

"Yes, he gave me his address when we broke cadet camp and I journeyed to Vermont to find him. By then, my father had been killed in the war. Even before that, my mother had chosen to sleep with another man while my father was at sea. She died, too, during the pandemic."

Abigail couldn't help but think Henry had become the original lost soul. Abandoned by all, but in the end, rescued by the lieutenant.

"But you found a home here."

Henry nodded, deep in thought.

A pause.

"What was it like training horses with the lieutenant?"

Henry sighed. "It was great, seems like I learned something new every day. He was a patient teacher. He never yelled or screamed at me." Laughing, he added, "Never threw anything at me, you know, like a horseshoe or a pitchfork."

That got them both laughing.

He hesitated. "He taught me how to be a better person."

"While training horses?"

Henry nodded. "Yes, the way we trained horses. Things clicked when we rode the horses on the trails or when we put them through the motions inside the corrals. This is why I wanted to get Mickey up here. I wanted him to discover how horseback riding could enable him to like himself more, to feel stronger, to find purpose. I wanted him to learn how to care for animals and to not feel so alone. I guess you could say I wanted him to discover who he was and not let his war injury get in the way."

Henry looked at her and smiled.

She reached over and touched his arm. Out of the blue, she said, "I'm glad we reconnected."

Henry replied, "So am I."

A minute or two passed between the two and neither spoke.

Henry eventually broke the silence. "You know, Abigail, he really liked you."

She did a double take. "What did you just say?"

"I said he liked you."

She paused. "You think so?"

"No doubt. He talked about you a lot. He brought up the diving horses in Connecticut many times, focusing on you. He was hoping he'd get to see you again and really hoped you'd come work with him in Vermont."

Abigail raised her eyebrows. "He said all that?"

Henry hesitated but continued. "Indeed, he did and a lot more. He was hoping the two of you would meet, free of distractions, and spend time together."

The words went straight to her heart and hurt.

Henry picked right up on it. "I didn't mean to make you sad," he said, "but you need to know I hurt too, Abigail."

"I know you do," she said, "and I'm truly sorry for your loss, Henry."

"We're in this together," Henry said. "We'll get through this."

"You're right," she replied. "No more of this sappy stuff, at least not now."

They were at least able to laugh, although strained.

Abigail said, "So back to you, Mr. Cameron. Let me see if I have my details right. You grew up in Boston in a naval family. You lived on the edges of Boston harbor. You vacationed with your parents on the seashore. You enlisted in a cadet camp sponsored by the Junior Naval Reserve. You gave thought to following in your father's footsteps and sailing the seven seas."

Henry dropped his chin to his chest and slowly shook his head. "Yep, and here I am," he pronounced.

"Yes, and here you are, living on a horse farm in Vermont." She smiled. "The horseman who came from the sea."

Nine

The next few November days passed by and before long, Thanksgiving was upon the Cooper farm. A few small sleet storms had pelted the area in the past week, nothing serious or damaging, but no one could deny how the temperature kept dropping, necessitating the need to button up and winterize the home, a rite of passage for Vermonters. Food preparations were made for the coming winter months as foods from the kitchen were stuffed and canned on a continual basis and stored in nearby root cellars.

Julia vividly remembered the brutal winter of 1917 and in no way wanted a repeat performance. Everyone played a part making sure windows were locked and tightened, attic insulation and shingling checked for snugness and fit, firewood stacked, plumbing inspected, and adequate water storage kept on hand.

The Cooper barn demanded separate inspection. Henry, Mickey, and Abigail assigned themselves such duties and spent entire days examining the roof, floors, and stalls of the five horses. All looked good. Bundled hay and straw arrived in abundance from a nearby farm and the bales of hay, straw, and grain were elevated and stored in the barn's loft. An ample water supply for the horses was kept nearby and in fresh supply.

All of the tack was in good shape: replacement straps, harnesses, bridles, reins and stirrups kept in a supply room. Lengths of lead rope hung from the barn's walls. After the barn and stable seemed safe and protected, the crew unraveled snow fencing from several giant spindles and spread it along the Cooper property line, providing a barrier against snow drifting and allowing motor vehicles to come and go from the farmhouse.

———————

As Thanksgiving neared, Julia's kitchen became a beehive of activity. Everyone helped with the preparations, even Abigail, although this was hardly part of her job visitation and interview. She insisted on being involved in the festivities and celebration.

She rolled up her sleeves and worked with Julia side-by-side, helping with any task needing an extra hand or two. Everyone later agreed Abigail thoroughly enjoyed being part of the family preparations.

Food preparation was a project in motion, with lots of moving parts, orchestrated by Julia and commencing at dawn. Julia was the first up and after stoking the kitchen stove, she would start stewing the neck and giblets for the turkey gravy. She would make her pie crusts that very morning so that they were fresh and flaky. She'd prepared apple, pumpkin, pecan, and mincemeat pies for all to enjoy.

While the pies were baking Julia would work on making the stuffing. Those just waking up smelled the aroma of onions and celery simmering in the turkey stock and the pies baking. The two turkeys went into the oven when the pies were done.

At this juncture, Julia's food preparations switched into high gear. She prepared turkey stuffing, turnips, sweet potatoes, squash, mashed potatoes, and vegetables. Julia also insisted on preparing cranberry sauce, honey glazed carrots, and cornbread. Julia knew that the delicious mixed scents of a Thanksgiving meal would trigger hunger pangs for those in the farmhouse. She was prepared for this, though. She made it a point to have the living room tables set up with crackers, cheese, mixed nuts, and fruit such as grapes and orange slices in anticipation of the gang trying to hold off until the big meal.

By late afternoon when all were seated at the table, Julia stood at the forefront of the table. She cleared her throat to get everyone's attention and clasped her hands in front of her.

She said, "Before we share this meal, I'd like to say a few words." She directed an extra social cough Carl's way, who was in the process of stuffing a buttered dinner roll down his dough hole. When Carl realized that all eyes were now upon him, he stopped and wiped the flaky crumbs and streaks of butter from his face.

After the admonishment, Carl sat ramrod straight. His head was down, listening half-heartedly to his wife but eyeballing a nearby loaf of pumpkin bread. He would strike soon.

Now that she had everyone's attention, lest Carl's hungry eyes, Julia continued.

She said, "In a way, a bountiful meal like this pays homage to those we lost. All of us at this table should be thankful because now you get to be with, at least in spirit, the family that started this farm. Mr. and Mrs. Cooper passed away years ago, and only recently did we lose their son, Tom, someone who was very dear to all of us." She paused for a moment or two. "But now we are in the capable hands of Henry Cameron, our new leader and visionary for the future of the farm and its stable of horses. We will do well under his sensitive guidance and direction. We will also do well with the compatriots he brought along with him: Hudson Delaney, and newcomers Mickey and Abigail. Our hope is that all of you will stay on and work alongside us during the coming year. We need you and would be thrilled to have you on board for a long time." She looked each of them square in the eye. "Please stay," she implored. "We don't want any of you to leave us."

She wasn't finished.

"To all of you, please recognize that ours is a family that cares about you. We never need big meals like today to be thankful. All we need to do is develop an appreciation of life and the people we cherish around us. Be thankful for what you share with us and always recognize how lucky you are to be around others who care about you."

As Julia sat, a moment of silence passed. A toast was offered, then Hudson went about the business of carving the two turkeys. He stood at the head of the table and went to work, quickly demonstrating that he was no stranger to the business. He immediately took on the first turkey.

With the platter still steaming, Hudson separated the leg and thigh from one side. He then separated the drumstick from the thigh bone. After that, he removed the breast and wing from the same side. When he was done with that, he repeated the same technique with the other side. When finished, Hudson sliced the breast and thigh pieces for the platter that took center stage of the table.

And when that was done, Hudson repeated his culinary expertise on the second turkey, following the same techniques. When he was finished, the platter was placed on a side table, ensuring that everyone would have more than enough to eat. His carving signature was to pile the white meat of the turkey on one side while the dark meat was stacked on the other. The drum sticks were placed on either side.

The turkey meat was succulent and mouthwatering, as were all the fixings. Julia was showered with compliments as everyone enjoyed the food and the efforts going into its preparation. As far as dessert was concerned, the pies provided a sweet ending to the meal. The crusts were fluffy and the fillings tasty.

Once everyone had their fill and the table was cleared, the group donned sweaters and went outside to enjoy a traditional Thanksgiving bonfire. Hudson had gone outside before the others were done eating to start the bonfire and place chairs a safe distance away from the flames and sparks.

It was a fitting way to end Thanksgiving. A true Thanksgiving. All felt safe and secure in the company of friends, and the stars twinkling above in the cloudless sky and a bright yellow full moon provided a scenic lullaby for the day.

At one point, Abigail decided to stand. "I'd like to say a few words," she said. "First of all, I want to thank you for letting me stay with you on this beautiful farm. My time with you has been wonderful. I've not had a single boring moment. I learned so much from each of you, and I thank you for putting up with my constant questions. I thank you for your wonderful hospitality, especially today's delectable and sumptuous Thanksgiving meal."

She broke out in a wide smile. "I've got to admit, cooking is no specialty of mine. Whatever I make is either too raw, too bland, or too spicy. Often I can't even eat the meal I've slaved over." She looked over at Julia. "You, Julia, are a master chef and I've never eaten food so delicious and satisfying. I hope the boys sitting around the table appreciate the food you always put on their plates and the hard work that goes into it."

A wide smile creased Julia's face when she met Abigail's eyes. Her cheeks blushed.

Abigail shifted her weight from one leg to the other. "Now on to business." She hesitated for a moment to gather her thoughts.

Henry held his breath, not knowing what to expect. Neither did anyone else.

Abigail scratched behind her ear. "We agreed a week or so ago that I'd stay for a week to get a feel for the place and for all of you to get to know me. Right from the beginning, I liked what I saw. Good people, good horses, good shelters, all sitting on beautiful acreage. Now, as I look at each of you, I can say that I know all of you better, and I hope the same goes for you when you look at me."

She took a deep breath and continued. "I've looked at the jobs to be done, big and small. There's nothing in my vision that I can't do here, and this goes beyond training horses." She spoke with conviction. "There's much work to be done, some jobs long overdue," she added, "and I can help."

She continued. "If I'm lucky enough to be your final choice, I pledge to provide your steeds with regular exercise, proper feed, and needed nutriments. I'll muck out their stalls with Carl, and make sure their bedding is always fresh. If it's cold, I'll remove blankets in the morning and replace them in the evening during the winter months. I want you to know, too, that I enjoy all of the caregiving aspects of this job, from currying and brushing to bathing the horses. I enjoy working with veterinarians, farriers, blacksmiths, and saddlers."

She continued, "Beyond this, I have ideas on how and what to add to the herd, plus ways to promote horse-riding at the farm, and ideas about expanding the existing corrals and trails. Also, if you are going to add additional horses to the herd, the corrals need expansion." She paused. "To think of such possibilities is exciting, and if you hire me, I'd like to be part of how you map out these plans."

She sighed. "So, I guess I'm saying, if you want me, I'm sold on all of you and this farm. With your backing, I'd like to stay on board and be part of your family." She finished and breathed a sigh of relief, shrugged her shoulders, and finished. "I want you to think about what I just shared and talk amongst yourselves." She smiled. "If an offer comes my way, I'm going to need plenty of help unloading my flatbed and moving into one of the upstairs bedrooms." Her smile widened.

No one spoke, and the bonfire continued to crackle.

Then, out of the dark surroundings, the peaceful bonfire was no more.

From the driveway, a pair of headlights sliced through the night and found its way to the Cooper farm, crunching the gravel driveway. No one recognized the car. Once it pulled to a stop, two strangers got out, one on each side. They left the car headlights on.

All around the bonfire, everyone rose from their chairs, startled to see a car stopping by the farm this late. Henry approached the strangers, followed closely by Mickey. Henry didn't recognize the first guy he approached. He was big and bulky, as tall as well as imposing. Henry guessed he was at least six foot four and three hundred pounds. His head was shaven and his brow furrowed as he took a few steps toward Henry.

"Help you?" Henry smiled. "You fellas lost?"

The monster just smirked.

The second stranger pulled up alongside his companion. "We ain't lost," he said. "Just stopping by to spread a little holiday cheer, is all." He held up a wicker gift basket containing two bottles of wine, decorative ribbons tied around the neck of each bottle.

The voice was unmistakable and even in the darkness Henry could see that the second man was no stranger, of that he was certain.

Henry felt his smile slide away and a bead of sweat jump off his brow.

It was captain Bill Cameron, his violent and despised uncle.

Ten

For a moment, everything was frozen. No one spoke, no one moved an inch. The night air was still. Henry began getting a sound buzzing in his ears. He was dimly aware of Mickey standing by his side and the rest of the group clustered in back of him, still around the bonfire. His vision blurred and he tried to stay focused on his uncle. The monster took a step closer to Henry.

Mickey looked at Henry and muttered, "What's going on here, boss?"

Henry said sideways to Mickey, "Go find Hudson. I'll take care of this."

Mickey stiffened at the request, but took off immediately. He returned to Henry's side in less than a few minutes. He turned his head and said, "I can't find him, but the others are searching, looking for him."

"Go back and find him."

"No, I'm not leaving you alone with these two derelicts."

The captain overheard the muffled conversation and the news plastered a smile on his face. He leaned forward and put the gift basket on the ground in front of them. "Sergeant Delaney is here, too?" He rubbed his hands together. "Perfect. I can't wait to see that clown. He was an insult to the military and now is up here shoveling horse manure. Such a storied career."

The goon next to the captain laughed when he heard this. He had a high-pitched laugh, one you'd expect more from a school girl instead of a bodyguard.

Henry looked at his uncle up and down. He'd aged considerably since he last saw him. He'd lost much of his hair and his eyelids were heavy and drooping. Bags under his eyes were puffy and dark. His nose and his ears were oversized, especially his honker. He was overweight and pasty, his shirt and pants pulling against a bloated belly. A few buttons of his shirt had popped open. Even at the slight distance they kept, Henry smelled rancid body odor and alcohol.

Mickey piped up, unafraid of either of them. He wasted no time taunting the captain. "Captain Cameron, is that really you?" He tilted his head sideways and laughed out loud. "Last time I saw you, you had your sorry ass knocked into the Thames River by lieutenant Cooper. You'd just taken a haymaker to the side of your head and you were out on your feet. I gotta tell you, you were dead in the water that day." Mickey laughed out loud and rocked back on his heels. "You looked like a drowned rat. The big joke was that not a single soul moved to toss you a life preserver. The camp's reaction was that you were a pariah, and no one wanted to save you."

The captain looked over and nodded to his bodyguard. The goon approached Mickey head-on and once there, slammed his fist into Mickey's ribcage, pummeling him to the ground. Mickey had tried holding an arm up to protect his body, but the punch was too powerful. He was hurt and he had trouble struggling to get back up on his feet.

The monster moved toward Henry as he balled his fists. "You're next, junior," he frothed at the mouth. "I'm going to kick your ass and give you a lesson on how to respect and listen to your uncle."

But the monster didn't reach Henry. In an effort to protect Henry, Mickey had gotten himself up off the ground and tried to tackle the giant from behind, but was easily elbowed and brushed aside. When he struggled to get up, the bodyguard turned and violently kicked him several times in his ribcage. The thug pawed at the ground with his feet, ready to inflict more pain, but the captain held him back.

When he finally was able to stand, Mickey held his arm and ribs where the blows landed, and returned slowly to Henry's side.

The blows hurt Mickey, but he pretended it was nothing. He straightened the best he could and looked at the lummox, tossing him a crooked smile. "That all you got, lard ass?" Mickey taunted. "Come on, let's have another go at it."

Henry looked over at the captain and said, "You know, my father always told me you were a pansy and a coward, even when you were a kid." He laughed. "No wonder you hired this dimwit to do your dirty work. God forbid if you ever had to do it yourself."

Out of nowhere came Julia, behind all of them. She cradled a shotgun in her arms, a Winchester M1897, one of the most common trench shotguns in World War I.

"You leave these boys alone right now," she hollered. "Who the hell do you think you are, trespassing on our private property and creating chaos? Get out of here or I'll start shooting." She looked at Mickey, who was hurt and hunched over in pain.

From behind her, another voice chimed in. "Julia, stop this."

She turned to find Hudson, moving quickly toward her. "Give me that shotgun, please, before anyone gets hurt."

Hudson stood by her side and gently took the shotgun from her. "It's okay, Julia," he said, "I'm here now."

They shared eye contact. She appeared shaken. "It's okay," he said, "let me handle this from here on, okay?"

She nodded slowly, tentatively, and relented. She went over to Mickey and put her arm around him. He grimaced in pain. No doubt, he was hurt bad.

"Take Mickey into the house, Julia," he said. "Let him sit and get his wind back. We'll be there shortly."

She nodded and helped Mickey to the door. They walked away slowly. Abigail and Carl decided to stay outside and stood off to the side to see what was going to happen next.

When Julia left, Hudson turned to the assailants.

Without any hesitation, he grabbed the shotgun and wrapped his right hand around the barrel while his left hand grasped the wooden stock. He calmly walked over to the goon and said, "I'm sorry. I apologize for the crude talk from the woman and her threats while holding this shotgun. No hard feelings, okay?"

The caveman nodded.

"Good," said Hudson. With that he slammed him viciously in the mouth with the butt-stock of the shotgun. The guy was knocked backwards and his legs buckled immediately, causing him to collapse and fall to the ground. He'd been knocked out and lay there unconscious.

Hudson walked over to the captain, Henry following.

"Why'd you do that?" the captain asked, his eyes widening.

"I'll give you two reasons. One, he hurt my friend. Second, I never liked baboons."

"He's hurt," replied the captain, looking at his fallen escort. "Can't you see that?"

"He's hurt? How terrible. He'll hurt more in the morning, trust me. I suggest you organize a search party as soon as you get home to locate the teeth he's missing. He might like his new hillbilly look, but who knows? Either way, he's gonna have to get used to eating soup through a straw for quite some time."

Hudson summoned Henry to search the bodyguard for weapons and Henry returned with a pistol, a heavy sap and a switchblade. Hudson collected all the weapons and shook his head. "First thing tomorrow morning, I'll be dropping these off at the sheriff's office, along with a complaint that you were trespassing on private property and threatening this family." He scoffed at the captain. "I'm gonna put you behind bars. Both you and that idiotic knuckle dragger over there will be taken into custody."

The captain shook his head. "Who the hell do you think you are, Wild Bill Hickok?"

Hudson tilted his head. "Nope, I was thinking more along the lines of Doc Holliday."

The captain just sneered.

"So, fill me in you drunken sot. Why are you here?" asked Hudson.

"I need to talk with Henry."

"About what?"

"It's private," said the captain, "plus it's none of your business."

Hudson replied, "Talk now, while your mouth still works." He held up the shotgun for emphasis. "You'll never have privacy so long as I'm around."

The captain looked over at his partner who was still knocked out. He'd be of no help.

Hudson said, "Let's be clear about some matters. I want to say that I can't stand the sight of you, never could. I was told everything by lieutenant Cooper. He shared how you threw a punch at Henry in Boston when he discovered that you and Henry's mother slept in the same bed. Henry intervened and stood up for his mother and you decided to teach him a lesson. You decided to deliver a punch to the side of the kid's face. The bruise left behind a black and blue mark that looked like an eggplant for over a month."

He continued. "You're a real tough guy, beating up a teenager. You never checked on him, you never visited. Hell, you never even checked on his mother when she was dying in a Boston hospital. You stole from her, you used her. Plus, you stayed in her apartment without her permission when she was gone. Lieutenant Cooper told me you trashed the place, you drunken derelict. And if that wasn't enough, you snuck up on the lieutenant and knifed him, sending him to the hospital."

The look on Hudson's face was pure hatred, dark and dangerous. His eyes narrowed and Henry could see the tendons in Hudson's neck bunched in anger. "So, what are you after here? What do you want?"

The captain coughed up some phlegm and spat it on the ground. "I want to arrange a financial settlement with Henry."

Hudson gritted his teeth. "You're after Henry's money? You're joking, right?"

"I just want what's fair, I want what's mine."

Henry was stunned. "What do you mean, you want what's yours?" Henry asked.

The captain looked at Henry, acting as if Henry had just appeared out of thin air. "Here's why I needed to talk with you. When your father went out to sea a few years ago and you were away at that summer midshipman's camp, your mother and I fell in love. Your mother and father hadn't been getting along for a long time. She was lonely in Boston and wanted companionship. I was available and we spent a lot of time together. One thing led to another, and we ended up sleeping together. That's how you found us that Sunday morning when you and your old girlfriend Lily Corwin unexpectedly dropped in to visit."

The captain continued. "I'm sorry things turned ugly that morning and I shouldn't have hit you. But you were giving your mother a lot of backtalk and guff. All I was trying to do was protect her."

This angered Henry and he snarled, "And this gave you the right to punch me in the face when I wasn't looking?"

The captain cast his eyes downward. "I'll say again, I'm sorry."

Henry glared at him. "You're not sorry, and you're a liar. If you were really sorry, why didn't you visit her in the hospital? Why didn't you attend her funeral? And now, why would you show up here tonight with weapons and an animal to protect you? Why would you hurt my friend Mickey?" He stood there shaking his head. "You're dirty, you always were."

Hudson felt the need to cut in. "Do you honestly believe you have a right to any of Henry's inheritance?" asked Hudson.

"I do."

"Judas Priest, why would you think that?"

The captain looked back and forth at the two of them. He appeared to swallow hard, then continued, focusing on Henry. "You never returned home after your cadet camp was over. In fact, your mother never heard from you again. No letters, no phone calls, no visits. Nothing. You disappeared from her life. She didn't know what to think."

"I wanted nothing to do with her."

"She recognized that."

The captain said, "In the meantime, she started getting sick. She said to me she wanted to get her affairs in order. This prompted her to start revising her inheritance, which up until that time identified you as the sole beneficiary. She wanted to change that document since you'd disappeared from the face of the earth. She wanted me to receive half of my brother's pension and savings. I resisted at first, then realized without you, she had no one left to receive her inheritance. She hired a lawyer and the last I knew, he was in the process of finishing her last will and testament. My brother's pension and savings would be divided in half between the two of us."

"Bullshit," said Hudson in a huff. "Show me the legal backing for this."

"My attorney will have everything prepared in a legal document."

"And how much are you expecting?" asked Henry.

"I figured one-half of your father's pension and savings would amount to about ten thousand dollars."

Henry lowered his head in disbelief, chuckling softly to himself. This guy was batty.

Hudson looked the captain square in the eye. Hudson's whole demeanor was growing in severity by the minute. "You're a little late on the estate settlement, which was completed long ago. Under the current legal settlement, you are a nonentity."

"I beg to differ, Delaney. I'm entitled to reimbursement. You're wrong to say I get nothing. Papers being drawn up by my lawyer clearly state my case."

"I'll tell you right now, you'll get nothing from Henry's inheritance. I repeat, nothing. The inheritance is old news and so are you. It's done, it's over."

"You're not hearing me Delaney. Legal papers are being prepared."

"Our attorney will be waiting for them," countered Hudson.

Hudson added, "I'll say again that I will be paying a visit to the town's sheriff. I'll make sure he understands how you intruded and disrupted our Thanksgiving festivities. I will share how you and your goon showed up unannounced to our farm with firearms and other lethal weapons, plus how your sidekick resorted to physical violence."

Hudson handed the shotgun to Henry.

"In the meantime, get your huckleberry ass off of our property." Hudson reached over and grabbed the captain by the shirtfront up around his neck. "I've given you fair warning tonight. Don't ever set foot on this property again. Are we clear?"

The captain nodded.

"Plus, stop kidding yourself about this inheritance bullshit. You're a lunatic and a slobbering drunk." He paused. "And if you ever lay a finger on Henry Cameron or Mickey Parker again, I'll kill you with my bare hands. The same goes for anyone else you threaten in our family." He hesitated. "You got all that?"

The captain nodded once more.

Hudson said, "Now go pick up that cave dweller over there and the two of you get out of my sight." The ogre was stirring and was starting to sit up. His open mouth was a bloodied and swollen mess, as black as a darkened mine shaft.

The captain helped the bodyguard to his feet and steadied him as they walked to the car. When they walked past Hudson, the thug turned toward him and said, "I'm gonna kill you," but with his smashed mouth it came out, "*I gwana quil wu.*"

Hudson snorted and replied, "Really? Tell you what, once you get that mouth of yours fixed and you can speak proper English, give me a holler and I'll introduce you to the other end of that shotgun. In the meantime, keep moving, you toothless birdbrain."

Once they got in the car and started backing up, Hudson held up his hand. "Here's your gift of wine," he said as he threw both the gift basket and bottles into the back seat.

"Wait," Hudson said. "How'd you find this place anyway?"

"A female friend of Henry's," said the captain. "We're staying at an apartment this woman is renting."

Henry heard his name and sidled closer to the car. "What woman?" he asked.

"Her name is Maeve Adair. She has an apartment on top of a clothing store in town."

Henry's heart raced when he heard this. He remembered asking her about that apartment the last time he was in town.

She needed to be warned.

Eleven

Once the car left the driveway, everyone was told to go inside and gather in the living room. They were as quiet as they were numb as they shuffled along the pathway to the house. Julia observed everyone as they walked by, both young and old. Their faces reflected a wide range of emotion, from anger and resentment to shock and disbelief.

Julia went to the kitchen and made some coffee_and sliced some banana bread. Henry was the last person to enter the house and he immediately scanned those who'd taken a seat.

"Mickey," he announced as he scanned the room. "Where's Mickey? Is he upstairs in his bedroom? Would someone please go check?"

Abigail was the first to respond and took to the stairs. Her bedroom was two doors down from Mickey's.

After a short pause she shouted from the top of the staircase that she needed help. Henry went to the stairs immediately taking two at a time, and racing upstairs.

Mickey had removed his sweater and his undershirt was torn and bloodied. He was bare chested and still wore his prosthesis. The prosthesis was bloody. "I need help getting this off," he said, looking at both Henry and Abigail. "I've been sliced somewhere and any movement I make causes more bleeding. Can you help?"

"Of course," said Henry, "just let me look and see what you've got going on. Abigail, why don't you fetch us some hand towels from the bathroom across the hallway."

Henry carefully removed Mickey's undershirt and spent a few minutes inspecting the wounds. When he finished, he slid a chair over from a nearby desk and sat down facing Mickey. "Okay, you have at least two deep lacerations that I can see, maybe a few more. It appears that two of the buckles on the prosthesis straps broke free and sliced into you. I can see one that is embedded in you pretty deep. Your prosthesis also splintered and several splinters have pierced you pretty deep. We need to get the prosthesis off so that I can see the entire residual limb."

While Abigail used the towels to apply pressure to the visible lacerations, Henry and Mickey worked in tandem to carefully remove the prosthesis. It was soaked in blood on the inside and a third deep laceration was visible on Mickey's limb where the top of the prosthesis sat. Bleeding was heaviest there, largely because another buckle had broken off and embedded itself in another deep wound. Abigail immediately took another towel and applied pressure to that location.

While she stood next to him, Abigail looked at Mickey with heartache. In addition to the lacerations, Mickey's ribcage on the left side was already swollen and starting to discolor from the kicking. Sadness clouded Abigail's features and she had to bite her lower lip as she studied the trauma.

Henry felt the same, but for different reasons. He had a chance to observe Mickey from behind while Abigail applied pressure to his many wounds. He was shocked to see how damaged he was from the war, wounds that Mickey never talked about. He saw the back of his neck, how it was pitted with scars and burns. Some of the wounds had been stitched and scarring seemed to be everywhere. His back was peppered with larger scars in addition to several large burn marks. The most visible were around his shoulder blades, giving his skin a thick and leathery appearance.

"I'm sorry that you have to see me like this," Mickey said, lowering his head.

"Nonsense," Abigail replied. She shushed him quiet and gently squeezed his good arm. "There's just more of you to like and love, is all." Her eyes watered. "You were brave trying to protect Henry," she said, swiping a tear away, "and that wasn't lost on any of us."

Mickey spoke sideways. "You still there, Cameron?"

"I'm here." He stopped staring at Mickey's back. "How's the pain level, mate?" asked Henry.

"I ain't doing too good, boss man. Lower back is killing me. I was kicked pretty good after the first punch, but then that monster turned and kicked me all over. He liked to kick me with those high-rise boots of his."

"Dirty shots, but Hudson made him pay."

Mickey shot him a weak smile. "That he did."

Henry sent Abigail downstairs to fetch Julia, some whiskey, and bandages.

When she left, Mickey said, "I ain't going to no hospital, so get that out of your head right now. I know how your mind works, Cameron."

"That figures," Henry muttered. "Well, like it or not, I'm taking you to see Dr. Drake first thing tomorrow morning. He's our family physician and a good man. He's the one I was telling you about who treated the lieutenant when he fell sick. You'll like him."

The two exchanged a glance. Henry asked, "So do we have a deal that we'll go in the morning?"

Mickey hesitated, then nodded. "Okay, we've got a deal." He turned to Henry. "By the way, do you remember when that goon threw me to the ground and kicked me like a dog?"

"Who can forget that sideshow?"

"I just want you to know that I had him right where I wanted him, and he knew it."

That got them both laughing but Mickey had to stop because his ribcage hurt too much. He held his belly in pain and realized that it was getting harder to draw a breath. Deep down, he knew that he'd absorbed a savage, vicious beating.

By that time, Julia arrived with Abigail in tow, fresh supplies in hand.

Julia took one look at Mickey and her hand flew to her mouth. "What in the Sam Hill is going on here?" she exclaimed. She immediately took charge replacing the bloodied towels, using an antiseptic to cleanse the wounds, and applying bandages with tight wraps to the multiple lacerations.

Julia was fairly certain stitches would be needed for the wounds. She agreed with Henry that hardware was likely lodged in the deep lacerations, but admitted that removing these buckles was beyond her medical capability. When it appeared that the bleeding from all of the lacerations had ceased, she bathed the residual limb with warm soap and water. Once that was done, she inspected Mickey's bruised and swollen ribcage. She winced as she looked closer and surveyed the swelling and the discoloration that had already begun to spread. She didn't like what she saw. The risk of serious internal injury scared her.

Julia agreed that Mickey needed to be examined and treated by Dr. Drake in the morning. She told Henry that she would call his home phone in the morning and hopefully talk with him before he left for his office. Perhaps he could stop by, which he did almost every day when the lieutenant had been struck down by the Spanish Flu.

Henry added, "I've got to call Maeve and tell her what happened."

"I wouldn't call her now. It's late. Call her first thing in the morning."

Henry nodded.

They turned their attention back to Mickey and getting him into clean clothes. Mickey winced in pain as Julia helped him put on a clean undershirt and a sweater. Henry handed him a shot glass of whiskey, which he downed in one gulp. He winced, but opted for another shot and asked for drinking company. Henry obliged and took a shot, even Abigail knocked one back.

Almost immediately, Mickey's world became fuzzy, and the pain relaxed. He grimaced less and his frown lines smoothed.

Meanwhile, Julia focused her energies on Mickey's prosthesis. She picked it up and asked Mickey what the protocol was for cleaning it.

Mickey said, "You'll see everything you need in the bathroom across the hall. It should be easy to find. You'll also find everything laid out on the counter by the sink.

Julia was instructed to cleanse the outside of the prosthesis, most notably the blood that seeped from his residual limb. She then was instructed to clean the inside of the prosthesis with a damp cloth and mild soap. She was told to wash the part of the socket that touched his skin, but warned not to immerse the prosthesis fully in water. Moreover, she was advised to wipe off the soap with a clean cloth and dry the prosthesis completely. To prevent bacterial growth, Mickey asked Julia to use a scrub brush to get inside the socket to cleanse it even more, and once that was done, to leave it out to air-dry overnight.

When Julia was finished, she went back into Mickey's bedroom. The mood there seemed lighter and much more relaxed. Mickey was still obviously in pain, but enjoying the attention and company. Given his whiskey consumption, his eyelids drooped and his eyes glazed over.

Julia tidied up the bedroom and looked at Mickey. "Since you're all clean and bandaged, what would you like to do now?" she asked.

Mickey didn't hesitate. "I'd like to go downstairs and be with my friends."

He made an effort to rise from the bed, but once standing, needed Henry to steady his gait. He took the stairs slowly. He wore the pain on his face but made it to the living room and was guided to one of the favorite overstuffed chairs. Henry elevated Mickey's feet and placed them on a footstool. He looked comfortable, save for his left side, which he favored and protected with his right arm.

Hudson was the first to come over to him. For a minute or two he just stood with his hands on his hips in front of Henry. He finally broke into a grin. "I knew you were always a bulldog, but taking on a three-hundred-pound giant?"

"I tried, Hudson. I really did, but he was just too damn big." To talk was to hurt, so Mickey kept his comments to a minimum.

Hudson recognized Mickey's pain and reached down and tousled his hair with one hand. "You did good, Mickey. You can cover my back any day." He turned and walked to the middle of the living room. He had things that he needed to say and knew that Henry did too.

———————

Hudson raised his voice and said, "Everyone, let's gather around for a minute or two. Find a comfortable seat and get yourself into a relaxed position. Of course, as you can see, Mickey has already stolen the most comfortable seat in the whole house." This drew polite laughter from everyone except Carl, who instead of laughing politely, burst out in uproarious, side-splitting laughter. Julia let him carry on for a few seconds before she hushed him quiet.

Hudson was joined by Henry in the center of the room. Henry cleared his throat and spoke first. "What you witnessed tonight was unfortunate. Those men were wrong in terms of what they did and what they demanded. Furthermore, they did it in front of you, my family. I will protect all of you at all costs and I know Hudson will do the same."

Henry was silent for a moment, then looked at Mickey. "They inflicted pain and injury on my best friend. Mickey is like a brother to me, and when he hurts, I hurt." He paused again. "We'll take him to the doctor first thing tomorrow morning and he'll be back on his feet in no time. Just wait, you'll see."

Henry took in a deep breath and let it out slowly. "All of you had the opportunity to overhear what this fracas was all about. The captain you saw this evening is indeed my uncle, my father's brother. He is not a nice man. When my father was away at sea during the war, he took it upon himself to move in with my mother and she in turn broke her wedding vows by allowing this to happen. When both my father and mother died, this man felt he was entitled to part of our family inheritance but there is no legal basis for this. He's tried to strong-arm me several times for money, like he did tonight, but to no avail. I'll be visiting with my attorney to inform him what happened tonight. Both Hudson and I will also be visiting with the town sheriff to inform him about what happened."

Henry turned to Hudson. "I think you also have something to say."

"Yes, I do. I was over in the garage locking everything up for the night when the fireworks started. I rushed back to see what was going on. When I arrived, I saw Julia holding a shotgun pointed at the two intruders. At that point, Henry was stooped over helping Mickey to his feet. One was a giant and I knew I wouldn't be able to bring him down without a weapon." Hudson looked at Julia. "That's when I took the shotgun out of your hands and approached that big moron. To distract him and relax his defenses, I apologized for your behavior—overly so—and when he let his guard down, I clouted his ugly puss." He hesitated for a moment. "Everything I said about you to him was untrue and he fell for it hook, line, and sinker." Hudson sneered at the memory of it. "That circus clown was as stupid as he was dumb."

Hudson looked over at Mickey. "We have a real hero in the room, the guy who stole the most comfortable chair tonight." Mickey had to smile at that. Hudson said, "Here's someone who gets slammed to the ground by a three-hundred-pound ape, yet gets up and tries to tackle the bastard, all in an effort to protect his best friend and family. In the cavalry we call that gallantry, in the cavalry we say that when you bloody your knuckles for a fellow trooper, you've earned your keep." He looked at Mickey. "Son, you've earned your keep."

Mickey smiled again and heads nodded. It got quiet for a moment.

———————

Abigail stirred on the couch. She cleared her throat. "I don't want to speak out of turn but I believe there's another hero in the room."

"And who might that be?" Hudson asked.

"You."

Hudson hiked his brow, his cheeks blushed.

"Yes, you. You possessed the bravery to approach that evil man, knock him out, then dress-down the captain. That took strength, that took courage. He even threatened to kill you when he left." She shook her head. "Personally, I wanted you to hit that monster again."

Carl piped up. "Yeah, I wanted someone to punch him again too, then while he was on the ground, that jerk needed to be kicked in the gut. He needed a taste of his own medicine."

Hudson shook his head and replied, "No, Carl, only a fool would do something like that."

Carl's whole face lit up immediately. "I'll do it."

Henry and Hudson looked at each other, both trying hard to stifle a smile. Julia looked at the two of them and did the same. She touched Carl's arm and held a finger up to her lips, a gesture for silence. She said, "Let's settle down now, Carl. Henry has more to say."

Henry stepped forward. "Okay, we need to discuss just a few more things before we call it a night. It's approaching midnight and

I know you're all tired from a long day. Tomorrow will be hectic. We need to get Mickey to the doctor's office to get him patched up, plus we need to visit the town sheriff and report what happened. I want both of those men put behind bars. They apparently are renting an upstairs apartment above the town's clothing store. I think all of you except Abigail know Maeve Adair. She needs to be warned." Henry paused for a few seconds. "While all of this is going on, please watch over the farm, help each other out like we always do. Carl, I'd like to ask that you tend to the horses as usual but also to help move Abigail's belongings into her room from her flatbed."

All of a sudden, Henry stopped in the middle of a sentence and stared wide-eyed at Abigail.

"Wait a minute," he said, "Before the trouble tonight, you announced that you accepted the position. Given what happened this evening, I need to ask if you still want the job. Do you?"

She didn't hesitate, instead looking Henry square in the eye. "Do I still want the job? Are you serious? I want it now more than ever."

Twelve

Julia awoke to unfriendly dreams in the early morning, the sun barely up. She'd slept fitfully during the night. Carl was sound asleep next to her, snoring loudly, and didn't move as she swung her legs out of bed and got dressed. The events of last night weighed heavily on her. Of course, the violent interaction that took place in the driveway was terrifying to watch, as well as witnessing the brutal injuries to Mickey. Thanksgiving had ended in a true nightmare.

Julia snapped out of it. She left the caretaker's cottage and walked briskly to the farmhouse. Once there, she found both Henry and Mickey in the living room. She'd later discover that Henry had stayed awake the entire night tending to his friend, having moved a cushioned chair and an extra hassock next to Mickey. Both were wide awake.

She took one look at the two of them and smiled. "Well, good morning gentlemen. I didn't expect to see both of you up."

"I wanted to keep this guy company," replied Henry. "He's a big baby, still afraid of the dark."

Mickey grinned a bit, but it came across as a feeble and frail attempt. His color was off, pasty bordering on ashen. Julia sat down on the armrest next to him. "Tell me how you're doing, Mickey." There was a calm demeanor in the way she spoke.

Mickey tried to straighten in the chair. When he did, the movement created a sharp pain that cut into the left side of his rib cage and below his breast bone.

"I hurt all over, Julia," he said. "I can't lie."

She asked if he could stand. He did so, even though his blanket was bunched around his waist. He did his best to try, but needed Henry's assistance to stand straight. He tried standing on his own, but was wobbly.

She asked if he could lift his sweater so that she could examine and assess the damage. He did so, exposing the contusions on his body. She winced when she surveyed the damage. Overnight the bruises had turned purple with dark blue coloration encircling the primary contact points. The bruises were grotesque, both swollen and inflamed. Julia gently touched his areas of injury. Mickey winced when she did.

Julia helped him to sit back down in the cushioned chair. He did so with great effort.

When Julia looked over at Henry, they exchanged nervous glances. Both recognized the severity of the damage as well as the need for immediate medical attention.

Julia excused herself to brew some coffee and make some phone calls. She first called Dr. Drake from the telephone in the hallway, and spoke in hushed tones. She expressed her concern about Mickey's injuries and asked that he stop by on his way to work.

She returned and announced, "Good news. Dr. Drake will be here on his way to his office. He's concerned about Mickey's injuries. He'd like to take a look at him before we do anything."

Dr. Horace Drake was no stranger to the Cooper farmhouse and was always a welcome guest. He'd treated the Cooper family for years. In years gone by, he went out of his way to stop by and check daily on the lieutenant, who'd been stricken with the Spanish flu. He stayed with the lieutenant until the very end, and with his gentle persuasion and medical guidance, enabled the family to create a peaceful and humane way of letting go.

Mickey had never met the doctor, a fifty-something, hardy-looking man. He'd been Julia's family physician for years and according to her was a good, reliable family doctor. Julia greeted him at the front door and ushered him inside to meet Mickey, who was sipping a glass of juice in his chair.

Dr. Drake entered the living room, and immediately recognized Henry and went over to shake hands. They hugged each other. They'd grown close caring for lieutenant Cooper, a grueling stretch of time that knitted the two together.

The doctor was in his fifties, in shape and hardy-looking. He wore a red plaid flannel shirt, khaki pants, and hiking boots. He'd lost his wife a decade ago, but rather than mourning his loss, he instead invested his energy into his patients. His unrelenting care and support earned high marks within the community. He was as trusted as he was worshipped. He'd also earned high marks when he cared for Julia's husband, Carl, when he fell and incurred serious head wounds tending to a landscaping project on the Cooper farm.

Dr. Drake introduced himself to Mickey and pulled up a footstool next to him.

"Julia tells me you're having a rough go of it, lad. Said you were punched and kicked pretty good last night."

Henry nodded.

He looked at both Mickey and Julia. "Was this reported to the police?"

Julia replied, "Hudson is in town with the sheriff as we speak."

"Did this violence happen in town?"

"No, this happened in our back yard. Two thugs trespassed on the property and did this to Mickey, along with other invasions of our privacy."

The doctor shook his head and returned his attention to Mickey. "Is it okay if I look at the injuries?" he asked, promising that he wouldn't inflict any more pain. "I won't hurt you," he promised. He asked Mickey to stand, both Henry and Julia helping to steady him. Dr. Drake asked that he remove his sweater and undershirt, and he needed help with this too.

The sight of Mickey's naked upper-body made Dr. Drake furrow his brow. As Julia observed earlier, Mickey's swelling on his left side had increased, the bruising more pronounced. The discoloration of the bruising had spread to his abdominal cavity and upwards to his chest. Most of his residual limb was also starting to discolor.

Dr. Drake immediately reached into his medical satchel and withdrew his stethoscope. He said to Mickey, "This will give me a better idea of what we're dealing with in terms of potential internal damage. The stethoscope will help me listen more closely to the sounds generated by your heart, lungs and intestinal tract."

Mickey nodded. "Go ahead," he murmured.

Dr. Drake began his examination, pressing the diaphragm of his stethoscope against Mickey's chest with an emphasis on his heart and lungs. When he was done, he moved behind Mickey to further examine his lungs. He looked at Mickey's back before continuing, seeing first-hand a soldier's battle scars from shrapnel, burns from phosphorous bombs, as well as deep lacerations from barbed wire.

He paused to look at Mickey's residual limb. "Bullet wound cause this?"

Mickey shook his head. "Artillery shelling."

Dr. Drake looked over at Henry. He knew the two of them shared the same sentiment, the atrocious death of millions, the sadness of damaged survivors, the futility of war.

When he was finished with his examination, Dr. Drake put his stethoscope away in his satchel and dug around until he found a container of pills. He gave Mickey two and handed the container to Julia. "You're in charge of these, Mrs. Dawson. Put them in a safe location. The directions are on the label."

"Take these two now?" asked Mickey.

"Yes, wash them down with the rest of that juice you're drinking. They're pain pills and will help with your discomfort and distress."

Dr. Drake sat back down on the footstool facing Mickey.

Mickey slouched in his chair. He winced from the pain. His brow was dotted with beads of perspiration.

———————

The doctor leaned forward, fingers knotted together. "So, where were you stationed?"

"Cambrai, France."

"You're young, I must say. How old were you when you enlisted?"

Mickey hung his head and hesitated. "Seventeen, sir."

"I'm told horrible warfare took place in those trenches."

Mickey nodded. "A living hell everywhere, not just in Cambrai."

Dr. Drake took a deep breath and his shoulders sagged. "You are a patriot and I bow to your bravery." He paused and slowly shook his head. "But you shouldn't have been over there."

"I realize that now, sir. I regret enlisting, I made a huge mistake."

The doctor leaned forward and asked Mickey to extend his right arm, checking his pulse on the underside of the wrist. He was silent for a minute, then frowned. Finally, he asked about the lacerations on Mickey's residual limb. Julia described them as well as the imbedded buckles. Since the bleeding had stopped, Dr. Drake chose to deal with the three wounds later.

Julia asked, "If his wounds need sutures isn't it too late for this procedure?"

"When did this altercation take place?"

"Last night close to midnight."

The doctor did a quick calculation in his head. "The wounds are still suturable this morning."

He told Mickey it was okay to put his sweater and undershirt back on. This time, both Julia and Abigail helping him.

Dr. Drake waited for Mickey to sit back down. He cleared his throat. "Mickey, you're banged up pretty good inside, I think you know that." He hesitated a bit. "You're going to need help beyond what I can offer."

Mickey didn't respond, instead, he tilted his head to one side and stared out the window.

Everyone in the room looked at each other, waiting for Mickey to respond.

Finally, he did. "What kind of help are we talking about?"

"You're going to need hospitalization. I'm worried about your left lung on the side you were traumatized. You need to have your lungs examined with equipment that I simply don't have available."

"No," Mickey said firmly. "No more hospitals. I had enough during the war." He stiffened in his chair. "I hated the hospitals, the pain, the medicine, the doctors. I hated all of it. I still have horrible memories of my time there, the crying and shrieking of others in my ward, the stench of the place, my own pain, the bedpans, the nightmares. Nope, I won't go back."

Dr. Drake said, "Mickey, listen to me. Please hear me out. You aren't going back to any of those war hospitals overseas. I'm sure they were awful but you're home now. Our hospital here is a good one and all I'm recommending is for the medical staff there to run some diagnostic tests on you, that's all."

All became quiet.

"Do you think I'm in harm's way?" asked Mickey.

"I'm concerned with what I'm seeing." He forced a smile. "I think you're exhibiting classic symptoms of a punctured lung. You've suffered blunt trauma to your side and chest, and the pain has apparently spread to your shoulder and back. You're exhibiting shortness of breath, made worse by your coughing. If it is indeed a punctured lung, your body is receiving reduced oxygen levels, which can explain your increased heart rate. Of course, we'll know all of this better after some tests are run on you."

Mickey folded his arms across his chest. "So, what's the plan?"

"I'll call from here and we'll get an ambulance to transport you to the hospital."

"Now?"

"Yes, now."

"Why do I need an ambulance?"

"Because I'm not sure how damaged your left lung is, plus I don't want to risk any further damage. I also don't know if you have any other internal injuries."

Mickey bit his lower lip. "What will happen at the hospital?"

Dr. Drake was both patient and truthful. "The folks at the hospital will take X-rays, which will produce images of the structures inside your body. It will give us a better idea as to what kind of damage your left lung experienced compared to your right lung. They'll be able to see any other internal damage." He paused. "Your lacerations will also be treated. If the cuts are as deep as Julia described, you're going to need sutures."

"What about my shortness of breath? Sometimes I feel like I'm panting."

"That's what concerns me. If that continues, they may hook you up to what's called a pulmotor, which is a device that helps you take breaths if you're struggling."

"How does it do that?"

"It creates what's called positive pressure ventilation. Basically, you will be fitted with a face mask and oxygen is disbursed until a set pressure is reached in the lungs, at which point the device switches to exhalation, thus creating breaths for you."

Mickey looked puzzled.

Dr. Drake said, "Let me push aside the medical terms. The device will blow fresh air or oxygen into your lungs."

Mickey nodded and appeared weary. The pain pills were beginning to look like they were taking hold.

"You okay, lad?" asked the doctor.

Another nod.

"Okay, let's move on. We should address your residual limb. Do you have a prosthesis for it?"

Julia located it in the corner of the living room and brought it over to the doctor. Although it had been thoroughly cleaned, it had broken straps, missing buckles, and splintering at the top.

"Do you know of anyone who can fix this?" asked Julia.

"As a matter of fact, I do. A friend of mine. He's done quite a few of these. If you wish, I could take this with me when I leave and drop it off. He'll fix it."

"We'd be grateful if you could do that."

He looked at Mickey. "You know, they're making lightweight metal prostheses now. Much easier for you to manage. This wooden one is quite heavy. I'll see what I can do about that."

With that he asked if he could use the telephone to call the hospital. When he returned, he announced that an ambulance would arrive in fifteen minutes or so. He asked Julia for his overcoat, slipped it on, and gathered his belongings.

He huffed at the suggestion of payment for the home visit, then said goodbye to everyone in the room. He told Julia he had patients that he needed to see at his office.

Before leaving, though, he sat back down on the stool facing Mickey. He looked at Mickey and held his gaze for a long moment, then reached for his right hand. They shook and the doctor held the grasp while he talked. "Listen to me, son. You're going to be okay, trust me. You'll also meet some fine people while you're at the hospital. I'll bring the doctors up to speed when I get back to my office. Let them proceed with their testing. In the meantime, I want you to keep your chin up and stay strong. You're going to be okay."

He squeezed Mickey's hand. "Can you do that for all of us?"

Mickey smiled. "Yes sir, I can do that."

"That's good," he replied, satisfied. He patted Mickey's knee as he stood and headed for the door. As he paused to button his overcoat, his heart suddenly felt heavy, his mood gloomy. He'd been profoundly touched by this boy soldier, a youngster who had no business fighting in a grownups' war, but who nonetheless enlisted and now carried disfigurement for the rest of his life. The doctor realized tens of thousands of other underage boys had met with the same fate and ended up being shipped home, broken and damaged. What he saw this morning truly saddened him, a scarred survivor now being forced to deal with yet more physical injury, this time at the hands of local ruffians. The doctor's once-upbeat mood crumbled, sorrow now draping his face. He sighed and let out a breath.

He looked back at the boy soldier, gave him a little half-wave, and departed.

He would never see Mickey again.

Thirteen

Before the ambulance arrived, Mickey was given a sponge bath and dressed in clean clothes. Although he said he wasn't very hungry, Julia nonetheless prepared a cup of tea for him along with several slices of buttered toast sprinkled with cinnamon. Mickey ate most of it despite his earlier brush-off. By the time he was finished, the ambulance had pulled into the driveway.

The two ambulance attendants who entered the farmhouse were polite and as gentle as they were kind and efficient. They exchanged pleasantries with Julia and assured everyone that Mickey would have comfort and safe-keeping while journeying to the hospital. He was placed in a single cot affixed to the inside of the ambulance.

Before the ambulance left, the family gave its good wishes to Mickey.

Henry clenched his right hand around Mickey's, holding it close to his chest. "You'll mend, *compadre*," he said, "I know you will. You're tough and strong, plus I need you. Get better and come home where you belong."

Mickey nodded as he looked to Henry for strength. It was difficult for him to speak as he was laboring between breaths more markedly, all of which made his words unclear. His forehead still glistened with perspiration and his voice was hoarse. Henry raised his hand to indicate that he understood and backed away. Mickey nodded his approval. In turn, Julia, Abigail, and Carl shortened their goodbyes.

They watched as the ambulance backed out of the driveway then disappeared down the country road. Henry pulled away from the others and shared with Julia that he needed to contact Maeve Adair by phone. He retreated into the farmhouse and for the sake of privacy, unraveled the cord to the telephone until it reached into a nearby room.

Everyone came in from the outdoors and sat at the kitchen table while Julia and Abigail prepared breakfast. The group was quiet and spoke in soft voices. The silence in between was awkward, it was almost as if the house had become deserted. Of course, their minds were on Mickey's injuries and his well-being, but ever present were the sequences in last night's horrible attack.

All were terrified the strangers would return.

Henry returned from his telephone call. He came over to the kitchen table, pulled out an empty chair, and slumped in it. He was exhausted and like the rest of them, he'd managed little sleep. He rubbed his eyes with his fists.

Julia brought him a cup of coffee.

Before he had some, Henry coughed into his hand and shared that he'd just spoken to Maeve.

Everyone stopped what they were doing.

Henry said, "It is true that my uncle and that monster checked into Maeve's vacant apartment above the clothing store a week or so ago. We need to investigate this."

He took a sip of coffee.

"So how did these strangers interact once they arrived?" asked Abigail.

"They were alone, and admitted they were unfamiliar with the county. Maeve said she felt sorry for them. She added that the captain was polite and courteous, and very thankful for the accommodation, especially since it was a holiday. The big guy, on the other hand, said nothing.

Julia piped up. "But what about us? How did they find us? But then, Julia stopped. She threw her hands up and exclaimed, "I'm sorry, I didn't mean to interrupt. Please continue."

Henry nodded. He said, "They went up to their apartment, but not before asking where the Cooper farm was located. Apparently, the captain had visited the apple orchard as a child. She gave them directions and after that, they went upstairs to their apartment. It wasn't too long before they got into their car and disappeared during the late evening. She said she had no idea where they were going."

Henry had some more coffee. "According to Maeve, a few hours passed."

"Then what?" asked Abigail.

Henry cleared his throat. He hesitated, looked down at his hands, steepling his fingers. "Maeve said the two returned after an hour or so. It was late. She could clearly hear their car pulling into the driveway. She heard them up in their apartment talking and after a while the captain knocked on her door. He asked for some extra towels along with some water and some ice. He said they had to return to Boston for a little while. That was the last she heard from either one of them. She heard their automobile disappearing into the night."

Henry shook his head, then looked around the table at all of them. He lowered his voice. "You should know that Maeve feels terrible about all of this."

They all nodded. "Of course, Henry," Julia said. "But no one is blaming her. She had no idea what she was getting into."

They finished their breakfast quietly, heads bowed as they ate. Conversations were still quiet, laughter nonexistent.

————————

After a short while, Hudson arrived with the town sheriff. The group at the table straightened themselves as the two walked into the kitchen. Hudson introduced the sheriff around the table. The sheriff made an effort to approach Julia, but all he received from her was a clipped greeting. Julia turned away from him and busied herself clearing the table. Henry found this to be strange exchange and most unlike Julia.

The sheriff was a beefy fellow, about fifty-something, dressed in a forest green uniform. He had a hang-dog look about him and his lips naturally curled as if he were sneering at those around him. He wore a sheriff's badge attached to his front flapped pocket as well as a Sam Browne belt with a pistol stuck into its right-side holster. Handcuffs dangled from the side of the belt along with a bundle of keys on a ring.

The sheriff's name was Cormac Whittaker, a lifelong resident of Compton who served as sheriff for over 25 years. His father served as town sheriff before Cormac came on the scene. Cormac had the reputation of being a temperamental, gruff, no nonsense law officer. Henry had never met him before, while the lieutenant spoke of him sparingly while he was still alive.

The sheriff reported that Hudson had filled him in on the violence that occurred, in addition to bringing to his office the collection of weapons gathered that night. He also indicated that he'd be returning to the farm to gather more details and to complete an official police report.

As they sat at the table, Whittaker asked a flurry of questions so that he could learn more about the trespassers before he visited their apartment. He listened attentively to the events of the night as shared by everyone in the room. Henry noticed that he took a particular interest in Abigail and her version of the attack. He maintained eye contact with her and sported a wolfish grin a few times when she spoke.

After listening to the witnesses, the good news was that although the strangers had trespassed, nothing was stolen or damaged. The bad news was obviously the violence inflicted on Mickey. Whittaker said, "When they're found, both will be arrested. Until that happens, I'll be releasing warrants for their arrest."

The sheriff furrowed his brow and let out a breath. Henry thought he caught a whiff of liquor. The sheriff rose, adjusted his gun belt, and turned to leave. Henry got up as well. He and Whittaker looked at each other for a minute. "I'd like to go with you," said Henry. "I know Maeve Adair and I think I can help," he said.

Whittaker hesitated and straightened a bit when he heard Maeve's name, then said, "If you think you can offer assistance, your help would be appreciated." He added in a smug and smarmy way, "I know Maeve Adair, too."

Henry approached Hudson and thanked him for what he did. He also gave marching orders for the day, a wide-range of duties and responsibilities previously outlined to his crew. Henry added that he wanted Hudson to pick him up at the clothing store within an hour and together they'd drive to the hospital.

Henry climbed into the sheriff's police car and the two of them left the farm and headed for the clothing store. The first words out of the sheriff's mouth were, "Rumor has it you inherited the entire Cooper farm."

"That's true."

"Everything? Orchards, cornfields, horses?"

Henry nodded.

"All fifty acres?"

Henry nodded again.

"How'd you manage that? You special or something?"

The questioning irritated Henry. "I'm the property owner at the farm and that's all you need to know. The lieutenant got himself appointed as my legal guardian and willed everything to me after he passed."

The sheriff released a soft whistle. "You indeed must be special, Cameron. How're you doing with all that acreage and all the cash that goes along with it? I'm told you're now one of Compton's wealthiest citizens. You gonna turn this place over and sell it? You'd make a pretty penny on it, that's for sure. Hell, I'd even be interested in buying it."

Henry said, "I'm not going anywhere and the place is not for sale." He was starting to dislike the abrasiveness of this guy.

Whittaker looked over and smiled.

"What?" Henry said.

"You're a real pistol, aren't you? You some sort of tough guy?"

Henry didn't respond.

They drove for a few more miles.

Whittaker said, "You know, you look just like him."

"I've been told that."

Whittaker smiled, stole a look at the road, then looked back at him. "I mean it, the resemblance is amazing."

"So they say."

They kept driving.

The sheriff said, "Tell me about Mr. Parker. How'd you two meet up?"

Henry drew a deep breath and let it out slowly. "We met at a junior midshipman's camp in Uncasville, Connecticut. It was called the Junior Naval Reserve, one of the first of its kind. Mickey and I were close. We both wanted to enlist in the navy when we were done with our training, but that changed when the war broke out. Mickey and a few other cadets wanted to enlist in the American Expeditionary Force even though they were underage. They signed up and were shipped off to France."

"What about you? Why didn't you join your buddies?"

"Lieutenant Cooper talked me out of it. Plus, I'd just lost my father and my mother was stricken with the Spanish flu. I ended up losing her, too. The lieutenant offered me a job up here." He stopped for a moment, then said, "I had no family until I came up here."

The sheriff offered no sympathy or regrets.

The sheriff pushed on. "So, your pal Mickey Parker went to fight the Germans overseas and for his efforts came back home as a cripple."

Henry aimed a glare directly at him. "Calling someone a cripple is pretty harsh, actually pretty mean," he said.

"What, using the word cripple? Maybe you'd prefer gimp, or stumpy?" He snickered to himself.

Henry couldn't believe what he was hearing. "Were you ever sent overseas to fight the enemy, sheriff?"

The sheriff hesitated and after a few beats said, "No, can't say I was."

Henry muttered, "It shows."

"What's that supposed to mean, Cameron?"

"What I mean is simple, sheriff. Mickey Parker fought in France and came home a patriot and an amputee. His whole life was turned upside down. No help anywhere to be found." He let that sink in. "The last thing he needs in his life right now is someone calling him derogatory names."

The sheriff shot him a dirty look, accompanied by a smirk from that curled lip of his.

They drove a few more miles. Henry asked, "So, how'd you meet the lieutenant?"

Whittaker replied, "Tom Cooper and I grew up together."

Henry was surprised and hiked his eyebrows. "Really? It's funny, he never mentioned your name."

"Well, we hung out some. I lived about a mile down the road. I'd always hike up to the farm, find Tom, and together we'd terrorize the neighborhood, explore the woods, and of course, spend time with the horses. God, Tom loved those horses and had a special knack with each of them. Believe it or not, he'd whisper in each of their ears and I swear each horse understood what he was saying. The bond he created with each was incredible." He shook his head. "No wonder he became a pony soldier."

Henry said, "I was transfixed by the stories he'd tell. Especially when he joined up with Hudson."

"Hudson seems like a good man."

Henry nodded.

Whittaker continued with his recollections. "We also had some fun climbing up to the top of the barn roof." Whittaker dropped his chin to his chest and laughed. "Man, that rooftop was a sacred place. No one ever ventured up there, except the two of us. We spied on everyone up there." Whittaker laughed. "Tom would hide there so he wouldn't have to work. We'd hear his father calling out for him but Tom wouldn't budge. He'd just slink lower on the roof and laugh."

Henry said, "He once told me that someone dared him to pee from the edge of the roof, which he did. Were you that someone?" asked Henry.

"Can't lie, that was me," he said with another smirk.

"He still remembered those times. A while back we were repairing the roof and adding some new shingling. He told me how he didn't want you calling him a coward, so he did it. He said he was scared to death, but he didn't back down."

"I don't know what scared Tom, I mean, it was only a thirty-foot drop." Whittaker laughed heartedly at his own humor.

Henry didn't laugh. Instead, he said, "So when he got older, he left the farm."

Whittaker nodded. "Yep. He didn't have much of a relationship with his parents, and hated getting up to do farm chores." He scratched underneath his chin. "His father was an old coot, Henry couldn't stand him. So, when Henry got older, he took off one night, didn't tell anyone, and disappeared into thin air."

Henry remarked, "So he moved out West and joined the 7th cavalry."

"Right," said Whittaker. "Plus, he stayed away for what seemed like an eternity."

Henry said, "Did you know the lieutenant married and brought a baby boy into the world."

"No, I didn't know that."

Henry added. "But he lost both of them in a fire."

"I didn't know that either."

They lapsed into another silence as they continued the drive toward Compton.

Henry asked, "Did you see much of the lieutenant after he returned home?"

"Not really."

Henry had to admit, this had become a strange and strained conversation. The more the sheriff spoke, the less Henry was convinced that the two men were actually friends. While they might've grown up together, this hardly translated into an enduring and meaningful neighborhood friendship. Rather, they were acquaintances who'd drifted apart over the years, including the sheriff being oblivious to the tragedies besetting the lieutenant's life. This, plus the cold shoulder given by Julia to the sheriff mere hours ago as well as Whittaker's cruel and callous reference to Mickey's amputation cast him in a suspicious light.

The sheriff was odd and Henry couldn't figure him out. As they neared their destination, Henry was left guessing as to what the sheriff's motives were and what his deal really was. His behavior was both peculiar and slippery, perhaps duplicitous. An inner voice told Henry to stay away but to keep a watchful eye on this guy.

Fourteen

They pulled into Compton's main street. There weren't many people walking the sidewalks and those that did stopped and waved to the sheriff as he passed by in the police car. He looked at each and returned the greetings. They parked in front of the clothing store, and the two climbed out and entered the building. Maeve was waiting for them just inside the door.

She was first drawn to the sheriff. She grasped his hand with the two of her own. "Always good to see you, Cormac." She then gave Henry a friendly hug. Henry wasn't expecting the embrace, but didn't refuse it. She looked especially pretty this morning. She wore her auburn hair up in a bun and her green eyes were sparkling. She carried a scent of lilac.

"We've had some trouble and we need to talk with you," said the sheriff.

"I've heard," she said. "Why don't we go back to my office for some privacy."

It was quiet in the store, just a few customers milling around. They walked to the back of the store to her office and closed the door behind them. The office was arranged the same as it was when Henry visited a little while ago. The sheriff and Henry took a chair while Maeve settled in behind the desk.

"I'm sorry about the circumstances bringing us together this morning," Maeve said. She looked at Henry. "I'm truly sorry about Mickey." She hesitated. "How is he?"

Henry replied, "He's hurt pretty bad. He was taken by ambulance from the farm to the hospital early this morning. We think he has a punctured lung and probably some other internal injuries, but we'll have to wait and see. We're worried. I need to go to the hospital and check on him shortly. Hudson will be picking me up."

The sheriff took out his notebook and looked at Maeve. "What can you tell us about last night?" He hesitated in mid-sentence.

"Better yet, can you start at the very beginning and tell me how you met these two?"

Maeve thought for a moment. "Their telephone call came out of the blue. The upstairs apartment had just been vacated and given a fresh coat of paint and thorough cleaning. The captain was the one making the call and his timing was perfect. He inquired about the rental fee, deposit, and our location. He also asked if the apartment was located anywhere near the Cooper apple orchard. He said his family would often come up here to go apple picking."

Henry cut in. "Did he give you his full name over the phone?"

"What do you mean?" she asked.

"Did he just identify himself as a captain?"

"Yes, that was all."

"He never mentioned his last name was Cameron?"

Maeve shook her head.

"Never identified himself as my uncle?"

"Not once," she answered. "I had no idea he was your uncle."

Henry frowned. "Did he ever mention that he was looking for me?"

"No, Henry. Your name never came up."

The sheriff interrupted. "Let's not get too far ahead of ourselves." He looked at Maeve. "Okay, so what was your next contact with the captain?"

"He asked me to hold the apartment, which I did."

"Did he schedule a time when he could drive to Vermont and see the apartment?"

"He did, and said they would be up here in a few days."

"Who are 'they?'" asked the sheriff. All the while he was scribbling in his notebook.

Maeve hesitated. "The captain showed up with another guy. A big, burly man. Didn't speak, but looked imposing and dangerous. Scary, really."

The sheriff said, "Tell me how they made contact with you up here in Compton."

Maeve nodded. "They didn't make contact ahead of time. The two of them just arrived in a nice car. A big car. Once they parked, the captain introduced himself and I showed him the apartment."

"Was he satisfied?"

"Oh my, yes. The captain loved the apartment and expressed his satisfaction." She hesitated. "But the big, burly guy never left the car."

The sheriff and Henry looked at each other.

The sheriff said, "So I'm assuming the captain signed the register as well as the leasing documents needing his signature, yes?"

She didn't answer.

The sheriff said, "Maeve, I asked you a question. We need to see these documents." His expression changed as he frowned at her.

A few moments passed. Maeve hung her head. "I don't have any documentation on either one of them."

The sheriff was clearly perplexed. "What do you mean?"

She replied, "They never really registered."

The sheriff was taken aback. "How can this be? Everyone has to sign in, especially when entering into a rental agreement. Are you telling me you have no documentation on either one of these characters, yet you allowed them to stay on your premises without proper identification?"

She answered sheepishly. "I took them at their word."

"What does that mean?" asked the sheriff.

At first, Maeve didn't answer. She looked back and forth at the sheriff and Henry, realizing she had no choice.

Finally, she spoke. She tried to keep her voice steady but knew she appeared nervous. "They wanted the apartment, but only on a short-term basis, just a week or two. When I asked for a rental fee along with a deposit, the captain balked. He indicated that he was waiting on his monthly pension from the navy and would pay me in full when the check arrived."

Henry shook his head. "He was never in the navy."

It got quiet in the office.

Maeve was clearly embarrassed. "I made a mistake. I was wrong. I should've asked for personal identification and a deposit."

The sheriff asked, "Why didn't you?"

"I don't know. He said he was short of cash after the long drive to Vermont. He seemed sincere, convincing." She coughed politely into her hand. "He told me he traveled up here because he was about to come into a tidy sum of money." She hesitated. "I believed him, plus I needed the money after refurbishing the place."

The sheriff took a deep breath and let it out slowly. "Let me see if I have this right. You let the two of them stay on your premises, not knowing their identities, history, or intentions? And, you let them stay."

"That's correct," she mumbled. "How I handled things was wrong. Like I said, I took this man at his word and made a bad mistake." She looked at Henry. "I had no idea that all of this was connected to you." She swallowed hard. "I'm sorry." Her face reddened and she sighed with exasperation.

Henry chose not to respond. His shoulders sagged as he looked away.

The sheriff once again asserted his presence. "Okay, let's move on. Why don't you bring us up-to-date as to what happened last night."

Mauve hesitated at first, glancing at the ceiling. "It was late. I was not expecting any visitors. The captain was outside the door and said his friend had just experienced an accident."

"Did you see the injury?" asked the sheriff.

"Only a partial view," she replied. "His partner was standing behind the captain and holding a hand towel over an apparent wound to his mouth. I could see that quite a bit of blood had soaked the towel, plus he was in obvious pain."

"Did you ask how he received the injury?" asked the sheriff.

"I did, but I didn't get an answer."

"What happened next?"

"They requested ice and fresh towels, which I provided. The captain thanked me and the two of them left. I could hear their car driving away in the distance."

The sheriff asked to see their apartment.

Maeve hesitated at first, but then led them up a staircase to the apartment's entrance.

———————

When they opened the apartment door, the smell of old cigarette smoke and nicotine hit them square in the face. The bed was unmade, dirty linen piled in a corner. Empty liquor bottles were scattered about, bloodied towels left here and there along with droplets of blood on the hardwood floor.

"They've moved out," said Maeve.

"How can you tell?" asked Henry.

"They checked in with two duffel bags." She looked around again. "The bags are gone."

The sheriff asked, "Duffel bags?" He turned to Henry. "Didn't you say your uncle never served in the navy?"

Henry scoffed at the question. "That's what I said. My uncle never served in the navy."

Maeve acted surprised. "But wasn't he a naval captain?"

Henry straightened. "He was never a captain, although he liked to say he was. He was placed in charge of teenage cadets learning how to sail in that junior midshipman's camp I told you about. He was fired from that position and given a dishonorable discharge."

The sheriff and Maeve exchanged glances.

They walked around the apartment looking for clues but found nothing.

The sheriff rummaged through a desk and a bureau but came up empty-handed. No bills, no letters, no documents. He placed his hands on his hips and looked around, then walked to the center of the apartment.

"There's nothing here," he said. "Maeve's right, they're gone."

Henry continued to walk around the apartment. He followed the sheriff's tracks and double-checked his trail, looking under the bed, inside the closet, and underneath the furniture. He found nothing.

The sheriff was ready to leave and told Henry to meet him outside later. He'd finished his search, in Henry's mind a colossal, half-ass effort. The sheriff and Maeve both left, and went downstairs.

Henry was about to do the same when he spied something that caught his attention beneath the pile of dirty linen tossed in the corner. At first, he thought it was a piece of trash but as he got closer realized it was the curled edge of a photograph. He scooped it up and brought it over to the window for a better look. Henry looked at it and the images of people captured in the photo stared back. He recognized everyone, and seeing the images unnerved him.

It was a photo of his uncle Bill, who had his arm draped around his mother's shoulder while Henry stood by her other side alongside his father. The picture was taken at a picnic in a local park, and all four were smiling and happy. It was taken several years ago but Henry recognized it immediately, a moment frozen in time before his father was away at sea during the war. Since then, his mother had succumbed to the Spanish flu and his father had perished at sea, his ship having been torpedoed by a German submarine.

He remembered the photo and how it sat framed and sitting on shelving in his mother's old apartment in Boston. She kept it there forever, or so it seemed. The frame was obviously missing and the photograph, now worn and curled, had obviously been removed from the picture frame. It was a family keepsake that had been stolen from his mother's possessions, yet another cruel blow delivered by his uncle.

The photo brought back a flood of memories. It reminded Henry of the happy times he once shared with his family, when everyone got along and watched over each other, when love was absolute and unconditional. But looking at the photo now, the image reminded Henry of moments he tried hard not to think about. His uncle had become the enemy, his mother an unfaithful wife and mother. Henry could only imagine why this photo had traversed to Vermont, perhaps for no other reason but for his uncle to create a charade of familial closeness while pressing for a beggar's share of an inheritance.

He decided not to share the photo with the sheriff or Maeve, at least not now. Instead, he placed it in the pocket of his overcoat. He took one last look around the apartment and chose to leave. He turned off the lights, closed the door behind him, and descended the stairs.

He heard soft voices and occasional giggling from below.

At the bottom of the landing, Henry saw a partially opened door, apparently the location of the voices. He arrived unnoticed as the voices continued in hushed tones. He craned his neck a bit and peered inside, although later he wished he hadn't. The sheriff and Maeve were doing far more than quietly conversing. They stood inches apart as they spoke. Her arms were up and around his shoulders and his were around her waist. Hugs and kisses were being exchanged.

Henry didn't want to see any of this. He backed away quietly, but not before Maeve looked up and saw him retreating. The two locked eyes. She knew beyond a shadow of a doubt that Henry had seen everything.

Henry left the store and waited outside on the sidewalk. The sheriff eventually arrived, Maeve not too far behind.

"You all set to go with your ride?" asked Whittaker.

Without mixing words and no eye contact, Henry nodded.

Whittaker returned the nod along with a crooked grin, got into his car, and left.

Maeve looked at Henry quickly, cast her eyes downward, and didn't way a word. She didn't stay long and beat a hasty retreat through a side entrance to the clothing store.

While Henry waited for Hudson, his hands tightened into fists and he clenched his jaw in frustration. The tension was so great he felt as though his teeth were going to break. The last few days had been a succession of troublesome and disturbing fragments, vignettes such as today representing storm clouds ready to collide with his life.

Fifteen

Henry didn't have to wait long for Hudson, and once on board the two quickly parted for the hospital. Henry filled Hudson in on what he'd learned from the sheriff and Maeve, but kept private the romantic interlude he'd observed between the two. They drove to the hospital with few words spoken along the way. Both were exhausted from the last few days and both were consumed with thoughts of Mickey's well-being.

They turned off at a tree-lined street that led to the county hospital. The hospital was an older, two-story brick structure with elaborate landscaping covering its front lawns, ivy creeping up the chimney. The two got out and swiftly walked to the main entrance but were stopped by hospital guards who issued face masks and advised them of the protocol for entering the hospital.

The two were not aware that pandemic restrictions were still in place. Once the 1918 surge had wreaked its havoc, most citizens thought the worst was over, but the hospital setting was a grim reminder that the Spanish flu continued to kill, especially from a variant of the influenza emerging in 1920. Few recognized the lingering threat of the Spanish flu or took notice of the safety precautions. Hardly anyone realized that most pandemics throughout history lasted between two and three years and in America, the final toll was yet to be tallied.

Beyond the face masks, the two couldn't help but pay attention to the hospital precautions along the way to Mickey's room. Postings everywhere included guidelines and precautions related to quarantine, isolation, disinfection, ventilation, and personal hygiene designed to limit droplet infection. No exceptions were allowed.

At the intensive care desk, they asked for Mickey's room location. Once known, the two walked the hallway leading to his room. When they arrived at their destination, Mickey's door was closed and a notice posted outside of it spoke clearly that visitors were not allowed.

Instead of walking away, they waited. They notified a nurse that they were Mickey's guardian keepers and needed an update on his condition. They were told to be patient and that a doctor would soon be sent their way. While waiting, Henry sat in a chair outside the door while Hudson stood against the wall, one foot in back of him for balance as well as comfort.

Eventually, a nurse appeared along the hallway with a doctor. The doctor introduced himself as Phil Kincaid, and the nurse simply as Rose.

Hudson barged right in. He expressed that he needed to know the extent of Mickey's injuries, medical interventions, and recovery prospects. He didn't mince words.

The doctor was just as forthcoming. "I understand your concerns. Mr. Parker experienced a profound chest trauma. He's suffered a significant punctured left lung and has two fractured ribs. His spleen also appears to be damaged, although for now we can't be sure. He's scheduled for more diagnostic tests tomorrow."

Hudson asked, "Can we see him?"

Dr. Kincaid forced a smile and said clearly, "Absolutely not. Right now, we have Mr. Parker hooked up to a pulmotor, which will help him take breaths when he's struggling. Mr. Parker has been fitted with a face mask and oxygen, which makes it near impossible for him to talk."

"Understood," said Hudson, who exchanged glances with Henry. "How can we help? Is there anything we can do to lend a hand?"

Dr. Kincaid shook his head. "No, there's nothing you can do at this point. He needs to rest. I suggest going home knowing that he is receiving the best possible care." He paused. "We'll call with updates. Once we get his damaged lung back up to speed and remove the breathing apparatus, we'll allow visitations. You can call at any time to see if the visitation restriction has been lifted. It would be in your best interests to call first before you travel here, only to be turned away. Please recognize that at the present time, he's fragile."

"We completely understand," Hudson replied.

It was time for them to leave.

On the way back home, they were more talkative. Topics were swapped, from the Red Sox to the upcoming winter weather. Hudson also brought up how Abigail needed more direction and purpose as to her role as horse trainer at the farm. In the midst of her acceptance of the training position days ago, he proposed that she needed more guidance on how she fit into the farm's daily operation. Speaking bluntly, Hudson suggested that she needed to spend more time with Henry, learning the ropes along with his expectations.

When they arrived back at the farm, they were both worn out, two tired souls looking for relief and rest.

While Hudson chose to crash for a while in his bunk, Henry filled Julia in on Mickey. She was concerned, of course, but disappointed that no one could enter his room and visit. She'd heard of Dr. Kincaid and knew that his reputation was excellent. She knew Mickey was in good hands.

They talked back and forth a little more, but Henry was restless. Julia suggested that he walk the property to get some fresh air into his lungs. He acted on the suggestion and ambled over to the main corral where Abigail was putting the horses through their routines. He hooked his arms on the top railing and watched her working the herd.

She noticed him out of the corner of his eye and walked over, smiling. But as she got closer, her smile drooped, and concern draped her face.

"How's Mickey?" she asked.

"We couldn't get in to see him, but he's stabilized. No visitation privileges for anyone. The doctor treating Mickey told us he definitely has a punctured lung along with fractured ribs. Tests are still being run on him to assess any other internal injuries."

She looked at Henry and held his gaze for a long moment. "I'm worried," she said.

He lowered his voice and it dropped in volume. "I am too, Abigail."

She could detect his frustration and uncertainty. They watched the horses quietly as the minutes passed.

Henry finally broke the silence. "What do you say we go for a ride? I've been wound too tight ever since the other night."

She smiled, a grin that sliced itself from one cheek to the other. "I'd like that very much, Henry." She wore her hair in a pony tail and her big brown eyes sparkled in the sunlight.

Abigail started walking away but shouted over her shoulder, "Which of these rascals do you want as a mount?"

Henry opened his mouth to speak, then stopped. "Surprise me. You're the horse trainer now, you pick the mounts. Your judgement counts the most."

She nodded and then hurried off, a warm sense of confidence washing over her. Henry had just affirmed her presence on the farm, and she felt comfortable and elated with his opinion. She almost skipped her way to the barn.

After a while, she led two horses to Henry, Lola and Monte, both saddled and ready to go. She'd mounted Lola and offered Monte's reins to Henry. Before he mounted, he approached Monte from the side. He talked quietly to the horse, whispering almost, stroking its neck and gently touching its ears. Two friends, connected as ever. From his coat pocket, he dug for and found a small, slender piece of a peppermint stick for Monte. The horse slurped and gobbled from Henry's palm. Meanwhile, Henry stroked Monte's forehead a few times before he mounted.

They rode for at least a mile before the two of them spoke.

They slowed and Henry looked over at her. "You ride like the lieutenant once did," he said.

"Meaning what?"

"You're moving as one, rider and horse." When he thought about it more, his mouth twitched. "It makes me realize you carry the same traits the lieutenant used to preach to me. He used to tell me,

over and over, *'Develop a synchrony between you and the mount.'*
I mean, his love and knowledge of horses was drilled into me." He
paused a beat. "I know he'd be happy that you are here now."

The two stopped at the Cooper tree farm, blue spruces
everywhere.

Abigail hooked a leg around her saddle horn. "Tell me what
he was like, Henry."

"Well, everyone knew about his horsemanship skills as well
as his cavalry glory. He was legendary and he taught me what he
knew about horses."

"You learned your lessons well."

Henry nodded. "Yes, he taught me so much."

"Like what?"

Henry straightened himself in the saddle. He smiled, the kind
that surfaced from warm memories about to be shared. "He taught
me to be a better person."

He continued. "We shared a lot during his dying days. We had
a routine where I would spend dinner time with him. He insisted
upon my joining him and we had many heartfelt conversations. I
wish we could've had more."

Henry wasn't done. "I don't want to make you sad, but from time to time, the lieutenant brought up the diving Arabian horses and you. He reminisced about the night he walked you home along the Niantic River shoreline, and how much he wanted you to come work at the horse farm."

She listened, head bowed. She dismounted from Lola to check and tighten her cinch, although Henry knew she was using that as a ploy just to gather herself. Abigail kept her head down and after circling Lola, got back in the saddle.

She shot Henry a humorless smile as she gathered her reins. Her words at first were quiet, some fumbled. She eventually asked, head down, "Were you with him in the end?"

"I was," Henry nodded

"Was it a peaceful death?"

He nodded. "It was, Abigail. I'll always remember our last night together. We were having dinner together in his bedroom. He didn't eat much and he was experiencing considerable pain. Never once said 'ouch,' though. A real warrior. He had a few sips of some turkey broth, a cracker or two, and some sweetened tea."

When he finished his broth that night, he told me it was time to get the bottle. Of course, both of us knew 'the bottle' was a bottle of rum he'd received a while back from Dr. Drake."

"Dr. Drake gave him that?"

"He did. He said many of his patients were using it for the pain. We used it off and on for a month or so. He refused any other pain medication."

Henry said, "Dr. Drake and the lieutenant shared a special friendship. Dr. Drake took an immediate liking to the lieutenant, wanting to hear all his war stories. I remember how he was particularly fascinated by how the lieutenant's company helped chase Pancho Villa back to Mexico."

Henry continued. "So, when I uncorked the bottle that night, he said he'd be honored if I'd join him for a drink. So, I poured two shot glasses. We clinked our glasses and sent the rum down the hatch."

"Could he hold it down?"

"Yes, he could, and did."

"Then what?"

When he'd get a drink under his belt he'd often ramble. For example, that night he reminded me for the umpteenth time to take good care of the farm and the horses. Stuff like, make sure I harvest the apples, grow some corn, feed the chickens, keep the family protected from harm."

Henry stopped and stared at the ground.

"Henry? Are you okay?"

"I just remembered something."

"Tell me."

"You weren't working here when he died." He raised his head and looked at her. "He said if I ever saw you again, he asked that I say goodbye to you for him."

"He really said that?"

"He did." He paused. Henry eventually broke the silence. "As I just said, Abigail, he really cared for you."

She paused. "The feelings were mutual."

"I thought all along the two of you would've made a good couple. No doubt."

Abigail shifted in the saddle and looked down. "Thank you, Henry," she mumbled. She felt her eyes beginning to water and didn't want that to happen in front of Henry. Her feelings for the lieutenant and their doomed romance still lingered and hurt. The lieutenant was the kind of man she always wanted in her life, gentle but rugged, tender but protective. She cursed her heart for letting love and hope bloom so easily.

Henry pressed on. "So anyway, after our shot of rum, the lieutenant got drowsy and fell asleep. I turned in a little bit later, sleeping on a couch in his room in case he needed me. At one point, I heard some slight coughing coming from him, nothing out of the ordinary. We found out later he died during the night, without struggle or resistance."

He hesitated. "So, to answer your question, he slipped away from all of us quietly and peacefully, which more than likely was the way he wished to leave."

Sixteen

The two of them decided to keep riding and swung along the outskirts of the Cooper property. Along the way they spotted two yearling fawns crossing the trail about twenty-five yards away. The riders slowed to a stop and didn't say a word. A few minutes later, a doe emerged from the woods chewing on a few pods from the branches of a tree. At that point, Henry and Abigail were spotted by the mother and all three turned tail and bounded back into the woods.

They eventually came to a gulley, a dusty ravine of sorts that might've first been created by the action of water. But as they led their horses around it, it became apparent that the gulley had been widened and cleared so that it was as wide as it was flat. It was longer that it was wide and at its far end was a raised shelf of gravel around ten feet tall.

"What's this place?" Abigail asked.

"This is a shooting range the lieutenant made piecemeal growing up. He and I spent lots of time out here shooting rifles as well as pistols." He pointed out distance markers marked on the side.

"Okay, got it," she said. "So, the raised end of the range stops any stray bullets."

"Exactly."

"Was he a marksman?" asked Abigail.

Henry took a deep breath and let it out slowly in the form of a laugh. "A marksman?" he said. "I would say so. I've never seen anyone shoot a rifle or handle a pistol like he did, his accuracy was extraordinary. He was a sniper when the cavalry tried chasing Pancho Villa in Mexico." He shook his head as he reminisced. "Down in this shooting range I personally saw him hit targets with long guns that were three hundred yards away."

"You're joking, right?"

"Nope. He was that good." Henry stared for a few seconds at the shooting range, resurrecting days gone by. The cracking of the long guns, the reloads, the smaller discharge from the handguns.

He turned in his saddle. "Have you ever fired a weapon?"

She nodded. "I was taught how to shoot my father's 12-gauge shotgun when I was growing up. My father was a hunter. He took me out hunting several times, but I hated every minute of it." She hesitated. "Do you hunt?"

"Nope, I'm like you. Hunting never appealed to me."

"How about the lieutenant?"

"He probably did when he rode with the cavalry, but I never saw him hunt up here."

Henry paused for a beat or two. "Abigail, even though you won't be hunting you still need to learn how to shoot. We'll give you lessons down the road."

"Why?" she asked.

"Because you need to be ready and alert out here. When the lieutenant first showed me the property, he told me that in the spring, especially, the woods are rife with wild life, and most creatures take to prowling."

"Creatures? she asked. "What kinds of creatures?"

"Black bears and bobcats are especially active up here."

"Do they attack?"

"Rarely. You don't bother them, they don't bother you."

"Then why the guns?"

"Your horse could get spooked by unknown noises or by sudden movements near their home. So be prepared and keep your eyes open when you ride, especially during the spring. I ride with a rifle in my scabbard, and I will see to it you ride with the same whenever you go out." He coughed in his hand. "Just a precaution, mind you."

She nodded.

Henry looked her way. "What do you say we dismount and walk the horses. You got any problems walking?"

"Nope. I like walking. Hiking is one of my favorite outdoor activities."

They dismounted and led the horses by their reins.

After a while, Abigail stopped. "Is it okay if I ask you some questions?"

"Sure, what's on your mind?"

"For starters, are you okay?"

Henry did a double-take. "Yes, I am. Why do you ask?"

"It's just that you seem out of sorts, preoccupied I'm guessing is the right word."

"Well, I'm worried about Mickey and would feel much better if he wasn't hospitalized. I've been thinking about him a lot and I guess it shows. No offense to you or anyone else."

"None taken. Is there anything I can do to ease the burden?"

"No, I'll be fine. I'll just be happy when he's back home with us."

"Of course." She waited. "Nothing else going on?"

"No, but thanks for asking."

But, the fact of the matter was that Henry had a lot more going on in his head than just Mickey, but he was holding his cards close. He was preoccupied with his uncle Bill and the vicious Thanksgiving eve attack on the family. The scoundrel wanted inheritance money and Henry refused to budge. Beyond that, Henry was still reeling from his visit with the sheriff to his uncle's apartment, where he stumbled upon a steamy liaison between the sheriff and Maeve. That rocked him back on his heels and sent him into a downward spiral of confusion. Maeve, of all people, was drawn to the town sheriff and she left Henry by the wayside. Henry's misgivings about the sheriff were a fly in the ointment and further complicated his mental irritation.

They kept walking. The fresh air felt good.

Abigail said, "What do you say we change the subject?"

"Good idea. Got a topic in mind?"

"I do. Let's keep walking and talk about the farm and what you intend to do with it."

"Sounds good. I'd like to hear your thoughts."

She rubbed the side of her neck, then pursed her lips. "I'll start with some basic ideas. First of all, we're shorthanded here, Henry, especially so since Mickey's been hurt. We need at least one or two more hands to help clean the stalls and see to the horses. Plus, you're going to need more help planting sweet corn in the spring. Carl is not getting any younger. I've witnessed his pace slowing down as well as his needing to stop and catch his breath, which I've not seen before. If you're going to add more horses, the increased workload will far exceed his competency. The guy needs help, not only in the barn but also in his handyman duties around the house."

Henry nodded. "You're right. I'll tend to that. You got someone in mind?"

"I don't, but I'll keep my eyes and ears open."

They kept walking along the trail. They startled a bit when a rabbit scampered from underneath a thicket, high-tailing it ahead of them and disappearing down a hillside.

"Anything else?" Henry asked.

"Yes," she replied. "What are you going to do with all these pretty horses, the ones you have now and the ones you want to add?"

"What do you mean?"

"Well, you've mentioned several times that you want to add more horses to your string, right?"

"Yes, that's the plan. The lieutenant wanted that."

"Right, I understand that." She hesitated. "But what's your plan for keeping them?"

Henry stopped walking and turned to face her. He bunched his eyebrows together.

She said, "What I mean is, what's going to happen once you acquire them? Keeping that many horses is an expensive venture, you know, grain and feed, routine farrier and vet visits, and the like. You've already constructed a new set of stalls in the barn for the new horses, but I'd suggest you think about expanding the size of the corrals."

"Good idea," he said.

"You sticking with quarter horses?"

"I believe so. They have great temperaments. They're a calm breed and like being ridden."

"Are you thinking of breeding them?"

"Well, Lola's a mare and Morning Star is a stallion, so there's one opportunity. If we add more horses, I was thinking of buying another mare and stallion. But I'll need your help along with Hudson to think that idea through."

Abigail got quiet.

"I didn't mean right now," Henry said.

"Sorry I got quiet on you. I wasn't thinking about breeding. I was thinking about the other horses. Norman, Rufus, and Monte are gelded, right?"

"Correct."

"And the entire string is how old?"

"Between six and eight years."

"That's young and a great age to sell if that's the route you want to take. Is it?"

Henry rubbed his chin. "I need to also think that option through with you and Hudson. Any initial thoughts?"

She let out a breath. "You've got a beautiful herd here. They're young, healthy, and well-trained. The records kept by the lieutenant indicate they all have great lineage. You'd get a pretty penny for any one of them. Of course, letting go would be the hard part."

He sighed. "Exactly. Those damn horses have grown on me. Why is it that we get so attached?"

She smiled at him. "Because that's the way we're made, Henry. And, it's two-way. They get just as attached to us."

Henry said, "The lieutenant once told me that the cavalry stressed early on that riders needed to bond with their mounts. In so doing, horses will differentiate their riders from strangers. The eventual bonding that takes place is based on olfactory as well as auditory and visual cues. In other words, bonding is fostered by seeing and smelling us as well as hearing our voices."

They continued to walk at a leisurely pace, the horses obediently trailing them.

"What else have you got for me?" he asked.

"A few other thoughts. I'll just toss them out and let you think about them."

"Fire away."

"First, we need to get you off this farm once in a while to have you rub elbows with other horse owners, trainers, and riders. You need to mingle with others, see what they're doing with their horses. Along these lines, you need to connect and become part of the equestrian community. You need to tell others about your horse farm, where it's located, what kind of horses you're training, and so on. You've got a hidden gem of a farm up here and need to upgrade its visibility. You need to show it off, not live in isolation."

She continued. "Some ranchers will want to come and visit and look the place over. That's good. Establishing this kind of contact will yield many benefits, especially when you're seeking professional advice and opinion. Bottom line, it puts you in the loop."

"How can I make this happen?"

"You look for contact opportunities, like horse shows or horse auctions. You check for upcoming events advertised in newspapers and magazines. You pick the brains of farriers, blacksmiths, and veterinarians. You attend social events sponsored by local owners. You visit equestrian facilities. Basically, you keep your ear to the ground."

She stopped in mid-step. "Wait a minute, here's something to think about. Why not host an equestrian social event right here? Once you have everything in place the way you want it, extend an invitation to other horse owners and trainers to come visit. Offer some food and liquid refreshment. You could put your horses on display as well as offer trail rides in and around your beautiful wooded property. Maybe plant the seed that you're thinking about, you know, offering horseback trail riding, provided you want to pursue that as a business venture."

"You're good, Ms. Emory. Very good. You've got some great ideas. We've got lots to talk about over the winter."

She nodded in agreement.

———————

They stopped to remount their horses. Abigail was up in her saddle while Henry was adjusting his stirrup. After a few minutes he was satisfied, and he put his left foot into the stirrup, ready to mount. But Abigail held out her hand and interrupted his movements.

"One last thing," she said.

Henry unhooked his left foot from the stirrup. He looked at Abigail and paused, surprised. He thought they were done.

"I have one more idea, a proposal really," Abigail said.

Henry waited, rolling his eyes.

She was firm in her delivery, as if something had been brewing for a while inside her head. She didn't hesitate. "Henry, I won't hold back here, especially since we have the privacy of the trails." She cleared her throat. "You need to ride competitively. I've watched you for some time now and you have the skill set necessary to become a champion. I've told you before, your riding skills are as good as, if not better, than the riders I've seen on my circuit. You've got the talent and now you've got the horses. Time for you to step up and show off your stuff."

Henry was floored with the idea. He walked over to Lola and held her bridle while he looked up at Abigail. "You want me to compete against professional riders? Are you serious?" He laughed out loud. "Compete as what, the rodeo clown who jumps out of a barrel to entertain the crowd?"

She laughed out loud, then got serious. "Oh no, Henry. There's no attempt on my part to be humorous. All I wanted to convey is that you're ready to compete. Believe me, you're ready."

Henry retreated back around Lola and draped his arms over Monte's saddle. He looked over at Abigail.

"Tell you what," he said. "I'll give some thought to your proposal on two conditions. One, we've got to wait until things quiet down around here."

She replied, "Of course, and I didn't mean to add to the bustle. I was just adding some food for thought, more chatter for around the winter fireplace."

They remained quiet for a few moments.

"What's the other condition?" she asked.

He grinned. "If I agree to some type of competition, I ask that you do the same and come with me. You are a gifted rider and have all the experience with these kinds of events."

She glowed inside. Henry's affirmation meant everything to her.

He climbed aboard Monte and when he did, used his legs to gently squeeze the middle of Monte's ribcage, cuing him to move forward.

But not before Henry looked Abigail's way and winked. "Wouldn't that be something, I mean, the two of us showing up as a team? Now that's what I would call a real hoot."

Seventeen

Mickey recovered from his wounds but had to remain in the hospital for a week for observation and rehabilitation. As the week wore on, he slowly regained his strength and mobility plus his appetite gradually returned. He was not feeling as much pain nor was as tired as he once was. The medical staff noted significant improvement in his walking ability and upper-extremity muscle strength. His respiratory recovery was much slower, though, and his doctor urged patience. His cough still had a raspy sound, making it difficult for him to converse with visitors. It was as though he was trying to clear fluid with each cough.

Before Mickey returned to the farm, Henry thought it wise to bring the family together for some important news and information. They met in the living room after dinner one night. Earlier that day

Henry and Julia had visited Mickey, who was champing at the bit to ditch the hospital scrubs and return home. Of course, that was to be expected. Henry pulled a small notebook from his shirt pocket. He read from it. He reported that one of Mickey's doctors explained that Mickey had experienced a traumatic pneumothorax, a serious pierced lung injury, and that it would take six or seven weeks for Mickey to reach full recovery. He also had two fractured ribs, multiple contusions, and serious sutured lacerations on his residual limb.

That led to murmurs, and Henry interrupted the small-talk going on.

"Please listen," he said, and the voices around him quieted down. "Losing Mickey for an extended period time impacts everyone, but his recovery is the main focus for all of us now." He paused. "We're lucky that this misfortune occurred as we're entering the winter season and we're buttoning up the farm for whatever comes our way this winter."

Heads nodded.

Henry cleared his throat. He didn't know how to best proceed, but he said, "The temporary loss of Mickey means we need to hire more people to operate the farm."

Hudson was leaning against a corner wall and was taking in everything. He piped up and added. "You also need to recognize that we're sounding an 'all-hands-on deck alarm,' for the time being. Changes will be made as we figure out our best plan to assign duties and new responsibilities."

More head nodding.

Henry fumbled with the notebook. "I'm adding two new workers to our fold." He flipped a page. "I was fortunate to find a brother and sister, both in their late teens, looking for work. They live not too far away, have their own transportation, and really need the work. They'll be starting at the end of the week after we get Mickey home."

"Names?" asked Julia.

"Jacob and Ariel Winsted."

"I know the family," said Julia. "They're nice people, always polite and courteous. They own a small home a few miles from here. Good neighbors and very civic-minded people when the community reaches out for help. The mother is a food chef and the father was a custodial worker in the school system, but injured himself not too long ago. I think he's still out of work." She

214

paused. "The two kids were brought up right and I'd be willing to bet they're dependable, hard workers."

A silence.

Julia spoke up. "You need to tell us what the new help will be doing."

Henry looked directly at Julia. "First and foremost, we need to offer assistance to you, Julia, and provide some long overdue support."

"I don't need help," she replied rather brusquely. "I do fine on my own."

Henry replied, "Yes, you do, but your workload will be increasing."

Julia raised her eyebrows.

Henry said, "I've watched you since I've been here and you do an incredible job preparing meals, serving meals, and cleaning up after everyone is done. You are also an excellent housekeeper and an expert accountant managing our bills and expenditures. With your work-load increasing, that's why I want Ariel Winsted to pitch in and offer help. This means for meals as well as housekeeping chores, and of course, book-keeping."

Julia nodded, although her eyes were downcast.

He picked up on this immediately. "Julia, please don't get upset about any of this. This is in no way a demotion. I'm just trying to help you."

She nodded again and then looked up. "What about Carl?"

He looked over at Carl, who was sitting on a couch with his arms folded on his lap. Henry said, "He won't be demoted either. We need both of you more than ever. Jacob Winsted will work alongside Carl to keep the stalls clean and assist Abigail with whatever needs exist on any given day. Carl will be in charge of directing Jacob, tutoring him really, to manage the horses, tending to household repairs, and teaching him to pitch in whenever extra hands are needed."

"I understand, Henry," Julia said. She hesitated a bit, but then said, "It's a good plan."

Carl was rubbing his hands together in great delight. "I'm really going to be put in charge of someone?"

"That's correct," said Henry. "You'll be the one giving orders. Jacob Winsted seems to be an eager worker and is very enthusiastic about coming on board." Henry smiled. "You'll be the first to meet him so you might want to start working on some words of welcome."

Carl immediately stood up and adjusted his toolbelt, which he wore everywhere. Henry had given it to Carl as a Christmas gift a while ago and he wore it like a gun belt from the old West.

Henry looked at him and said, "Well, what are you going to say? Pretend that I'm the new hand."

Carl hooked his thumbs in his tool belt and tilted his head just so. He grinned and said, "Howdy stranger, welcome to the Cooper farm. Why not come inside and stay a while? I've been waiting for you and we've got lots to talk about."

The room got quiet. Then Hudson started clapping his hands and everyone else joined in.

Henry looked at both Hudson and Julia and shot them a deep, heartfelt smile. He went over to Carl and patted him on his shoulder.

Carl was a man unique in his simplicity. Brain damaged by a blunt trauma accident early on in his marriage with Julia, he was an uncomplicated man, a mainstay of the farm ever since he injured himself. He'd become a trusted laborer, happy and content with each and every chore assigned to him. Henry wished that he could be that simple and satisfied.

Carl looked squarely at Henry, shooting him a lopsided grin. "Is what I said okay?" he asked.

"Perfect," replied Henry. "Don't change a thing. You've just become our official greeter."

Carl pumped his chest out, pleased as punch.

———————

When Mickey eventually came home, everyone rejoiced. Led by Henry, they gathered around Mickey while he climbed out of a hospital transport and steadied himself to get his feet on the ground. He was tentative at first but quickly regained his footing. He walked slowly.

He looked tired and had lost weight. But he was the same old Mickey, joking and wise-cracking all the way into the house and settling himself on one of the living room's overstuffed chairs. Henry and Julia stood next to Mickey and made sure he was comfortable. He was hungry and hadn't eaten, prompting Julia to prepare small sandwiches and tea, accompanied by a few buttered corn muffins. He wolfed everything down and thanked Julia profusely. He proclaimed that hospital food was unfit for human consumption.

Mickey had strict marching orders from his doctors. They advocated that he stays active, but not in terms of strenuous exercises. He could get up and walk, but not over lengthy distances. He was told to wear loose-fitting clothes and avoid putting unnecessary pressure on the ribcage. At night, he was advised to sleep in an elevated position for the first week or so. Mickey agreed to the entire regimen.

Shortly after Mickey got settled, the sheriff's patrol car pulled into the driveway. Henry was out in the corral exercising Morning Star while Abigail was doing the same atop Norman, the seven-year-old Sorrel.

Out of the corner of his eye, Henry could see the sheriff leaving his car and walking toward the corral. He had a stiff posture, very square shoulders and a very lurching walk. He still wore the same stony expression he had in place when they first met.

He came right up to the corral fencing and aimed a glare directly at Henry. The sheriff faked a smile, one punctuated by his sneering upper lip.

"I need to talk with you, Cameron," he said, his eyes void of friendliness.

"What's this about? asked Henry.

The sheriff snorted loudly. "Why don't you get off that nag of yours and I'll tell you."

Henry snorted back. "You certainly don't know horses, Whittaker. This 'nag' is a thoroughbred horse," he scoffed. "Your comments about horses are comical."

The sheriff stuck his chin out toward Henry at a fierce angle. "That's sheriff Whittaker to you, son."

Henry didn't hesitate with a retort. "And that's Henry Cameron to you, sheriff, not son. Let's show some mutual respect since you're standing on my property."

They stared silently into each other's eyes for a minute or two, neither breaking the contact.

The sheriff finally said he had to talk with Henry in private.

Henry whistled for Abigail to ride over next to him. Abigail pulled up on Norman with her usual smile and buoyancy. She nodded a hello to the sheriff, then said to Henry, "How can I help out here?"

He held his reins out to her then slid off the saddle. "Abigail, take Morning Star with you while I tend to some matters."

She did so without hesitation, and the sheriff and Henry watched as she trotted away with the horses.

Henry and the sheriff left the corral and walked toward the patrol car.

The sheriff looked back over his shoulder. "I'll tell you, that horse trainer of yours is a fine-looking woman."

Henry didn't respond. In fact, he didn't even look up.

"That cowgirl married?"

Henry simply shook his head in animosity and kept walking. He still didn't answer.

"I asked you a question."

"Why don't you ask her yourself."

The curl in Whittaker's puss became even more pronounced.

They got to the driveway. "What is it you want?" Henry asked, hands on his hips.

"I need for you to tell me how this assault played out. I've got to create some kind of diagram for my police report."

"Have you found these guys yet?"

The sheriff shook his head. "Not yet."

Whittaker retrieved a small notebook from the inner pocket of his jacket. He turned to a blank page. "Help me diagram where everyone stood the night of the assault, where the attack took place, where their car was parked."

Henry did as asked and once finished, handed the notebook back and the sheriff slipped it into his jacket. He never looked at what Henry wrote nor thanked him for the help.

Henry assumed they were done and started walking back to the corral.

"Hold up there, cowboy," exclaimed the sheriff. "We're not done here."

Henry walked back.

The sheriff said, "I have one more issue." He cleared his voice. "The clothing store ..." Whittaker said haltingly.

Henry cut him off. "What about it?"

"You shouldn't have seen what was going on there between me and Maeve."

Henry smelled alcohol again. He stood still and silent and stared at the sheriff while the sheriff stood still and silent and stared back. Neither budged. They stayed that way for a while.

Eventually, the sheriff's shoulders sagged. With a crooked smile he leaned into Henry, cupping his mouth close to Henry's ear. "You see, Maeve and I have this little thing going on..."

Henry kept staring at him, not about to blink.

The sheriff scratched the back of his neck. "Now don't go around telling people what you saw, got it?"

Henry shrugged. "Now why would I go and do something like that?"

The sheriff straightened and poked Henry in the chest with his index finger. "Just make sure you don't." He gave Henry a sinister grin. "You won't like me if you make me angry, Cameron."

Henry replied, "I don't think I like you even when you're not angry." Henry turned away and started walking back to the horses.

He left the sheriff standing there by himself.

Eighteen

Henry sat at the kitchen table by himself looking out the window while nursing a cup of coffee. He was waiting for Julia, who'd asked him to spare a little time this morning. Over the years, the kitchen table had become special when not bearing meals, a cozy and snug location for the family to reminisce, make plans for the future, catch up on the latest news, or bring peace to the soul.

Julia arrived and after pouring herself a mug of coffee, sat down in a chair next to Henry. She reached over and gently squeezed Henry's forearm. "Thank you for finding some time for me. I only have a few things on my mind."

"I have all the time you need."

She thanked him and took a sip of coffee. "First, I want to thank you for what you did for Carl."

224

Henry hiked his brow, not sure what she meant.

"Putting him in charge of the new hand, Jacob."

"Oh, that." He smiled. "Carl can handle that and Hudson will always be around for consultation."

"Well, you didn't have to do that, Henry. It meant the world to him and he hasn't stopped talking about it. He took it as a real feather in his cap."

"As it was intended. There will be a bump up in his salary to go along with the new assignment and responsibilities."

She sighed. "It hasn't been an easy road for us."

"I know that."

"Some days I wonder if I have the strength to handle all the challenges he presents."

"You're a saint for what you do and how you do it."

"He's a good soul, Henry, even though he's limited with what he can do. We've always been a team and we're both in it for the long run."

That statement moved Henry. A lifelong commitment to each other.

Henry perked up and said, "The lieutenant told me early on that Carl is a workhorse. His advice to me was for me to keep his chores simple, don't overwhelm him with tasks, and provide lots of feedback."

"That's always worked for Carl." She had some more coffee. "Thank you, Henry."

He nodded.

She waited for a minute or two. "Now what's going on with you?" she asked.

Henry's brows knitted. "What do you mean?"

"That's one of the reasons I wanted to talk. Something's bothering you. You've got a burr under your saddle, I can tell."

"How can you tell, dare I ask?"

She replied, "Henry, I've known you for some time now. I've learned to read you."

He bowed his head a little then looked back at her. He spoke softly. "Can we keep all of this just between the two of us?"

"Absolutely."

"Okay, I trust you." He finished his coffee and pushed it away. He looked down at his hands and picked at a cuticle.

Henry asked, "How well do you know Sheriff Whittaker?"

She scoffed at the question. "Hardly at all," she replied. "You having trouble with him?"

Henry nodded but stayed silent. "The guy is really starting to bug me."

"What's he doing?"

Henry straightened in his chair. "Okay, for starters he and I never really hit it off. I felt like he was always looking down at me, like he was better than me."

Julia nodded.

"If you remember the circumstances, he arrived after the assault on Mickey to gather notes on the crime scene."

"Oh yes, I remember. Go on," she implored.

"I went with him to the clothing store to interview Maeve and investigate the apartment occupied by the two hooligans."

"How'd that go?" Julia asked.

"Horribly. He barely investigated anything. He tried to look like he knew what he was doing but he was out of his element. He found nothing of importance. He'd also been hitting the sauce."

"Drinking on the job?"

Henry nodded, shifting in his chair, trying to find the right words.

"What?" asked Julia.

"There's more. He and Maeve left abruptly, leaving me alone in the upstairs apartment."

"Did you follow them?"

"Yes, in due time."

He swallowed hard before he told Julia. "They were in a separate room with a partially opened door, hugging in a lovers' embrace, kissing, touching, and all that stuff."

"Oh, my dear God," said Julia. "With Maeve? He's old enough to be her father for cripes sake. What did you do?"

"I just tried to slip away without being seen. I walked backwards, away from the two of them, but Maeve saw me."

Henry let that sit for a while before continuing.

"A day ago, Whittaker returned here, I think you and Carl were at the market. Whittaker came back to the farm under the pretense that he was further investigating the crime scene."

"Was he?"

"No way."

She drank her coffee and got silent.

Henry picked up where he left off.

"The truth of the matter? He came here to threaten me."

Julia was shocked.

"He made it clear that if I talked to anyone about what I saw, there would be a price to pay."

"He threatened you?"

"Yes, he did."

"Anything after that?" asked Julia.

Henry shook his head. "Nothing," he said.

They looked at each other without speaking.

Julia got up, went to the stove for the coffee pot, and returned to refill their two mugs.

"Continue," she said.

"That's it, replied Henry.

She stood in front of Henry and shook her head. "No, that's not it, and you know that."

———————

Julia sat back down.

"Okay, you're right," said Henry. I'm holding back on you."

"Please don't," she replied.

"Okay, I won't. Anyway, I liked Maeve. The more I saw her, the more I liked her. We talked about getting together for quite some time, but things never worked out, at least from my end. Now that she's hooked up with the sheriff, I've lost total interest."

Julia let that sit for a while, but then spoke up. "If it's any consolation, Cormac Whittaker has always been a womanizer. The stories about him have abounded for years, and the marriages he's destroyed lay strewn upon the rocks. He's slimy and despicable. It's a wonder that he's kept his position this long."

"Is he married?"

"Oh yes. Married with two children. Disgraceful," she uttered.

"So that's why you turned your back on him when he first entered the house."

She nodded. "I suggest that you keep your distance from Maeve."

"I'll do that."

Henry bowed his head and ran his fingers through his hair. "I need your help, Julia. I won't go into that store, at least not now. Abigail needs to be outfitted with cold weather gear, including coat, boots, scarves, warm hats, flannel shirts, and so on. Since I don't want to see Maeve, will you take Abigail shopping?"

Julia replied, "All good," she replied. "We'll go shopping tomorrow."

Henry thanked her. They stayed quiet for few moments.

Julia looked at him. "Whatever came of that gal you dated from Boston?"

"Lily Corwin?"

"Yes, that's her, Lily Corwin. Did the two of you ever stay in touch?"

"No, I lost out on that one, too. She wrote to me several times but I didn't reply. We eventually got caught up when the lieutenant and I visited Boston to see my mother, but Lily informed me she was dating a doctor so I backed off."

"You liked her?"

Henry's face softened. "Yeah, I really did. She was a fine person, you would've liked her."

He waited for her to say something.

"The two of you met at the Connecticut midshipman's camp?"

"Yes, with Mickey. Mickey was dating another gal, a friend of Lily's."

"Sounds like you and Lily Corwin were serious," she said.

Henry blushed a bit. "I guess we were. We saw each other almost every weekend. We had dances every Saturday night at the camp and we spent those nights together.

"Nothing came of it?" Julia asked.

A long and painful silence fell.

Henry needed to think about her question. It took a while to dust away the cobwebs and revisit jagged memories while in Boston.

He struggled to gather his thoughts. "I made mistakes, Julia." he said.

"What kind of mistakes? Is there something you wish to share?"

He looked at Julia square in the eye and nodded. She was a trusted person, and he had no problem baring his soul in front of her, knowing that she would always keep it secret.

He swallowed hard and continued. "I visited her family one weekend and on a whim Lily and I decided to stop by and check on my mother. My father was away at sea, so we hoped our visit would be a welcome surprise. Instead, we found my mother and my uncle in bed half naked, aghast that we'd invaded their privacy."

"Uh-oh, what happened?" asked Julia.

"Tempers flared, insults abounded, threats and fisticuffs followed. It was awful. I didn't want Lily exposed to this. I demanded that she leave the apartment. I yelled at her with horrible language."

"And you? What happened to you?"

"I stayed and was physically beaten, bloodied and bruised at the hands of my uncle. I fled the apartment, alone and frightened in the city of Boston."

"That must've been awful."

He nodded. "It was pretty horrible."

"But you made it back to the midshipman's camp?"

"Just barely. Yours truly returned bloodied and bruised."

"Did you get help at the camp?"

"The lieutenant took care of me. Watched over me like a hawk."

"Did you hear from Lily after that?"

"No."

"But she tried reaching out to you."

Henry squirmed in his seat, trying to find a comfortable position. "She did, but I never responded."

Julia used a napkin to dab at her mouth. "Why not?"

"I was going through a cyclone of mishaps," he replied. "I was a mess. My father died at sea, my mother died from the Spanish flu, my friends had set sail for France, the lieutenant went home to Vermont, and suddenly I was alone."

"And Lily Corwin got lost in the shuffle."

"Exactly."

"Do you still miss her?"

Henry was ruffled and didn't hear the question. "What was that?" he replied.

"I said, do you still miss her?"

He bowed his head once again. "Yes, I miss her. I wish I could rewind my life so that I could go back and change things."

"Why did you burn her letters sent here not too long ago when she was still seeking contact?"

"I was embarrassed by my mother and uncle, plus I was ashamed by how I spoke to her on that horrible day. Truly embarrassed."

"But you got a chance to see her again when you were in Boston with the lieutenant, right?"

"Yes, that's correct. But she made it clear that she was involved with another partner, a medical guy."

"At the hospital where she worked?"

He nodded.

"So, it was really a goodbye."

He sighed wearily. "Yes, it was a goodbye. She made that clear. That was the last contact I had."

They sat there for a while, the two of them, sipping their coffee.

Julia reached down and retrieved an envelope from her apron and placed it in front of Henry. "This arrived yesterday," she said. She nudged it forward so that it was directly in front of Henry. "I'm not hiding mail from you, and I fully recognize that I don't have that right. But I wanted to make sure the letter was in safe keeping. I didn't want you to rip it up, even though I didn't know what was inside."

Henry stared at the envelope, the handwriting in particular. He knew immediately it was from Lily. Her handwriting was the giveaway, he'd recognize it anywhere.

After several minutes, Henry decided to open it. He stared at the contents, both of his hands trembling. He was nervous and it showed.

"Do you want some alone time?" Julia asked.

"No," he replied. He decided to slide the letter over to Julia and asked her to read it.

She was more than accommodating. She slipped on a pair of reading glasses and read the contents out loud:

Dear Henry,

I hope this holiday greeting finds you well and happy.

As the holidays approach, I've been thinking of you and hope this letter arrives safely.

These are difficult times for all of us. I lost my partner and for now, I'm living with my parents. They both send their best.

I'm hopeful you and your new family are rejoicing and eagerly awaiting the new year.

How is the lieutenant? The last I saw, he was recovering from that terrible stabbing wound incurred in the city, one that I helped to treat. I hope he's healed and continues to protect your nest.

I think of you often, and the many good times we shared. If you ever travel to Boston, I'd love to connect and catch up.

Warmest regards,
Lily

Henry sat there for a moment or two, letting Lily's words sink in. Henry and Julia looked at each other, but neither spoke.

Finally, Julia got up from the table. She worked her way over to Henry and stood behind him, resting her hand on his shoulder.

Julia said, "Henry, I was taught long ago that everyone in the world deserves a second chance." She squeezed his shoulder tenderly. "Sounds to me like you just received yours."

With that, she turned and left him alone with his thoughts.

Nineteen

Winter took its time heading for Compton, but all indications were that it wouldn't stay away for much longer. Quiet crunchy mornings were now commonplace as frost covered the ground. The last of the deciduous trees had dropped their leaves and the winter skies would soon pelt Vermont with snow, sleet, and hail. Wildlife could be seen scampering for their winter locations, and townsfolk broke out their winter coats, boots, ski caps, and scarves. Houses were buttoned up, firewood stacked, and country roads plowed. Toboggans, skis, and snowshoes stood at the ready.

Mickey gradually regained his strength. He'd come home from the hospital with strict marching orders from the attending physicians. This meant he had to take all medications, consume ample nourishment, engage in an exercise regiment, and get adequate rest. A visiting nurse named Thelma Wainwright visited the farm twice a week to assess Mickey's recovery, and she was pleased with his progress. During one of her early visits, Thelma paid particular attention to the lacerations on his residual limb. The wounds were deep and prone to infection and required a lengthy healing timeline. Complete healing was needed for the residual arm to carry the weight of the wooden prosthesis. Mickey was warned that any surgical wound has the potential to become infected, and he had to be on the lookout for redness, fever, and swelling.

For the first few weeks, he was sedentary most of the time. Nurse Wainwright told him that fatigue was the body's way of signaling that it needed to rest and heal. In due time, Mickey sat at the family dinner table, which boosted his spirits immensely. The conversations at the dinner table were always lively and upbeat, the laughter loud. Julia's food never tasted so good. Mickey remarked later that mealtime with the family was without a doubt the best medicine ever.

With his strength growing, Mickey began walking outside. The early December air was cold, but not frigid, and its freshness felt good. He increased his endurance every day by walking up and down the long driveway, and it was only a matter of time before he headed for the corral to watch Abigail work the horses. There was a magical pull toward the horses and each day he ambled over to the main corral, leaned against the railing, and watched Abigail put the five horses through their routines.

On one of his early visits, Abigail took a break and wandered over to Mickey.

She smiled. "How're you doing, Doughboy?"

He smiled back. "Doughboy, haven't heard that nickname for a while. I like it."

Abigail scrunched up her face and asked, "Where did the expression 'doughboy' come from anyway? What does it mean?"

"I'm not sure, but I heard several explanations for it while I was overseas. One was that American soldiers loved fried flour dumplings and this contributed to the expression. Another explanation was based on America's delayed involvement in the war. For three years prior to American involvement, our allies voiced that the doughboys were 'kneaded' in 1914, but didn't 'rise' until 1917."

"Makes sense," she said.

"You got nicknames for everyone here?"

"Just about. Let's see, Hudson is 'Sarge' because of his former cavalry rank, Carl is 'Gunslinger' because of the toolbelt he wears like a holster, Julia is the 'Wagon Boss' because everyone knows she's the one who really runs this outfit."

Mickey nodded. "And what about Henry?"

"Henry is the 'Horseman Who Came from the Sea.' Now here's a guy with tons of boating experiences but instead chooses to become a horseman, a magnificent one at that."

"I would agree. And you? What are you called?"

"Henry calls me the 'Arabian Vaquera' because of my work with the diving horses."

A knowing smile creased Mickey's face. "Ah yes," he said, "of course."

While they were talking, Abigail's back was turned away from the herd. She didn't see Monte, the dusty gray gelding, pull away from the other horses and slowly approach Abigail from behind.

Mickey touched Abigail's arm and spoke softly. "Whether you know it or not, Monte is creeping up behind you, a few steps at a time."

"I know," she casually replied without even turning around.

"You know? How do you know?"

"He and I have a special relationship." When she turned around to face him, Monte nickered and whinnied. Abigail looked over to Mickey. "Hear that?" she asked. "For this guy, a nicker and a whinny are signs of connection, a friendship." She reached into her barn jacket and produced a small carrot, which Monte gobbled from the flat of her hand." Afterwards, Monte used his head to nudge and nuzzle Abigail. "He's one of our brightest stars," Abigail said as she snuggled up against Monte's neck. "Quick learner, gentle disposition, great saddle horse."

Mickey said, "I'm going to ride that horse someday." But deep inside he had second thoughts and paused to look around the corral. He looked at Abigail. "Be honest with me. Do you think I'll ever get up on a saddle and ride him?"

She didn't hesitate. "Absolutely, no question about it, you'll ride with us. It will happen a lot sooner than you think."

This buoyed Mickey's spirits. He reached over and rubbed Monte's neck. "You like this boy a lot, don't you?"

She nodded. "I can't lie, I do."

"Why Monte?"

"It's hard to explain. But I can tell you this. Monte was a castaway traumatized by losing his parents at an early age in a fiery accident. He was a skittish and high-strung horse. He was brought here by the lieutenant, who couldn't find the time to work with him, but he saw potential, so he handed Monte off to Henry for relaxation and comfort. In due time, the two orphans connected and became inseparable. Now, this beautiful animal longs for attention and tender loving care, and that's where you're going to step in and pick up where Henry left off. You're just what Monte needs and if you ask me, he's just what you need." She hesitated. "I look at this horse having a connection to the lieutenant, to Henry, and now to you and me. That kind of bonding really melts my heart."

Mickey chewed on this for a few moments. "I don't think I can begin riding without my prosthesis. The visiting nurse said I need to be fully healed before I can even think about wearing it again. Plus, my prosthesis needs to be repaired and fitted. Dr. Drake was going to take care of all that. I hope he doesn't forget about me."

"I'm sure he won't forget. You're unforgettable, Mickey."

They both laughed.

Abigail cocked her head to look at Mickey. "Is there something else worrying you about your prosthesis?" Abigail asked.

He paused before responding. "Yeah, I suppose there is." He cleared his throat. "I just hope I don't need a new prosthesis. The process of creating a new one can take forever. I waited a long time for mine. Fittings, therapy and maintenance took months to refine it so that it met my needs." He sighed. "Most of the one-size-fits-all limbs are as uncomfortable as they're ugly. I just want to look normal again."

She flashed a dimple at him. "You look pretty normal to me. In fact, I'll bet you looked quite handsome and dashing in your uniform."

The two grew quiet as they watched Monte wander off to join the other horses.

———

Mickey spoke quietly as if talking to himself. "Horses are such beautiful animals."

"Do you mean these horses or horses in general?" Abigail asked.

Mickey didn't answer. Instead, he lowered his head and seemed to drift away, lost somewhere. When he raised his head, a single tear trickled down his cheek. Abigail was unprepared for that.

He quickly swiped the tear away. "Sorry," he said.

Abigail opened the corral gate, came around, and walked over to him. "Hey, you okay? What just happened?"

He blinked his eyes a few times as if to see more clearly. "Sorry, I didn't want you to see that."

She gave him a few moments to gather himself. "Mickey, talk to me."

"It's just that I saw some terrible things over there."

"In the war, you mean. In France."

He nodded. "Awful, really awful things. Every so often I'll get a flashback."

She let a minute pass. "About what? Let me help you."

He hesitated, shifting his weight from one leg to another. "The men dying around us was horrible, I mean all the blood and gore was grisly and terrifying, but the thing that I couldn't shake was the horror of all the horses getting killed. Millions of them destroyed in the most awful ways. The guys in my company said death was something I'd get used to, but that never happened. The horses we have here in Vermont are so beautiful and make me smile, make me so appreciative of how we care for them, but then memories of those killed over there grab me by the throat and won't let go. So many innocent and pure animals sent to their death."

Abigail waited for a second. "Was that what triggered things a minute ago?"

He nodded. "I watched you cozying up to Monte and I got a flashback of a gelding attached to our company that looked a lot like him. Same dusty gray. He was part of a string of a dozen or so horses that we kept behind the lines. We used them as pack animals to carry supplies and weapons to the front and rear lines, and of course riders served as messengers on horseback. Anyway, I'd go over to see this horse whenever I could and bring him apples and carrots. I'd even ask the guys in my company for their apple cores. He loved the treats and would whinny and nicker when he saw me coming."

Where's he going with this? she thought.

Mickey continued. "One day the Germans decided to shell us with mustard gas, a poison we all feared. Gas masks had to be put on and adjusted immediately because sulfur mustard was bad stuff. When we heard shouts of, 'Gas,' 'Gas,' panic broke out in the trenches." He looked over at the herd for a second or two then returned his focus to Abigail. "Do you know anything about mustard gas?" he asked.

"A little."

"It was both gruesome and frightful. Barbaric and inhumane. Depending on your exposure to the gas it could cause fatal skin burning, blistering, respiratory disease, blindness, and death."

A pause.

"But gas masks protected you, right?"

"Yes, to a degree, but there were still casualties. We also had other victims. When this particular shelling took place, all of our horses had broken free from their restraints and experienced full exposure."

"Weren't the horses protected?"

"Gas masks for horses did exist, but soldiers had to save their own lives before they could turn their attention to their steeds. The panic in the trenches wasted precious time."

———————

Mickey continued, his head bowed and his voice noticeably weaker. "When the handlers found some of them, I eventually got to see the gelding, but wished I hadn't. He had severe burns to his head and hindquarters, and most of his gray coat had been reduced to bare skin with large yellow blisters. The mustard gas had sealed his eyes shut."

Mickey put his hand over his mouth to cover a cough, a weak and raspy one, and his eyes watered.

"Did the horse recognize your voice?"

"No, most of the horses were unresponsive to voices and commands. I brought some carrots and apples along with me but he wanted no part of them. He tried to bite me a few times."

She reached over to touch his shoulder. "I'm so sorry, Mickey."

He shook his head in sadness. "That's not even the worst part. After a few days, the Germans mounted another attack, this time a frontal assault with flamethrowers. My guess was the Germans thought we were in a state of disarray after the earlier barrage of poison gas, which we were, making this an ideal time to attack." He took a deep breath and let it out slowly. "The prospect of being burned alive was terrifying for all of us, especially as we watched the German infantry getting closer, sheets of flame breaking out in front along with clouds of thick black smoke."

She listened while dabbing at her cheeks with a handkerchief.

"But our line held. We stopped the assault and the enemy was pushed back." He hesitated. "Then something really sad and nauseating happened."

She waited.

"Out of nowhere came three of our wounded horses, having somehow broken free again." His voice quieted. "Including the gray horse."

"Where were they going?"

"I don't know. I don't think they even knew. They hobbled across the battlefield petrified. The Germans saw them as the troops retreated back to their trenches, including two armed with flamethrowers." He sniffled. "Before disappearing, the soldiers decided to set the horses on fire. Two of the horses collapsed immediately while the third tried getting away, its mane and shoulders on fire."

Abigail pulled in a long breath. "Was it the gray horse?"

"It was. He was set on fire and began shrieking, gasping for life. He finally fell and while still on fire, tried getting back up. Its hooves pawed violently at the ground. The German approached him, the flamethrower still ignited. There was little question as to what he was going to do."

Abigail was completely mesmerized and stunned by Mickey's narrative, but no words came to her mouth.

"Meanwhile, our company captain scrambled over to our trench location and shouted, 'Put that poor horse out of its misery, then blow that Kraut son of a bitch up. Aim for the tank on his back.' We followed orders and the company cheered the explosion."

Mickey was finished and he looked down at the ground, his eyes darting back and forth. His chest heaved as he tried stifling a sob.

"Have you shared this with anyone else? Henry perhaps?"

He shook his head.

"Come here," Abigail said, and when he did, she wrapped her arms around his waist and rested her head on his shoulder. "It's okay, Mickey, let it out. It's okay to be sad. I'm right here with you and I'm sad too." As she spoke, her eyes welled up.

They both wept and held on to each other for several minutes. When they separated, she spoke. "What you witnessed over there was something no human being should ever have to see. All of the war must've been terrible, but especially that. But please hear me, being sad doesn't mean you're not coping or losing your grip. On the contrary, you'll discover that over time sadness is a natural part of being human, a part of your uniqueness. It will get easier for you to come to terms with this over time. You'll find ways to adapt and persevere, trust me."

He nodded.

"Just look over there," she said, using her chin to point out the horses. All five of them were grazing together, quiet and peaceful. "Those pretty horses are content and happy, as safe and protected as they are unconditionally loved by all of us. We will keep them out of harm's way and never mistreat them. You were meant to be here, Mickey, to bond with another gray horse and to forge new memories."

He opened his mouth to speak then closed it. Then he tried again. "You know, I was always hoping that it was my bullet that took the life of that gray horse. I saw him lift his head one last time and I fired a shot at that very moment."

"You were hoping your shot was the coup de grâce."

"That's right, the mercy kill that ends the suffering of the fatally wounded."

She smiled grimly. "Who's to say it wasn't?"

They watched the horses for a little while longer before Mickey announced he was getting tired. He had to continually remind himself that he was still on a fairly strict exercise regimen. A brief embrace followed, and their eyes locked. "Thank you," he said quietly.

She watched as he slowly made his way back to the farmhouse, the boy soldier who came home from the war alive but wounded. He'd enlisted to join his pals on what was being touted as the great overseas adventure, but instead found a terrifying journey filled with suffering, sorrow, and painful regret. While Abigail was pleased to provide Mickey with emotional support, his haunting war recollections gnawed away at her, and she wondered how long it would take for him to reclaim a life of peace and serenity.

Twenty

Life on the Cooper horse farm had many traditions throughout the year, including finding the best Christmas tree to celebrate the holiday. Everyone got involved in the Christmas tree hunt, eventually choosing a blue spruce tree with the perfect shape. It would stand in the corner of the living room waiting to be decorated, its scent carrying throughout the house and creating a cozy holiday ambiance.

The hunt for the tree took place a day ago with everyone riding horseback to the property's tree farm except for Mickey, who was advised to stay home given the strenuous nature of the outing as well as the weather being quite blustery and chilly. Mickey didn't mind being left behind and to fill his time was given the assignment of retrieving boxes of Christmas tree ornaments and other holiday decorations from the attic and basement.

In the meantime, the hunting crew rode two abreast, Abigail and Julia out front, followed by Henry and Hudson. Searching to find that perfect tree, the debate of who found the best one, and the teamwork it took to get it back to the farmhouse was all part of the enjoyment. Abigail's choice was the winner, and once it was cut down and a length of rope attached to its base, the blue spruce was pulled along the trail by Julia's horse.

Along the way, Hudson took the opportunity to talk with Henry alone. The women had pulled ahead and were out of earshot.

Right from the start, Henry surmised something was wrong.

They stopped the horses. Hudson hemmed and hawed a bit before he spoke. "I need to bend your ear about a few private matters."

"Is that so? So long as it doesn't involve you leaving the farm and heading someplace else." He chuckled softly. "I can't run this place without you on board, sarge."

They stopped their horses.

Hudson laughed. "No, it's nothing like that. I'm happy and content here. I'll stay as long as you want me around, or until you decide to put me out to pasture."

"Well, that ain't going to happen. So, what's on your mind?"

"Mickey is on my mind."

Henry stiffened when he heard Mickey's name.

"This isn't bad, so don't fret. Just something to put in the back of your mind, is all."

"Go on."

"Apparently Mickey had a talk with Abigail the other day and Mickey got to share some of his war experiences. He shared some of the skeletons he's got stored in his closet."

Henry was puzzled. "You mean, about his wounds, about losing his arm?"

"No, different stuff. I guess he saw the enemy doing some brutal and sinister things to the war horses attached to his company. "Bad stuff, killed them in some terrible ways. Said he sometimes gets a flashback or a nightmare regarding what he saw."

"Is he okay?"

"Yes, he's more than okay. When this happened, Mickey needed to vent and Abigail was the sounding board, she just happened to be there."

Henry mulled things over. Eventually, he turned to Hudson. "What do you think I should do?" he asked.

Hudson said to Henry, "At this point, nothing. Just be aware and keep an eye on him. You and Mickey are obviously close, so I think sooner or later Mickey is going to share everything with you."

Henry said, "I feel left out of what he shared."

Hudson said, "Don't feel that way. The only reason this came out was because our horse Monte bore a resemblance to the horse being tortured on the battlefield. It triggered a flashback to the war and had nothing to do with him hiding things from you. You shouldn't feel left out."

"Should I approach him about any of this?"

"No, I don't think so, at least for right now. Plus, I don't think you should tip your hand and tell him we spoke, nor that Abigail shared a sensitive conversation. I'll do the same and of course, I will keep an eye on him too."

"Okay, my lips are sealed."

"War is hell, Henry. I'm sure the lieutenant told you that repeatedly."

Henry nodded. "He did, and then some."

A moment of silence passed between the two of them.

Finally, Henry sighed and they prodded the horses along. "You said you had a few other private matters to discuss. What else is going on in your mind?"

Hudson scratched his chin. "Well, this one is much more personal."

"I'm listening."

Hudson hesitated at first, then opened up. "I want you to know that Abigail and I have started seeing each other. We like each other. We both felt it was important to tell you and hoped this would be okay with you."

Henry heard this, then used leg pressure to stop his horse. Hudson did the same. They turned their horses so they could be facing each other.

Henry sat still in the saddle, puzzled. "What did you just say?" he asked.

"I said I'd like to see Abigail and we both hoped it would be okay with you."

Hudson waited, no doubt looking for Henry to say something. He didn't. The two just stared at each other.

Finally, though, Henry broke the silence. "So, are you looking for my permission?"

Hudson looked at him sheepishly. "I guess I just wanted you to know. We didn't want it to be a secret, least of all to you."

Henry shook his head and grinned. "You old horn dog. I didn't think you had it in you. You like her, eh?"

Hudson's face softened and then lit up. "I do. Liked her right from the start."

"Well, you don't need my permission to date her for crying out loud. The two of you are no longer in high school. Next thing you'll be asking me for your curfew time." Henry flashed a wide grin. "Seriously, this is great news, Hudson. The two of you make for a nice couple. I'm happy for both of you."

Henry reached over and shook Hudson's hand. "Pay heed of sheriff Whittaker, though."

"Why's that?"

"He was eyeballing Abigail the other day when he stopped by. Wanted to know if she was married. Said she was a fine-looking woman." He hesitated. "Julia doesn't care for the guy and said he was always a womanizer." Henry chose not to tell Hudson about Maeve and the sheriff, at least for now.

Hudson scoffed. "That boot-licking turnkey had better watch his step. I didn't like that bumbling flatfoot right from the get-go and I'll tell him so right to his puss." He let loose with a bitter laugh. "By the way, Abigail doesn't like him either. Said he gives her the creeps."

"Okay, calm down. I just wanted to give you a heads-up."

"I appreciate that Henry, I really do." He straightened in the saddle. "Listen, before we head back to the house, I've got one more thing to run by you."

Henry rubbed at his forehead and said, "Go ahead."

"I got a telephone call the other day from Ty Griffin."

"The breeder from Chicopee?"

"That's him. His ranch is where I found Morning Star and Lola a little while back. Gave us a good deal on both horses."

"I remember. What'd he want?"

"I asked him to call me after we bought Morning Star and Lola. Said we were looking to expand our herd and would be interested in adding a mare and a stallion. Anyway, he told me over the phone he'd just acquired two American quarter horses and thought of us. The mare is six years old and the stallion seven. Both measure fifteen hands and both are palominos. Pretty horses.

Healthy, friendly, gentle, easy to ride, effortless walk, trot, and canter. Griffin doesn't think he can hold on to them for very long."

Hudson tilted his head to one side. "What do you think?"

"I always wanted to own palominos. I think you should go take a look-see before they're sold to someone else. Chicopee isn't that far away. Why don't you give him a call and try to set up something before the holidays."

Hudson nodded. "How 'bout you come with me?"

"Sure, I can do that."

They were about to head back to the farmhouse when Henry suddenly stopped his mount and held up his right arm. "Whoa, hold up there, sergeant. You should be taking Abigail with you, not me. After all, she's the horse trainer." Henry winked at him. "Besides, it will give the two of you some time together."

"Is that an order, chief?"

"Yes, that's an order, sergeant," Henry replied, a sly grin on his face.

Henry then leaned forward in his saddle. "*Sígueme de vuelta,*" he shouted. This a spirited, "Follow me," often barked by lieutenant Cooper to Henry when the two of them were out horseback riding.

They galloped along the trail leading back to the barn. By the time they got back, the wind had picked up and brought a strong bite of winter with it. The sky had turned gray and a few snowflakes started to fall. They unsaddled their horses and put them in the corral.

The two joined the others in the living room. Much to their surprise, the tree was already in its stand and decorations were being hung. Mickey had retrieved all the ornaments from the attic and the basement, an assortment of wooden, hand-painted toy soldiers, angels, snowmen, trinkets, and toys, along with red and silver bows and lots of garland.

Julia remarked, "We thought the two of you got lost and were ready to send out a search party."

Mickey agreed. "Complete with a dogsled and emergency flares," he said lightheartedly.

Henry was apologetic and replied, "Sorry, Hudson and I had a lot to talk about and didn't realize how much time had passed."

"Isn't it a beautiful tree?" Abigail asked, folding her arms across her chest. "I'll have everyone know it was yours truly who picked it out, all by my little old self." She laughed out loud, poking fun at her inflated self-admiration. She got a good laugh from the others.

They were interrupted by someone knocking at the front door.

Mickey jumped to his feet to answer it, Henry deciding to follow.

The door was opened and two people, a young man and woman, stood outside.

They stared at Carl and Carl stared back.

The man said, "I'm Jacob Winsted and this is my sister Ariel. We're here to say hello and see the farm. Mr. Cameron said to stop by."

Carl continued to stare blankly at the two of them, frozen like a statue.

Henry nudged him from behind.

That brought Carl to life. He looked at the man, tilted his head just so, then grinned and said, "Howdy stranger, welcome to the Cooper farm. Why not come inside and stay a while. I've been waiting for you and we've got lots to talk about."

He'd memorized his welcome perfectly.

Henry introduced himself then ushered Jacob and Ariel into the living room to meet the others. Once the Winsteds had shed their coats and boxes had been moved out of the way, everyone sat down to get acquainted.

The two had just finished high school and were handsome, clean, and well-mannered. Ariel was tall and graceful with striking hazel eyes while her brother was broad shouldered and rugged, and owned a disarming smile. They sat up straight, asked good questions, and listened intently as Henry described the history of the farm, the horses, the cornfield, and the orchard. He shared some general features of their job descriptions, which for Ariel would be household and cooking chores while for Jacob it meant tending to the horses along with assorted maintenance assignments. Henry then rattled off a number of work habits he deemed essential to the farm's successful operation. These expectations included being punctual, completing tasks before leaving, being respectful to everyone, taking pride in one's work, being receptive to constructive feedback, and valuing honesty at all times.

Henry said, "If you have questions, I suggest you write them down. I know I've given you a lot to think over, and I encourage the two of you to talk and then let me know if you're still interested. If you are, we can talk wages and schedules. In the meantime, I'm going to have Carl show Jacob around the horse farm and Julia will take Ariel around the house so that you can get a feel for the place."

Ariel and Jacob stood and grabbed their coats, then went around the room shaking hands with everyone. They saved Henry for last.

Jacob said to Henry, "I know our purpose today was to just stop by say hello, but I want to say we'd both be honored to work for you. With our father out of work, money is tight back home, so this job means a lot to us."

Ariel added, "By the way, your Christmas tree is really pretty," said Ariel. "We haven't gotten ours yet."

"We will, though," added Jacob. Jacob stumbled with his words, making Henry wonder if they were really going to bring a Christmas tree into their home.

"Okay," Henry said, "why don't you come by tomorrow morning and we'll discuss details, including pay and work schedules."

"We'll be here, Mr. Cameron," said Ariel.

———————

The living room emptied with Carl putting his hand on Jacob's shoulder. "The first thing you need to do is buy a tool belt like mine. You'll never know when you might need a hammer or a wrench. It's good to have these hanging from your hip."

Julia looked at Henry and rolled her eyes while trying to hide a smirk before leading Ariel upstairs to look at the top floor.

Hudson entered the living room having just finished a telephone call. He settled in an easy chair next to Henry.

"I just talked to Ty Griffin," he said.

"And?"

"Ty told me tomorrow was the best time to come and see his horses. After tomorrow, most of his crew was leaving for the holidays."

Henry looked over at Hudson. "You okay with doing a day trip to Chicopee tomorrow?"

"Ready and able," he replied.

Henry looked at Abigail, who was seated across from him in the living room. He said to her, "I'd like you to go with Hudson tomorrow. Two sets of eyes are better than one and I'd like you both to view these horses."

Abigail readily agreed, not that Henry ever doubted her willingness to tag along with Hudson.

Hudson piped up while looking at Henry. "Will you be okay without us being around for a full day?"

"Not a problem," Henry replied, not giving it a second thought. "Mickey and I can handle all that needs to be done around here, plus we have Carl and Julia as back-up. We'll be fine."

Henry asked, "Will the owner be expecting you? Are the two horses ready to show?"

"Once I get back to him, everything will be ready. I'll call him back after we talk and say we'll leave in the morning."

"Okay, good. Now, you still trust this guy, right?"

"Absolutely."

"Make sure you get a copy of the horses' general information sheets. That will give us the horses' general medical information and what type of training they've had." He looked at Hudson. "What else do you intend to inspect?"

Hudson replied, "Whenever I look at a new horse, I try to get a good look at their hooves, teeth, and eyes. All of these can tell me a lot about a horse. If I can pick up the horse's hooves, I look to see how concave and shaped their feet are. If the horse happens to have flat feet, where it looks like it might be walking on the sole of its hoof, this can be a sign that it will need shoes and may have other problems relating to its feet later on. This puts me on guard."

Henry asked, "Will Ty allow you to ride the horses?"

Hudson replied, "When there is a purchase pending, he wants to make sure the buyer and the horse make a good fit. He is open to buyers who want to ride or see someone put the horse through its routines."

Henry leaned forward in his chair. "So, bringing Abigail along is your ace in the hole."

"Exactly."

"Okay, let me know what you think, both of you. If you like what you see, inquire as to what his asking price is, and whether or not the figure is negotiable. See if we can board the horses at his place for the winter. Ask what the monthly boarding price is. It may be cheaper for us to go to Chicopee with our own trailer and bring them back home. We'll see. After all, we've already rebuilt the barn to accommodate five more horses." He looked at the two of them. "How does all of that sound?"

They both nodded in synchrony.

"Any last thoughts?" asked Henry.

"Full steam ahead," said Hudson, a wide smile on his face.

Twenty-One

With the absence of Abigail and Hudson, who'd left for Chicopee at daybreak, Henry and Mickey tended to the early morning chores, including mucking the stalls and tending to the horses. When they were just about finished, Jacob and Ariel showed up in their car, as requested. They stood outside the corral, waiting for Henry.

Once Henry was done, the Winsteds exchanged greetings from afar, then Henry removed his rubber boots and gloves, slipped into his regular boots and tossed the gloves aside, then walked over to his visitors. He grinned and said "Morning, Winsteds."

They were eager with their greetings and along with that, both scanned the property and the hills beyond. Ariel had never seen such beautiful and tranquil surroundings,

Henry said, "Abigail will show you the trails when she gets back, which we'll use, and you'll be trained as you follow the horse paths."

Ariel said, "These hills and woods are beautiful, breathtaking really. Is this property all yours? We don't have the view of the hills from our place like you do here."

Henry responded. "Yes, it's all ours. About fifty acres."

The two newcomers were swept away by the amount of land before them.

"You own the apple orchard, too?" asked Ariel.

"Yes, that's ours."

"Our parents used to take us here when we were kids for sweet corn and apples," she said. "This used to be the Cooper farm, right?"

"That's right."

"Are you a Cooper?"

"No, but lieutenant Tom Cooper was my legal guardian."

"You mean the cavalry officer?

"That's him."

"Didn't he pass away just a little while ago?"

"He did. He got infected by the Spanish flu a short while ago and didn't make it. This town lost one of its best in Tom Cooper but his legacy will live on."

"Is he buried nearby?" asked Ariel.

"He is," replied Henry. "Once we get you squared away, maybe we can go visit his gravesite."

A few moments of silence passed.

"And what about the soldier who lost his arm?"

"You mean Mickey?"

"Yes, the handsome one," Ariel said, blushing a bit. "Will he be working with us?"

"Mickey will be with you every day."

"Oh, good," said Ariel, trying hard once again to hide the blushing.

Henry switched gears. "Can the two of you ride horseback?"

Jacob answered for the two of them. "We've both been on horseback, not a lot, but we've both got some experience. Some bareback, too."

"We'll help teach you what you don't know." And with that he made sure all of the horses were secured, then invited Jacob and Ariel into the house.

They were as polite inside the home as they were outside.

Julia had anticipated the Winsteds and had prepared fresh, hot coffee along with warm biscuits with honey glazed topping. The biscuits were an immediate hit.

Everyone ate their fill, then Henry invited them into the living room.

Julia excused herself, and Micky and Carl were elsewhere on the property. Henry and his guests had the room to themselves.

Henry said, "Okay, let's talk about the jobs, shall we? You came back, so I assume you both want the jobs offered."

Both nodded.

"You've had the opportunity to walk around, see the place, and talk with our workers about the job responsibilities. I assume you've had time to talk with your family about it, too, plus you've had time to sleep on it."

"All good?" asked Henry. "Any reservations?"

Both replied exactly at the same time, "All good," almost like they'd rehearsed the timing of their response.

Henry grinned at them. "Does that often happen?" he asked.

Jacob replied, "What, speaking at the same time?"

Henry grinned and nodded.

"Yeah, that happens pretty often," said Jacob.

Ariel giggled. "That's because we're twins."

"Really? You guys are twins? I didn't know that." Henry slowly shook his head and grinned some more. "Is one of you more dominant than the other?"

Ariel looked at her brother. "He likes to think he is, but don't let him fool you. If you want things done, come see me."

Jacob just shook his head and muttered something to himself.

Henry picked up where he left off and covered the wages, days needed, and so forth. Finally, he said, "We'll get you started after the holidays. I'll call you about a start-up date."

Rather than elated, their faces became sullen.

"What's wrong?" said Henry. "Did I say something wrong?"

Jacob said, "We were hoping to start today or tomorrow. We really need the money, Mr. Cameron, especially given the holidays. Our mother works, but our father doesn't. He's been pretty much limited with what he can do for over three months now. He's got a pretty serious back injury, but he's improving. Hopefully he'll be up and about by springtime."

Henry reached into the back pocket of his dungarees and produced two envelopes. He held them up in front of the two. "These are for you. Call it an advance against future wages. I want the two of you to work here, to stay here and be part of our team, so let this be an incentive for the two of you to come back and stay on board."

He handed the envelopes to them, his smile broadened. "Like I said, I don't expect either of you to work until the first of the new year. For now, enjoy the holidays. Be with your family, help them, and be patient with your father."

Inside each envelope was two hundred dollars in cash.

They looked wide-eyed at the bills and thanked him profusely for his kindness and generosity. Tears filled Ariel's eyes. They left wishing Henry a Merry Christmas, the words spoken, of course, at exactly the same time.

———————

Later that afternoon, Carl and Julia drove into town to do some grocery shopping. That left Mickey and Henry alone. They tended to the horses for a while before high-tailing it to the house, a wintry breeze chilling their bones. Once inside, they heated up some leftover coffee and once they stoked the flames in the fireplace, pulled their chairs in close.

They sat there, relaxed, sheltered, and snug.

Henry told Mickey that he'd hired the Winsteds, although the two wouldn't be starting until after the holidays.

Mickey said, "That's good news, I liked them both."

"I did, too. But let me tell you something, mate. Ariel has her eye on you. She asked who that handsome soldier boy was, wanted to know if you'd be working with them. Even blushed when she asked.

"Go on, you're putting me on."

"No, I'm not. You'll see."

Mickey just shook his head.

"She's a pretty one, soldier," Henry added.

They talked a little more, then out of the blue Mickey straightened in his chair. "I've been meaning to ask you something," he said. "The other day I was asked to retrieve Christmas ornaments from the attic and the basement."

Henry nodded. "Popular consensus was you did a fine job."

"Thank you, but I'm not fishing for compliments. When I was down in the basement, I couldn't help but notice a large room sealed at the far end of the staircase. When I got closer, I could see that its doors were padlocked."

"I was wondering when you'd notice it."

"So, what is it?"

Henry said, "Why don't we go down there and I'll show you."

They got up, then descended the steep staircase down to the basement. The basement was spacious and chilly. Henry reached up for a bulb, turned it, and a few bulbs hanging along the ceiling directed a pathway to the locked storeroom.

Henry had the keys to the storeroom doors and after fiddling a bit with the lock, it snapped open. The two walked in the room and were affronted by the mixed scents of gun oil, saddle soap, and cedar. Henry walked the length of the room, pulling cords downward from overhead light bulbs, which when combined illuminated every crevice of the storeroom. There would be no secret as to where the delicious mixture of delicious scents originated.

Now that Mickey could see, he couldn't believe his eyes. Inside was the equivalent of a military storeroom, a sealed-tight room chock full of uniforms, weapons, ammunition boxes, canvas ammunition belts, flags and guidons, military horse blankets, sabers and scabbards, holsters, knives and bayonets, saddles, saddlebags, canteens, boots, bugles, binoculars, stirrups, Western regulation cavalry hats and AEF Stetsons, and boots, lots of boots.

Mickey walked through the storeroom, tentative at first, but then with his curiosity piqued. He ran his fingers along the horse blankets and saddles, slid the sabers in and out of the scabbards, tenderly touched the brass buttons of the uniforms, unfurled the guidon of the seventh cavalry, then the eleventh cavalry."

He turned to face Henry. "He's here, you know. I can feel him."

Henry nodded.

"You must feel this every time you go down these stairs."

"I do. You have no idea how often I've come down here just to sit and be quiet. You know, just sit and remember."

"Does it help?"

"Yes, it does. I think of all he's done for me."

"Do you I mind if I poke around down here?"

"No, I don't mind. You know, it helps me to remember how we met, how he helped me. I'm sorry I waited so long to show you this room. Besides Hudson, you're the only person who's ever seen this."

With that reassurance, Mickey found his way over to a custom-made, oak gun rack affixed to a nearby wall. It was huge. The wood was beautifully crafted and stained. It held three Springfield rifles, two Winchester 1873 lever-action rifles, a Sharps carbine with a telescopic sight, a Ross bolt-action rifle, three Colt M1911 handguns, and three 1873 single-shot Colt revolvers.

Mickey touched the stock of one of the Springfields.

Henry said, "You were issued a Springfield in the war, right?"

"Yep, that's right. A bolt-action, 30/06 Model 1903 Springfield."

"Did you fire at the enemy with it?"

He nodded. "I did quite a few times before I was injured."

"Did you take incoming fire from the Germans?"

"We sure did it, lots of it. I'll tell you, those German boys could shoot. Stick your head up out of the trenches at the wrong time and you were well on your way to meeting your maker."

It was quiet for a moment, then Mickey blurted out, "I shot a horse once."

"How'd that happen?" Henry knew full well how it happened but wanted Mickey to open up and share the story.

Mickey did just that, and Henry took it all in, letting his friend know that what he did was deliver a mercy kill, a humane act and a noble gesture.

"That horse was suffering while it was dying, Mickey, and you spared him from any more pain. You set him free, and I would've done the same thing."

"Honest?"

Henry replied, "Honest," and patted Mickey on his shoulder. "I want you to know I'll always make myself available should you care to share anything else on your mind."

"I want you to do the same with your misfortunes, Henry." Mickey knew his friend had taken his share of bumps and bruises and didn't want him to be close lipped about any of it.

They shook on it, holding the clasp for an extra minute. No words were needed.

Below the rifles on the concrete floor, just below the gun rack, was a large, locked, metal storage box. When it was opened, Mickey couldn't believe his eyes. It was an ammunition box, filled with dozens of magazines and boxes of ammunition labeled for the rifles and pistols as well as the single-shot Colt revolvers. Dozens of other boxes of ammunition for all the weapons rested at the bottom of the metal box. Canvas bandoliers and their leather counterparts were hung on pegs along the far wall, just above the ammunition boxes.

Obviously, this household was prepared for war, no matter the circumstances and no matter the foe.

Mickey stepped back a moment. He was perspiring and mopping his brow with a handkerchief. "There must be thousands of rounds in here," Mickey said.

"Easily," replied Henry.

At the rear of the basement were several uniforms worn by the lieutenant throughout his military career. During the Indian War campaign, he wore the standard blue blouse as well as the lighter blue regulation trousers with a yellow stripe running along the outer seam of the legs. A black, flapped leather holster held a Colt 1873 sidearm along with an ammunition pouch on the belt. He was also issued a greatcoat cape lined in yellow. Also issued by the war department was a regulation, double-edged hunting knife, nine inches in length and four inches in width. The knife was carried on the waist in a leather scabbard.

Another uniform worn by lieutenant Cooper was the standard issue for the American Expeditionary Force. It consisted of a broad-brimmed felt hat with a high crown, pinched symmetrically at the four corners. He wore a wool pullover campaign shirt that bore his rank bars on the collar. His pants were wool riding trousers, a darker olive drab color from his blouse. On his webbed gun belt was a .45 caliber, Colt M1912 semi-automatic pistol, secured by a long khaki lanyard looped diagonally around his torso. His M1912 gun belt also held a double pistol magazine pouch, and was itself supported by a pair of leather suspenders. The lieutenant carried two more regimental pistols in his saddlebags along with four extra magazines.

"Didn't he have a saddle holster made to carry the extra pistols and magazines?" asked Mickey.

Henry nodded. "He did. If a battle was looming, or if his command was riding into hostile territory, he'd attach it to the front of his saddle."

Mickey and Henry continued to explore the rest of the weapons trove before they decided to quit and go upstairs.

As they turned toward the stairs, Mickey stopped.

"I have another question to ask before we head upstairs," said Mickey.

"And what's that?"

"The lieutenant and Hudson rode in the same outfit, right?"

"Right, the eleventh cavalry."

Mickey scratched the back of his head. "Can you imagine the two of them charging the enemy together?"

"I wouldn't want to go up against either one of them," Henry replied.

"Me either."

"I'm told the lieutenant always led the charge while sergeant Delaney would bark the orders to the troops in formation. That must've been quite a show."

"But the troops never caught Pancho Villa and his army of renegades."

"Nope, never did. They pulled back into the mountains while the cavalry pursued." He paused. "But the lieutenant continued to engage down below in a battle with the outlaws who stayed behind as a rear guard. Even when he was stabbed in his leg while on horseback, the lieutenant fought like a tiger. Eventually, the few outlaws left retreated. The lieutenant lost a lot of blood and ultimately fell off his horse. Luckily a surgeon was nearby and after taking one look at the lieutenant's leg, had him whisked away in an ambulance."

"That's why he walked with a limp," Mickey said.

"That's correct."

Mickey said, "So, when the lieutenant and Hudson Delaney arrived at Camp Dewey in Uncasville, they'd just been discharged from the U. S. Cavalry."

"Right, when all of us arrived there, it was only a stopping point for them before they headed for Vermont."

Henry said, "But he saw potential in both of us and in his own way, invited us to join him. Unfortunately, he died before we got you to climb on board, but he knew you needed to be rescued."

Mickey lowered his head. "I never knew any of this."

"He wanted you to have a better life and he put that expectation on my shoulders. He died before he could search and find you, but knew I would continue the search."

It got very quiet in the basement.

Finally, Mickey said, "Is there any chance we can shoot any of these firearms once I get my prosthesis back? That might be a couple of weeks away, but maybe it's something we can plan on?"

"Sorry, absolutely not."

Mickey was shocked and glared at him. "Why not?"

"Because you don't need a prosthesis to shoot a sidearm in my army. We can start practicing as soon as you're comfortable."

Mickey balked. "What do you mean?"

"You're right-handed, right?"

Mickey nodded.

"Then we'll first get you a pistol and holster that's comfortable for your right hand. I'm thinking of starting you off with an 1873 single-shot Colt revolver. It has a decent kick but, manageable and accurate. You don't need two hands to fire it. After that, maybe we'll move you up to a Colt M1912 semi-automatic pistol. We'll see how that goes. It's a powerful handgun needing patience and practice. Then, once you get your prosthesis, we'll step up to the long guns. Sound good?"

Mickey grinned. "Can't wait."

Twenty-Two

By the end of the day, Hudson and Abigail had returned from their journey from Chicopee, Massachusetts, none the worse for wear. They were happy and lively, exiting the car with a bounce in their step and grins across their faces. It was great to be home among friends with good news to share.

Julia had taken the time during the day to prepare a pot roast with gravy and mashed potatoes along with steamed vegetables, and baked muffins, plus two apple pies, the latter cooling beneath a half-open kitchen window. The aroma of a mouth-watering, home-cooked meal filled the entire farmhouse.

The presence of both Abigail and Hudson back home was uplifting. Before sitting down to dinner, Hudson put the car away in the garage while Abigail went over to the corral and checked on the horses. When they saw her approaching, the horses sang forth a chorus of neighs, whinnies, and nickers. There was no mistaking their love for her. When she opened the corral gate and stepped inside, they approached her and engaged in some licking and kissing. Rufus and Lola gave Abigail some nudges and bumps to get her attention, and Monte even rested his head on her. Morning Star spent time sniffing her, no doubt detecting the scent of other horses.

At the dinner table the conversations were lively, animated, and entertaining. Of course, everyone wanted to hear about the excursion to Chicopee.

Henry said, "So, did the two of you find your way to the Wilcox Horse Farm?"

"Not a problem," Hudson replied. "We didn't get lost. I'd been there before, but this was Abigail's first visit."

Henry looked over at Abigail. "So, what did our horse trainer think of the place?"

"To be honest," Abigail said, "it took my breath away. It's huge, I'm going to guess the spread occupies well over eighty acres. It has two barns and twenty-some stalls, two corrals, a riding ring, paddocks, and a wash rack that provides a place to clean horses without a lot of setup work or creating a mess. Also, lots of trails for riding. I was impressed with it all, to say the least."

Hudson said, "Plus, the place was spotless, just as it was the last time I was there. That's when I purchased Morning Star and Lola."

"Did you get to see Ty Griffin?" asked Henry.

"Oh, for sure. He came bounding out of the house and greeted us with open arms. He was delighted to see us. He asked about you, Henry, as well as how Morning Star and Lola were doing. He was thrilled to learn that his horses had adjusted so well. But he became glum when I told him about the loss of the lieutenant. He didn't know the lieutenant had passed away. He was really crushed by this. He had enormous respect for the lieutenant and called him one of the finest horsemen he'd ever seen. The finest person, too."

Hudson added that they also talked about Monte, another horse purchased from Ty. This was before Morning Star and Lola were purchased, and both Ty and the lieutenant had reservations about Monte. The horse was jittery and high-strung, as well as distrustful. Monte was also ring sour, which meant that he got real onery when led into the riding ring. Ty shook his head and laughed, saying that he and the lieutenant didn't get to see much of a ring performance out of Monte that day. But the lieutenant bought him anyway, seeing potential and promise.

Henry chimed in. "When I first arrived here, I remember how the lieutenant told me that Monte had been in a fire that killed both his parents and left him traumatized. He was still spooked. The lieutenant paired us off and we spent hundreds of hours bonding, mostly my leading him through the trails. When I finally got him inside a corral, I used a lunge line, which enabled me to use a long rope to move him in large circles around me." He paused. "Exercise like that plus daily contact paved the way to riding him. Riding Monte came easier than I thought."

Hudson said, "Ty told us the lieutenant stopped by his ranch every now and then. He'd tell Ty about Monte's progress, due largely to Henry, the kid handler, as he was dubbed."

Henry dropped his chin to his chest and laughed. "Come on, man, he never said that."

"Oh, yes, he did," Abigail said. "I was there, I heard it."

Everyone had pretty much finished their meal. There weren't many leftovers, but everyone rose from the table to help scrape the plates. Silverware was separated from glasses and dinner plates, and Julia tended to the pots and pans. Hudson and Abigail took the tablecloth and napkins outside to shake the crumbs. Henry grabbed a broom and swept the floor. Carl just sat there smiling, cool as a cucumber, mainly because he'd managed to escape cleanup duties. He kept eyeballing the apple pies about to be served and kept licking his chops.

Julia suggested that once the kitchen was in order, they should all move to the living room, where she'd serve dessert. Abigail offered to help serve.

———————

Once they were settled, everyone dug into the delicious apple pie. It was tender and had flaky pie crust and juicy apple slices drenched in sugar, cinnamon and nutmeg. The aroma filled the room. It was a dessert made in heaven.

Finally, Henry asked Hudson, "Did you get a chance to introduce Abigail to Ty?"

"Of course, I did," Hudson said chuckling.

"What's so funny?" Henry asked.

Abigail interrupted. "Go ahead, funny man, tell him what's so humorous."

Hudson raised both his palms in the air, "Okay, okay, I'll confess. I introduced Abigail as the *Arabian Vaquera*. When I said that, Ty's whole expression changed. He furrowed his brow and scratched his head. He was totally baffled."

Everyone in the room looked at each other in puzzlement except for Carl, who was too busy jamming a second slice of apple pie down his dough-hole.

Henry said, "But then you told him that was just her nickname, right?"

"Of course," Hudson said. "I told him that her real name is Abigail Emory. I called her the *Arabian Vaquera* because she was the former trainer of the Arabian horses, King and Queen, of diving horse fame."

Hudson continued. "When I said that, Ty was shocked. He looked at Abigail and snapped his fingers and said, 'I remember, you were the horse trainer for J.W. Gorman's Diving Horse Show. I must've watched that show at least a dozen times whenever Gorman's show came our way. I want you to know that I thought you handled those Arabian horses with expertise and competence. I am so honored to meet you, Abigail.'"

Abigail blushed, then and now. She was overwhelmed with Ty Griffin's profuse recognition of her riding skills and accepted his compliments with grace and humility.

Hudson said, "Ty was flustered and happy, wanted to ask her a million questions."

Abigail smiled and took it all in.

"It got us off on solid footing," said Hudson. "All of us had a really good laugh over the nickname."

Abigail stuck her tongue out at Hudson and playfully punched him on the arm.

"So, what happened next?" asked Mickey.

Hudson said, "We were ushered into the ranch's largest barn, which had an indoor riding ring. Two of Ty's ranch hands went to a separate part of the barn and brought out the palominos. As Ty had told me over the phone, both stood fifteen hands tall. The mare is six years old and the stallion seven. As the handlers led the horses into the ring, the beauty and grace of the two horses were unmistakable."

"Oh my God," agreed Abigail, "they were breathtaking. Talk about pretty horses."

At that point, Hudson said to Abigail, "Let's show them the photos?"

"You have photos?" asked Henry.

Abigail excused herself. When she returned, she had a folder in hand.

Henry was handed the photo file and the others gathered around. He opened the file and the others gasped. The two photos of the palominos were in color, separately and together. They all stared at the photos.

Mickey asked, "How did they manage to get these photos in color?"

"Come on, man," said Henry. "Color photos have been around since Autochrome was invented in 1903. *National Geographic* was one of the early adopters of Autochrome photos."

Mickey nodded and continued to stare at the photos.

Hudson spread them on a nearby coffee table so that the others could see.

No one spoke while the photos were laid bare.

Finally, Hudson said, "The photos here don't do any justice to the grace and stature of these horses. You need to see them first-hand to appreciate their beauty, and Ty Griffin has extended an open-invitation for all of us to come down to Chicopee to see them and get a closer look."

He continued. "You need to be reminded, too, that a palomino is not a breed. These are quarter horses, and plenty of other breeds are palominos. Palomino is simply the coloring on a horse. The palomino coloring is most often described as "yellow." Palomino horses have a golden creamy coat that is accented by a flaxen mane and tail and potentially other white markings on the face and legs. While this coloring isn't found in every horse breed, it is more popular in quarter horses.

All eyes stayed glued to the two photos.

"Can you tell us which horse is which?" asked Julia.

"Okay," said Hudson. He pointed to the photos. "On the left is the stallion named Ronan. Ronan is a Golden Palomino. He is a beautiful quarter horse with a rich shiny coat that reflects like gold. We found him to be both friendly and curious. Ty told us that Ronan has a strong work ethic and a willingness to please. These traits make him highly trainable and adaptable to various riding styles."

Hudson continued and pointed to the mare on the right. "Tess is a Light Palomino. She has a softer creamy color, which shows a more noticeable yellow coat. She has a white mane and tail. Her temperament is captured in her gentleness. Based on Ty's reports, Tess is also easily trained and possesses a willingness to please."

"Where did these particular palominos come from?" asked Henry.

"Ty told us they were both born and raised in Newport, Rhode Island."

"Why are they being sold?"

"A sad story, for sure. The owner of the horses went to war as a soldier in the infantry. He died in the battle of Cambrai, France. He never came home. His body was never recovered."

Henry looked at Mickey. "You were in Cambrai, weren't you?"

Mickey nodded. "I could've been in the same trench line as this guy, but of course never realized it at the time." Just then, a wave of flashbacks flickered on and off in Mickey's mind, none of them quiet or peaceful. He bowed his head. The sounds and smells of gunpowder mixed with the stench of the muddied trenches. Burning flesh. Blood and vomit. A fleeting image of a horse set afire.

Henry looked back toward Hudson. "Tell me more about them."

"Before he went off to war, the owner said that if he didn't return home, he left specific instructions for his wife. He knew managing the two horses would be too much for her to handle by herself. Her husband wanted her to sell the palominos to an owner who could nurture and protect them, an owner who'd be able to let them run free. So, she contacted Ty Griffin."

Hudson added, "Ty mulled over the widow's desire and thought of our farm. Thanks to the lieutenant and Henry, our ranch was becoming known as a safe haven, a place where horses could go to find healing and strength, along with a quality training experience."

"How did the palominos perform in the ring?" asked Henry.

Hudson stumbled a bit and stared at Abigail. He replied, "Given her talents as a trainer, I'll defer this question to Abigail."

Henry nodded.

Abigail straightened in her chair. She said, Ty had one of his trainers there but had no problem allowing her to ride both palominos. "Ty said both horses were used to being ridden four days a week. At least two of the days included a more intense workout while the other days resulted in a slightly easier and less strenuous ride."

She continued. "It was easy to see right away that both palominos had received quality training. Tess and Ronan were alert and responsive. On command they walked, trotted, cantered. They picked up on my leads easily and demonstrated wonderful, effortless transitions. They exhibited beautiful stops, and were very responsive to leg cues. They stood patiently when instructed, which I'm sure translates to no fuss when approached by a farrier or veterinarian. Same goes for tacking or harnessing. Both palominos were easy to be stalled or turned out with other horses. They both got along with others, thanks to their gentle temperaments."

Abigail said both she and Hudson were impressed.

"Well done," said Henry.

Henry stirred in his chair. "Did you gather details on their preventative care and veterinary checkups?"

Hudson responded, "I have complete records on both. Nothing's hidden on either one. Based on the documentation I have in my possession, the palominos have received regular preventative care. They have been vaccinated against common equine diseases such as tetanus and equine influenza. A deworming program is in place to protect the horses from internal parasites, such as roundworms, tapeworms, and strongyles. They have received regular dental checkups and routine hoof care, including regular trimming and shoeing by a professional farrier."

Hudson finished up by saying, "Henry, we're looking at two healthy and robust horses. They've been the recipients of regular, general health checkups, at once or twice a year. These checkups have included a physical examination, blood tests, and any other necessary diagnostic tests. I'm convinced they'll remain monitored, healthy, and happy throughout their lives."

"You're satisfied?" Henry asked Hudson.

"I am."

He looked at Abigail. "And my trainer, *Arabian Vaquera*?" Are you happy with what you saw and how the horses performed?

She smiled. "I am. My gut tells me you won't regret bringing them on board."

"That's good enough for me," Henry said. He looked at Hudson.

"Don't you want to know the asking price?" asked Hudson.

Henry said, "Nope, that's up to you and Abigail to squabble over with Ty Griffin. You're my trainers and I'll back whatever offer or counter-offer the two of you deem reasonable."

Hudson took a long look at Abigail. He shrugged and their eyes locked. This was how Henry deflected responsibility and left major decisions to his lieutenants. He trusted those in his inner circle.

Hudson stood and took a step toward Henry. "One last thing. Ty said that given the time of year, with winter at our footsteps, we might want to consider boarding the two horses at his place until we're ready to transport them to Vermont when winter breaks. Should that be the case, he'd be happy to board them and transport them up to our place when we're ready."

Henry nodded and looked at Hudson and Abigail. "What do you say we chew on that for now, okay? Let's give it some thought before we make a commitment on boarding and transportation."

Henry held up a hand and paused. "But, In the meantime, I want the two of you to hammer out a deal with Ty Griffin to acquire these two rascals. Let's get their ownership under our belt first, then take it from there."

All three shook on it.

As they turned to leave, Henry said, "You might want to telephone Ty tonight and tell him we're interested in his horses and wish to make an offer. We don't want them sold out from under us."

Twenty-Three

The death of Dr. Horace Drake sent shock waves throughout the Compton community. Late Thursday afternoon, Dr. Drake's car skidded on a slick, icy patch on one of Compton's winding and narrow country roads, causing him to slam into a guard rail. His car flipped over several times, rolling and tumbling down a hillside before it reached a final resting place. Dr. Drake was thrown from the car and died from massive internal injuries.

Julia and Carl received the news while in town, leaving both shaken. Dr. Drake had been Julia's physician for years and a frequent visitor to the Cooper farm for various medical reasons. Carl first saw Dr. Drake when he fell and injured his head. His speedy referral to the local hospital was critical to Carl's diagnosis, surgery, and recovery. The doctor also visited lieutenant Tom Cooper every day when Tom contracted the Spanish Flu, and later passed away. And, he tended to Mickey when he was assaulted at the farm and experienced a punctured lung and fractured ribs.

When Julia and Carl returned, it was obvious the two were sad, but they expressed their grief differently. Carl was hard to read, mainly because he kept his emotions to himself. He didn't show his feelings outwardly, even though he was under a considerable amount of distress. As he walked through the house, his shoulders drooped and he fixed his eyes downward to the floor. His actions were slow and his gestures half-hearted. His breath faltered and fumbled when he tried to take a deep breath.

Julia, on the other hand, wore her emotions on her sleeve. She was deeply hurt and chose to openly show her feelings rather than keeping them hidden. She behaved in a way that made her pain and anguish visible to those close to her. She couldn't stop the tears from rolling down, and her voice cracked when she tried to speak. She got a lump in her throat. Her face got red and blotchy, and her eyes became bloodshot. She found herself edgy and getting angry for no reason.

The funeral was held in the town's Lutheran church. The church was a modest rectangular wood frame structure with a steep gable roof, clapboard siding, an entry portico, and a belfry. An antique church bell was rung for Dr. Drake's service and echoed throughout the hills and valleys of Compton. Inside, the church was packed with Compton residents. The ancient floor creaked with their overwhelming numbers, and the pews were packed, shoulder to shoulder. Many stood behind the pews as well as along the walls.

The service was performed by the same pastor who spoke at lieutenant Cooper's service. His name was Hobart Lambert, a stooped over elderly man dressed in black, tall and thin, who had thinning white hair and wore small gold spectacles. He looked too frail to stand behind the pulpit, but his voice proved to be booming as well as strong, and his delivery was as eloquent as it was impassioned.

It seemed as though everyone from the town attended the funeral service. Dr. Drake's only surviving relative was his brother, Woodrow, who lived in New Hampshire and drove to Compton for the service. After seeing him physically entering the church, there was no mistaking the fact that Woodrow was the brother of Horace.

The service included music, hymns, prayer, and readings from the Bible.

Once that was over, the pastor returned to the pulpit. His head was bowed. He breathed deeply. He looked up and faced the congregation.

He spoke. "Dr. Horace Drake made his life's work caring for others. He will always live in our hearts. He taught us the true meaning of love, laughter and family. As a family doctor, he was forthright, wise, and truthful while being caring, compassionate and thoughtful. He lived a selfless life by always caring for others ahead of himself. His compassion and grace were illuminated by his actions as a physician. His nurturing nature was the embodiment of the beautiful soul that he was and will continue to be in our hearts."

A few moments passed, the silence deafening.

The pastor called upon Dr. Drake's brother, Woodrow, to speak.

Woodrow didn't hesitate walking to the pulpit. He carried no notes. He spoke directly from his heart, brother to brother.

"The world is a little darker without my brother in it. I miss him, and I know you do, too. He was loved and respected here. He took pride in being a citizen of Compton and appreciated his hometown's familiarity and picturesque scenery. When he lost his wife, he took solace in adopting three dogs that brought him joy and companionship. These dogs were not just pets to Horace, they became his new family."

"Horace lived a life full of nurturance, courage and love. He leaves behind a legacy of strength, resilience, and a spirit that will continue to inspire this community. His memory will live on in the hearts of all who knew him, and he will be deeply missed. My brother had a calling for helping others and his compassionate manner was evident throughout his career as a family doctor. He would want you to remember how his arms were wide reaching because he held them open for all. He would want you to do the same."

Woodrow coughed into his hand and took the opportunity to swipe at tears wetting his cheeks. He gathered himself and said, "Horace cherished nature in all its forms and in its turn, nature loved him back. There wasn't a single bird, squirrel, chipmunk, rabbit, or deer in Compton that hadn't felt his touch at some point. That's because my brother's love for animals was boundless and he always had a soft spot for furry companions. He had an everlasting love of all animals, dogs and stray cats high on his list, and he regularly petted all four-legged pets on his daily walks in

Compton. He volunteered at animal shelters and donated whenever he could."

Woodrow looked up at the congregation.

"My hope is that the life of Horace Drake will always be an inspiration. My brother was exceptional in every way, and my hope is that this Vermont town will always love him and be grateful to him for his many kindnesses and care. He will be missed dearly but his spirit, warm smile, generosity and inspiration to make the most of every minute will live on in your hearts. Always hold those memories close."

Woodrow bowed his head at the pulpit, then returned to his seat.

Pastor Lambert asked if any members of the congregation wished to come forward and share condolences.

A number did and shared warm memories. It was only a matter of time before Julia stood and made her way to the pulpit.

Once she got there, she stood tall and straight. She looked elegant yet conservative in a dark blue suit and flowered blouse. She first introduced herself, then spoke.

"Thank you for coming, I thank you, Horace thanks you."

People smiled at that.

She continued. "After the tragedy of the Spanish flu, we've looked for heroes in our community, those who took risks every day helping the afflicted. Dr. Drake was one such caregiver and one of my heroes. This man got us through the pandemic and countless other sicknesses and diseases. He spent his entire professional life touching many lives through his unwavering dedication to medicine. He will be forever remembered as a doctor who forged a genuine connection with patients. I know this because he's been my family physician for over twenty-five years. He helped our family, he healed our family, he guided our family. And he's done the same with so many other families living here. His tireless attention to the residents of Compton will always be remembered. May his soul find eternal peace, and may his legacy continue to inspire goodness and kindness in Compton.

As soon as she left the pulpit, Henry rose to speak and found his way to the front of the congregation. He waited for Julia to take her seat before he talked. He began by telling the congregation who he was and how Dr. Drake helped care for lieutenant Tom Cooper, who contracted the Spanish flu.

"Dr. Drake was the first to identify the disease and because local hospitals were overflowing with patients, the lieutenant chose to fight the disease at home. Dr. Drake was a friend of the family and stopped by every single night to see how the lieutenant was faring. Such visits were made by a man who no doubt was exhausted after seeing multitudes of patients in his office." Henry paused and looked at the congregation. "But he came from the beginning of the lieutenant's diagnosis to the last breath he took. I ask you, how can you ever find sufficient words to thank a person for such incredible devotion to a patient?"

"I forged a unique bond with Dr. Drake during our many talks. We drank coffee together, even knocked back a few jiggers of rum." He got quiet for a minute, then smiled. "Okay, more than just a few." The congregation laughed.

Henry smiled, too, as a tear ran down his cheek. He didn't bother brushing it away.

"I'll always remember our conversations. Of course, talking about the lieutenant's condition was always at the forefront of our talks. Yet in between I learned a lot about this remarkable man and the character traits that made him so beloved around here. For example, his positivity and kindness were infectious, and he never ceased working to make life better for all of us. Dr. Drake represented the good that we all need every day in our lives. He was a beacon of righteousness and believed profoundly in the human spirit's ability to grow and change for the better. His patients knew they were loved and accepted because he was the epitome of empathy, especially towards the downtrodden, helpless, and maltreated. I'll tell you, this guy helped everyone and if you didn't like him, there's something seriously wrong with you."

More smiles and laughter from the congregation.

"I'll close with these thoughts. The light that Dr. Drake shared with us has touched many, and we will mourn his loss. Hopefully, we will take strength from his memory and be as loving, tolerant and gentle as he was. This man represented the good that we all need every day in our lives. He will be deeply missed, but I'm confident his spirit will continue to inspire and guide us."

Henry found his way back to his seat and sat down next to Julia. She reached for his hand and held it. "Bless you," she whispered.

———

Following the service, refreshments were served downstairs in the church hall. Henry and Mickey were hungry and headed for a large banquet table filled with casseroles, meatballs, pasta dishes, finger sandwiches, fruit, baked goods, sliced poundcakes, and beverages. Once Henry filled a plate for Mickey and got him settled at a table, he returned to the food table. Henry had to wait his turn at the end of a long line, but he didn't mind. He craned his neck to see if Mickey was okay and was delighted to see that Ariel and Jacob Winsted had joined him at the table. Mickey waved to Henry with a big smile on his face. That made Henry happy, especially Mickey's connection to Ariel. Meanwhile, he felt a light tap on his shoulder and turned around to discover the source.

And there stood Maeve Adair. She looked straight at him, smiling demurely.

"Hello Henry," she said.

"Maeve," he said, being taken completely by surprise. "Hello."

"I wanted to tell you what a fine job you did during the service. Your words were well chosen and touching."

"Thank you," he replied. "I was very fond of Dr. Drake and the care he gave the lieutenant."

"Everyone loved Dr. Drake."

"Did you know him?"

"Only casually. He came in the store every now and then. Very pleasant, nice man."

Henry nodded. He looked at her and wondered if she'd bring up the steamy incident at the store with sheriff Whittaker.

She didn't. Instead, she kept the conversation light. "So, how have you been Henry?" she asked. "How's everything at the horse farm?

"All good," he replied. "Just bought two new horses. Beautiful palominos."

"What are their names?"

"Tess and Ronan."

She smiled. "Ronan," she repeated. "You can't stay away from those Irish or Scottish names, can you Mr. Cameron."

"Nope, it's in my blood just like it's in yours, Miss Adair."

They both smiled then looked away and scanned the food line. It was still long.

Henry said, "Maeve, can we get away from this crowd for a few minutes? I need to talk with you about something."

There was some initial hesitation on her part, and Henry wondered if she thought he wanted to talk about the incident in the store. Nevertheless, she agreed and Henry led her to a quiet corner.

"What's on your mind?" she asked quietly.

"It's about my uncle. How many nights did he and his friend stay in your rental apartment?"

She had to think for a moment. "I believe it was three days and nights."

"And what is your daily rental fee?"

"Forty dollars a day." She paused. "Why are you asking these questions?"

"Because I know he didn't pay you when he left town and I want to square things with you."

She touched his arm. "That's not necessary Henry."

"Yes, for me it is, and I insist." He reached for his wallet and pulled out six twenty-dollar bills. He folded the bills and placed them in Maeve's hand.

She hesitated, but took the money.

"Please, Maeve." They looked into each other's eyes for a long moment. She put the bills in her purse.

"Was there a damage fee for anything broken?"

She shook her head, then put her hand on his arm again. "Henry, please, stop."

A loud voice behind Henry interrupted any further conversation or interaction. "You heard the lady, Cameron. "Stop."

He turned around to find sheriff Cormac Whittaker, armed and in full uniform, sneering at Henry with his usual smug expression. Whittaker got hold of Maeve's hand and pulled her away from Henry's arm.

"What's going on here?" Whittaker asked, stepping around Henry and standing next to Maeve.

Henry watched. "What's going on here is none of your business," Henry countered. Out of the corner of his eye, he saw the sheriff slip his hand around Maeve's lower back.

At one point, Whittaker leaned close and whispered in Maeve's ear. Maeve giggled.

That was all Henry needed to see, as bothersome as it was, and he turned to join the congregation to look for his family.

He didn't get very far. The sheriff raised his voice. "Cameron, I'm not done with you."

It got quiet, people turning and looking at the two of them.

Henry bristled, then turned and walked back to the sheriff. More people looked his way. Once there, he asked, "What is it you want, sheriff?"

The sheriff spoke in curt, churlish words. "You're going to come with me in my patrol car, back to my office."

Henry retorted, "I think not. I'm never going anywhere with you, and certainly not in your patrol car. If you've got something to say, say it right here."

Whittaker smirked. "Okay, I'll say it. I've got someone you might want to see back at the station. He was just delivered. We caught your uncle and he's now behind bars in my jail."

"You found him?" asked Henry in disbelief.

"Wake up, Cameron. We got him and he's now in my custody. You need to come with me now to identify him."

"Is he alive?"

"He's been banged around, but he's alive."

"When can I see him?"

"Now."

Henry hesitated, looking around the church hall. "You need to give me a few minutes so that I can notify my family as to my whereabouts."

"I'll be outside waiting."

He was able to find everyone, but he didn't disclose any details about his impending departure. Mickey had a ride home with the Winsteds, Hudson and Abigail had taken their own car, and Julia and Carl rode together. Everyone was in safe-keeping.

When he went outside, the sheriff was smoking a cigarette while leaning against his patrol car.

Henry walked up to him. "You made quite an impression walking into the church hall mourning a loved one, especially with your holster, revolver, and handcuffs. Nice touch sheriff. Where do you think you are, Deadwood?

The sheriff totally ignored the dig. He huffed a phony laugh, then said, "A word to the wise, hayseed. I'm gonna tell you just once more. Stay away from my property in Compton, and that includes Maeve. If you choose not to pay heed, you can count on facing my wrath."

Twenty-Four

It didn't take long to get to the county jail. Once there, the sheriff directed Henry to his office, a cubicle located about halfway down a long hallway. The sheriff pulled up a chair and sat behind a large, gray metal desk and Henry sat in a chair opposite him. The office smelled of sweat, old nicotine, and dust. There were no windows. The paint on the cinderblock walls was chipping everywhere, the linoleum tiles more broken than intact.

"We need to talk over some things before you can see your uncle," Whittaker said. He smelled of stale liquor and cheap cologne. He hadn't shaved.

Henry stared at him.

"Your uncle is not in good shape."

Henry kept staring.

"Five days ago, he caused a ruckus in a bar the other side of town. He was with an apparent buddy of his and got into it with three other guys sitting at the bar. According to the bartender, words were said between the two parties, insults were traded, and threats were made. The bartender told them to take their differences outside, and let me tell you they did just that and started swinging as soon as they left the place."

"A free-for-all," mumbled Henry.

"You got it."

"And my uncle and his friend got the worst of it."

"You got it. The other guys belonged to a rough crowd from out of state. Your uncle's pal, who was that?"

Henry shrugged. He didn't know the goon's name. The sheriff produced photos of the accomplice and only then did Henry recognize him.

"Yeah, that's him."

"He was shot and killed in the streets."

Henry gasped. "And my uncle?" he asked.

"He got roughed up and was knocked unconscious. Your uncle was hauled away in an ambulance."

"How bad?"

"He's been in the hospital for three days. He just got out today and was sent here."

"Why here?"

"Think about it, Cameron. You wanted him and the other stooge arrested. Then you were going to file charges once we had him behind bars."

Henry thought about such matters, then nodded. "Got it." Henry paused. "Where's his car?"

"Sitting outside in the station parking lot. The car's got two slashed flat tires, and who knows what other damage. We've left it there until you tell us what to do with it."

Henry nodded, then started to rise but Whittaker signaled that he wasn't finished. "Sit back down."

Henry did as told.

Whittaker continued. "Your uncle has no insurance and no next of kin, at least that's what he told the hospital staff. He's here to face the music about the trouble he caused. From what I can gather, it was the other guy who created the most havoc but he's pushing up daisies in some cemetery. So, it's your call as to how you want to proceed from here."

"Can I go see him now?"

"Follow me."

The sheriff led Henry down the hallway, then into the wing of inmate cells. His uncle was located in the last cell. When the sheriff opened the cell, Henry saw his uncle sitting in bed with his back flush against the cell wall. He wore hospital scrubs and a bathrobe. The sheriff left them alone.

He had a split lip, a laceration with visible sutures on his forehead, and a gash across his eyebrow, the surrounding eye socket purple and puffed.

Henry sat down on a stool and chose to just look at his uncle.

In time, Henry asked, "Can you talk?"

"I can," his uncle replied, although his words seemed jumbled.

"What's your plan for handling the mess you created?" asked Henry.

"I don't have any plans. All I know is that I'm broke and hurt. I have a bunch of unpaid bills. I can't even afford to get my car fixed. I can't afford my hospital bills, I can't afford paying my rental bill to Maeve Adair. All I want to do is get out of this town."

It got silent in the cell.

"Do you know what happened to my partner?"

"The same one who almost killed Mickey Parker?"

"Yeah, him."

"He got killed in your scuffle outside the bar."

"Dead?"

"Yeah, dead. Hope you're proud of that."

"He was a good man."

"A good man?" Henry laughed sarcastically. "You've got to be kidding. He was a total, unqualified imbecile."

"So, what does that make me?"

"Honestly? It makes you the dolt of our family, the halfwit who's embarrassed all of us for years."

"And where does that leave me?"

"It leaves you right where you sit. Behind bars."

"Come on, Henry, I need help. Get me out of here."

"You must be joking. You'll get no help from me or anyone."

"Hey," he said, "we're family."

"Really? We're family? After all the trouble you've caused, you now have the gall to tell me we're family?"

"I'm sorry, Henry. I'm wrong. I didn't know what I was doing. I apologize."

Henry stared at him. He asked, "What happened to you, anyway? Really, what caused you to turn out like this?"

"I got lost in the shuffle. My brother got all the attention, everyone in the family adored him. Everything was always directed toward him. Everything I did was wrong, every decision I made was criticized or condemned."

Henry made a face. "Poor baby. I should slap you across your face and tell you to grow up. You are nothing short of a sniveling coward and a crook in your family's eyes."

His uncle started whimpering through his swollen eyes.

Henry didn't buy the sob story. "My listening days are over with you. You're a drunk and a liar, a thief and a thug. You use people to your advantage. If you think I'm going to come and rescue you from this cell, you're crazy. I'm the only family you've got left, do you realize that? You burned your bridges with my father and you did the same with my mother. You helped kill the only other father I had in my life, lieutenant Cooper. Then you sicced your hired goon on my best friend and almost killed him. You're nothing but a monster."

Henry's uncle got into a coughing fit.

"Can't you help me, just a little?" he whined. "I'm broke, my car has been taken away, and I have bills I can't pay."

"Where are your clothes?"

He pointed to a pile of clothes sitting on a chair. The clothes were torn and filthy. "When's the last time you had a bath?"

"I can't remember."

"When's the last time those clothes were washed?"

"I don't know that either."

Henry said, "What you should know is this. You smell something awful. Don't you even have personal belongings? How about a suitcase?"

He shook his head. "Please, Henry. I beg of you. You're my last hope. I just want to get out of this town. I won't come back."

"You beg of me?"

"Yes, I beg of you. Please forgive me and help me."

When Henry got home, he got out of his car, went to the corral, saddled Morning Star, and took to the trails. He didn't see anyone and assumed all were in the house. He needed fresh air and wanted to be alone. He rode past the cornfields, the apple orchard, the shooting range, and eventually decided to stop at the family cemetery. It had been a long day and he was mentally exhausted. He tied Morning Star to a small, nearby tree and went to sit on one of the stone benches.

He didn't know how long he sat there. He was too busy watching a red-tail hawk soaring overhead, then he turned his attention to some cardinals foraging for what he guessed were wild berries, nuts and seeds.

Henry was too preoccupied to notice that Julia had ridden up behind him, having taken a different route from the house. When Julia called out, mainly because she didn't want to spook him, Henry turned around on the stone bench.

"May I come join you?" she asked.

"Of course," he responded. "Come aboard."

She hitched her horse to a tree near Morning Star and walked over, choosing to sit on a bench next to Henry.

Henry blew into his hands for warmth. "Winter is here to stay in Compton and the first snowfall is knocking on our door."

Julia smiled at him. "You sound like the lieutenant when you talk like that. At any rate, I don't think you rode up here just to predict Vermont snowfalls."

Henry lowered his head and smiled. "No, you're right. My mind's racing on me. I thought getting outside might help slow things down."

"Has that worked?" asked Julia.

"I think so."

He looked over at her. She was a rugged, robust, good-looking woman. She wore a long winter overcoat with a fur collar hiked up, calfskin gloves, and a tan, wide-brimmed hat pulled down low. She looked every bit the horsewoman, and certainly rode like one. She was among the best riders at the farm, always was.

"I was touched by your words at the service today, Julia. It hurt to hear them and I'm sorry you've been hurt. I know Horace Drake meant a great deal to you."

She nodded. "Thank you, Henry. And I'll have you know you made me cry today with what you said about him. You had our whole pew tearing up."

They got quiet for a while.

Henry said, "Want to talk about sheriff Whittaker?" At the time, Henry told Julia and the others that he was departing from the church reception to go to the police station with the sheriff.

Julia said, "I saw you talking with Maeve, then the sheriff showing up out of nowhere. Trouble?"

"No, no trouble. I paid my uncle's bill with Maeve when he stayed at her apartment. The sheriff showed up and essentially reminded me to stay away from his property, including Maeve."

"Another threat against you."

"Yep."

Julia said, "Henry, stay away from that woman. She's trouble."

"I intend to."

She hesitated, then said, "Have you heard from Lily in Boston?"

"No."

"Did you write back to her?"

"I sent her a Christmas card."

"That's it?"

"That's it. She's not going to write back."

"You're sure of that?"

Henry just shrugged.

Julia said, "Okay, let's move on. What did Whittaker want?"

"He told me my uncle had been found and arrested. He got himself involved in a street fight. He got knocked unconscious and the goon who was with him was shot and killed."

Julia just shook her head. "So, he's back in Compton."

Henry nodded. "He'll have to face the charges leveled against him."

"How is your uncle?" asked Julia.

"He's been punched senseless. His face is covered with bruises and gashes. He had trouble talking with me, but we managed."

"Did he ask for anything?"

"His usual plea for money." Henry fidgeted a bit. "He also asked for forgiveness."

"Is that something you'd be able to give, Henry?"

Henry let out a breath. "I don't know."

"Offering forgiveness is not going to cost you a cent, Henry. I want you to think long and hard about all that's happened to this guy. This is a person who doesn't know the harm he's brought to others. He never will because he has no moral awareness of the pain he's caused. His best friend has been killed. He has no home, no family, no income, no future pathway to anywhere. He's amounted to nothing in the world. Can you imagine living like that?"

"No, I can't," Henry said quietly.

They got quiet again.

"I feel like I lost touch with the farm these last few days. Is everything okay here?"

Julia said, "We're good. Everyone's doing their thing, plus helping each other out."

"Is Mickey okay?"

"He's in a tizzy over his prosthesis. Dr. Drake took it the morning he stopped over to treat Mickey, but never returned it. He was hoping to have it repaired. Since then, we can't find it."

"Was it in the car wreckage?"

"No, the car was destroyed and hauled away. It wasn't in the car."

"Do we know who was going to fix it?"

"No, and neither does his office. The office staff had no clue who it might've been but promised to keep looking. They weren't very optimistic about finding it."

"Well, we'll just have to get him a replacement. Where do we go for that?"

"Mickey told me the nearest VA hospital is somewhere in White River Junction, but he won't go there."

"Why not?"

"Too much past trauma in his head. Beyond the trench fighting, he was really rattled by the horror of the other soldiers in the field hospitals, all the disfigurements and amputations. You should talk to him, Henry."

Henry exhaled a deep breath. "I'll do just that."

"Be mindful. He still has nightmares of the war and the atrocities he witnessed.

They switched gears.

Henry asked, "Has Hudson approached you about our pending purchase of the two palominos in Chicopee?"

"He has. The check has been cut and ready to go. Ty Griffin knows Hudson is on his way."

"Great. Give Hudson the check and some cash and tell him to hook up the horse trailer and get ready to roll. Tell him to pack for two and have Abigail ready to join him."

Julia nodded and walked to her horse.

"Anything else?" asked Henry.

"Yes, one other matter. I was thinking of having a small Christmas Eve party and inviting a few of the neighbors over. Maybe we can shake some of the doldrums away from the farm.

Maybe have some wine, eggnog, crackers and cheese, hors d'oeuvres, that kind of thing. Would that be okay?"

"Great idea. Add the Winsteds to the guest list. I'd like to meet the whole gang."

She nodded. "By the way," Julia said, "I think Ariel has taken a liking to Mickey."

"I think she has, too." He looked at her and smiled, the first real smile he'd had all day.

She smiled back before mounting her horse and trotting back to the house.

Twenty-Five

The next morning, Henry helped Hudson and Abigail pack for their trip to Chicopee and the Wilcox Horse Farm. It was a perfect day to travel, the skies clear and the sun bright. Both Hudson and Abigail seemed happy to be getting away for the day, and equally excited to be bringing two new horses back home.

Henry went over to the driver's side to talk with Hudson. "All good?" he asked.

"All good. Now you're sure you want to do this?"

"I'm sure. I thought things over and decided against boarding the horses at Ty Griffin's ranch for the winter. After all, we've built new stalls and our barn is in good shape. Having them here will give them a chance to gradually meet their new family, hear the sounds and sights around them. We'll get them outside as often as we can, weather permitting of course."

Abigail leaned forward in her seat. "Plus, they'll get to meet us." She beamed. "I like the plan, Henry."

Henry straightened. "Have a safe trip." He smiled and playfully punched Hudson in the shoulder. "Keep your eyes on the road, cowboy."

After their departure, Henry gathered some tools, fired up the flatbed, and drove along the property line until he reached the Christmas tree acreage. He stopped the flatbed, grabbed a few tools and walked in between the blue spruce trees. Once he found a tree to his liking, he picked out a bow saw, huddled against its base, and began sawing. It didn't take long for it to fall and when it did, he dragged it to the flatbed and lashed it securely in place. The entire process took no longer than twenty minutes.

He drove away from the farm property and traveled along the back country road until he found the Winsted property. He found the place easy enough, a long driveway leading to a two-storied clapboard nestled against a backdrop of tall pines, the trees swaying in the early winter winds. A fairly large bubbling brook abutted the property from behind. It was a bucolic setting.

Henry approached a large heavy oak front door. A Christmas wreath hung on it. He rapped his knuckles against the heavy wood several times, then waited. When no one responded to his knocking, he assumed no one was home so he started descending the front stairs.

The front door opened half-way and he stopped midstep.

A woman appeared in the doorway. She was a slight, pretty woman. "May I help you?" she asked.

Henry turned to face her while back-tracking up the stairs.

"Yes, my name is Henry Cameron, and I own the farm down the road."

Her hands flew to her face. "Oh yes, of course, the old Cooper farm. Would you like to come in?"

"Yes, but rest assured I'll be out of your hair in no time," he said.

She extended her hand. "My name is Rebecca Winsted."

Henry shook her hand and smiled.

He was led into a living room, a fire burning brightly against the far wall. Mr. Winsted sat in an easy chair next to the fireplace. He was a handsome, clean-shaven guy.

Henry didn't hesitate and walked right over to him. "Mr. Winsted, I'm Henry Cameron from the Cooper farm."

He got up slowly and extended a hand. "I'm Leland Winsted." He hesitated. "You just hired my son and daughter, right?"

"Yes, I did. I wanted to meet you both so I thought stopping over would be the proper thing to do. I also wanted you and your wife to know how pleased we are with Ariel and Jacob."

Leland nodded and smiled. "Thank you. We think they're pretty good kids."

"Yes, they are. You brought them up proper."

"I'm glad," Leland said. He grinned at Henry. "So, does this mean you're gonna keep them on the payroll?"

"Absolutely," replied Henry. "Now what about you? How're you doing? The kids told me you hurt your back."

"It's been slow, and my doctor has told me over and over to be patient.

"When did you injure it?"

"Back in June. Unfortunately, this being December, the school I've worked at has since hired a replacement, which now looks permanent. Bottom line, I no longer have a job and my disability checks stretch us to our limits. We've had to cut a lot of things out of our life."

Mrs. Winsted walked into the living room bearing a tray of homemade cookies. All three sat down munching on oatmeal cookies and small-talking about Compton.

At one point, Henry asked, "So what happened to you anyway?"

Leland answered, "I fell from a stepladder trying to change an overhead light. Fell ass over tea kettle, right on the old keister. Ruptured some spinal discs. I'm still healing and I'm making progress, at least that's what my doctor says."

Henry chuckled softly. "'Ass over tea kettle,' my mother used to say that." Then he got serious. "When can you get back up and around?"

"I can walk pretty good now. The doctor tells me by early March I should be up and moving, ready to work again."

"And then what?" asked Henry.

"That's the problem. At this point, I just don't know," he said forlornly.

"What kind of work are you looking to do, Leland?"

"At this point, just about anything."

"Can you drive an Avery Bulldog?"

"An Avery Bulldog? I sure can. I was trained on an Avery Bulldog. Used to work on a farm before we moved up here. You looking to plant some crops?"

"Sweet corn, lots of it. I need to hire a driver and some workers to disc and harrow, drill, harvest, cut silage, thresh and shred. All that stuff."

"Thought you were a horseman. At least that's what Jacob tells me."

"That too."

"You gonna replant old Mr. Cooper's cornfields?"

"I am. I made a promise to his son before he died that this would be done."

"You're a real mover and shaker, ain't you?"

"I try my best."

They both smiled.

"So, tell me Leland. You interested in helping me out?"

"Yes, I am."

"Then I'll be back and we'll talk details." He looked over at Rebecca. "I'll just stop by and maybe get some more of these delicious cookies while I'm here." He smiled her way.

They talked a little bit more before Henry stood. He didn't have much time to spare if he wanted to get the rest of his errands done. He thanked the Winsteds for their hospitality and they, in turn, thanked Henry for the sunlight he'd brought into their lives.

As they stood by the doorway Henry realized he'd forgotten to share a few things. "By the way, we'd like to extend an invitation to all of the Winsteds to join us for a small Christmas Eve get-together. We're hopeful all of you can make it. We'll let you know the time."

"We'd be honored to stop by," said Leland.

"Good. And I left you a little Christmas gift outside your house." He laughed. "I was going to use it as a bribe to get you to come work for me."

After Henry left, Leland and Rebecca went outside and discovered a freshly cut blue spruce Christmas tree leaning against the house.

Henry walked in the main entrance of the police station and knocked on the doorframe of sheriff Whittaker's office. The sheriff had his feet up on the desk reading a newspaper while eating a banana. He lowered the paper when he saw Henry.

"Well, look at what the cat dragged in," he said with a smirk.

"Morning, sheriff. Sorry to interrupt your morning reading. I came to get the keys to my uncle's car. I'm going to move his car out of here."

"Really? The car has two flat tires because they were slashed by members of your uncle's fan club. Go see Jimmy at the corner gas station and tell him to come look at it." He scratched the top of his head. "I'd like to help you out Cameron, but I'm kind of tied up this morning."

Henry looked at the newspaper, then at Whittaker. "I can see that. You haven't read the comics yet or finished that banana."

"Smart ass," Whittaker growled. He fished in his desk draw for the keys, found them, and tossed them to Henry, who caught them one-handed.

Henry turned to leave.

"Not visiting your uncle while you're here?" Whittaker asked.

"Nope."

"Say, now that we got him in the slammer, we need to finalize the charges you intend to bring against him."

"I thought we did that already."

"Nope, not yet. Those two thugs have been on the lam since they left your house that night. I couldn't really file charges against them until they were apprehended. All I could do was issue an arrest warrant, which authorized police to take the two into custody. Of course, the bum who beat up your pal is now dead as a doornail. That means most of the complaints lodged that night were against the dead guy, not your uncle."

"So where does that leave us?"

"That's what we need to talk about. You've got to decide what charges you want to slap on your beloved uncle."

"How about if I come in tomorrow to square all of this away"

"Okay, but tomorrow is Christmas Eve day. I ain't gonna hang around all day waiting for you to show up, that's for dang sure."

"I'll come early."

Henry left the building and told the sheriff he was going outside to wait for the mechanic. He'd called Jimmy on his way into town and the guy said he'd meet Henry at the police station. His uncle's car was a 1918 Buick and Jimmy assured Henry over the phone that he had the correct tires in stock. He also said that once the tires were changed Henry could park the car on his slot for a flat rate, if storage was needed.

While he waited, Henry unlocked the car and inspected the interior. Litter was everywhere, including food wrappers, soiled shopping bags, empty booze bottles, cigarette and cigar butts, old race horse programs, a tattered sleeping bag, some girly magazines, a pair of mud-caked boots, old newspapers, and a pile of dirty clothes. The odor was a horrid mixt of mold, unwashed clothes, sweat, and dirty feet. In short, the car was a pig sty.

Henry had never met Jimmy, but a truck's backfire as it came around the corner told him that he'd arrived. He got out of his truck and walked over to Henry.

"You must be Jimmy," Henry said, extending his hand.

"Yep, the one and only." Jimmy was middle-age, rail thin, and dressed in greasy, full body coveralls. Perched on his head was a red plaid winter cap, the kind that comes with woolen earflaps. The flaps were not currently tucked in or down, but rather sticking out sideways like wings.

"I didn't catch your name," Jimmy said.

"Cameron, Henry Cameron."

"You live around here?"

"Yeah, I own the old Cooper farm."

Jimmy looked Henry up and down. "Ah yes, you're the horseman, the new rich guy in town."

Henry chose not to respond, instead just smiled.

Jimmy said, "You know, I always wanted to learn how to ride a horse but never got the chance." He looked over at the car. "That the car?"

"That's it."

Jimmy wandered over and inspected the tires, at one point dropping to his knees and looking at the tires from underneath the car.

He returned while brushing gravel off his hands. "The two slashed tires obviously need to be replaced but the other two appear to be okay. I can replace the two tires right here. I'll just need to grab some tools and parts over at the garage, then I'll be right back. It shouldn't take too long."

"Great. I have a few stops to make in town so that works out perfectly. Also, I need this car cleaned of all the junk that's inside."

"Everything?"

"Yes, everything. If by chance you find something that looks valuable, put it in a bag and hold on to it for me. Also, I need

the interior wiped down with a cleaner, and the outside washed."
Henry tilted his head to one side and looked at Jimmy. "Is that
something you can do for me?"

Jimmy nodded. "I've got a kid working for me over at the
garage who can do all that. When I'm done with the flat tires, I'll
drive the car over to the garage and he can get started."

"Good. While you've got it over there, please fill up the gas
tank and check the oil."

"You're gonna pay for all this, right?"

"Of course. Tell you what, you do a good job and I'll pay you
in cash and also teach you how to ride a horse."

"You got yourself a deal, Mr. Cameron."

They shook on it.

———————

Henry had business to discuss with his banker, which took
longer than expected, then had stops to make at his lawyer's office,
the pharmacy, the post office, and finally the clothing store. There
was quite a bit of mail to pick up at the post office, including a
fairly large package addressed to Julia. Maeve wasn't working at

the clothing store so he took his time poking around, selecting the items he thought were most appropriate.

When he was finished with his errands he pulled into Jimmy's garage. Jimmy and his helper weren't finished with the car but the new tires had been mounted and a large garbage can near the Buick was half-filled with his uncle's trash. Rather than wait, Henry told Jimmy he'd be back in the morning to square the bill. He asked Jimmy to hold the keys overnight.

As he drove home, his mind began racing as he contemplated what he needed to do tomorrow, his thoughts kindled by Julia's sentiments about forgiveness. She was right of course, as she almost always was about everything under the sun. He needed to come to grips with the issue of forgiveness, which meant learning to let go of the past. He also had to learn that while a person's sins can't be undone, forgiveness can become a gift for both the sinner and the person holding the grudge.

But how to best accomplish this was a steep and slippery slope. He had to take some chances and be willing to accept the possibility of making a wrong decision. The lieutenant always told him that the person who isn't courageous enough to take chances will amount to little in life. He was often reminded that making a wrong decision was far better than remaining saddled in indecision.

Henry would see about all this tomorrow.

Twenty-Six

T he two palominos were as beautiful as Henry expected. He was watching them from outside the small corral, resting one foot on the bottom rail. The horses were both graceful and muscular, short and athletic. They had expressive eyes, short necks, broad chests, and large round hindquarters. The two stayed close together as they surveyed their new surroundings, both demonstrating a calm, gentle demeanor and a general nosiness about the farm's other horses contained in the separate main corral. Occasionally they'd nicker and rest their heads over the neck of their partner, other times they'd gently nudge each other.

Hudson had been in the barn and walked over to Henry. "Well, what do you think?" he asked.

"Champions," Henry replied. "Definitely pretty horses to complement the rest of the herd. Their coloring is stunning. The pictures we have of them really doesn't do them any justice. Their golden creamy coats are accented by their white manes and tails."

"I knew you'd like them once you saw them outside."

Hudson and Abigail didn't get home until fairly late last night, limiting the amount of time and contact Henry had with them. According to Hudson, they were good travelers and didn't make any kind of ruckus in the trailer on the way home.

Hudson said, "The previous owner was at the ranch to say goodbye to them."

"The widow of the soldier lost in the war?"

"Yes. It was a tearful moment for her. Sad to watch, but she honored her deceased husband's wishes. Lots of hugs to the horses. She asked if she could come up here and visit them from time to time."

"Of course," replied Henry.

"That's what I told her. I gave her our address and telephone number. I didn't think you'd mind."

"You did good, Hudson." Henry looked around the grounds. "Where's Abigail?" he asked.

"She's in the barn gathering up her bedroll."

"She's doing what?"

Hudson smiled and supplied more detail. "She slept in the barn last night to be with them. She unfolded a cot, got her sleeping bag and a lantern, and slept in the empty stall next to Ronan and Tess. Wanted to check on them during the night, including talking or singing to them if they needed calming."

Henry smiled back. "I'll tell you Hudson, she's quite a woman."

Hudson nodded his head. "That she is. Abigail even talked Ty Griffin out of a week's worth of grain, hay, and water so that Ronan and Tess could be drawn to the familiar up here rather than a sudden change in their nourishment. She intends to gradually introduce our water and feed to them."

As if on cue, Abigail emerged from the barn and approached them. She was carrying two lead ropes.

"Morning Ms. Emory," Henry said.

"Good morning to you, Mr. Cameron," she cheerfully replied.

"Did the newcomers pass muster last night?" he asked.

She nodded. "Once the palominos settled into their stalls and were given some food and water, I wanted them to start getting used to the sights, sounds and smells of the barn and the other horses around them. It may take a little while for them to get used to their new environment, but for the most part, they did remarkably well the first night."

"Were our current horses there?" he asked.

"Not when I first got there, but they filed into the barn later. As they were brought in, the herd took immediate notice of the two palominos. They knew something was different the moment they arrived."

"What did you do about that?"

Hudson replied. "When the others arrived, each paused going into their stalls, several with their necks and backs tensed. Some tucked in their hindquarters and flattened their tails, and their noses. They knew strangers had arrived and they looked around with a mixture of surprise and suspicion."

"But in due time you expect everyone to adjust?"

"Absolutely. Already, they're finding comfort being here."

With that, Hudson went inside the corral and helped Abigail attach lead ropes to Ronan and Tess. Once they did that, they took them out of the corral and walked them around some of the property.

Henry turned and was surprised to find Julia standing close by.

"Good morning, Julia," he said.

She greeted Henry with a smile while sipping a cup of coffee from a mug she'd swiped from the kitchen. "Look at those two," she remarked.

"They're something else, right? Beautiful horses."

"I meant Abigail and Hudson, not the horses."

Henry did a double-take.

"There's something going on there, Henry."

"You're right." He paused. "Whatever it is, I like it."

"So do I. I'm happy for both of them."

Henry asked, "What about Mickey and Ariel?"

"Something brewing there, too, Mr. Cameron."

"Think so?" He looked over at her.

She smiled, the big radiant kind.

Henry straightened up after leaning against the corral. "I've got to run into town. Can I pick up anything for you? Anything for our Christmas Eve party?"

"No, we're good for that. Not a big group, plenty of snacks." She looked up at the sky. "Looks like snow is coming, maybe our first big one. We might have a white Christmas this year."

"I'll be back before it starts." He turned to leave and Julia reached for his arm. "Henry, hold up." She took a step closer. "I want you to know that I can see what you're doing."

He did a double-take but it didn't last for long. "That doesn't surprise me. Is there something you want to share with me?"

She pulled him close and planted a kiss on the cheek

"The lieutenant would've been proud of you," she whispered.

———————

He had business at the bank and once he was done with that, he stopped at Jimmy's gas station. His uncle's Buick stood by itself in a corner lot, shining and polished, ready to drive off the lot.

He turned and saw Jimmy, out of his coveralls and sans his winter cap and flaps. He was actually a good looking fellow, now clean-shaven and wearing a crisp and clean office outfit.

"Hey there, Mr. Cameron." He swung an arm around and pointed toward the Buick. "What do you think?"

"It looks great, mind if I take a look inside?

"Not at all."

Henry did just that, opening the driver's side and sitting inside. The horrid smell was gone. He inspected the front seat as well as the back seat. The car was free of filth and rubbish, the leather polished. He got out and closed the door. He walked around the car, carefully inspecting the car's exterior. He then loaded some items from his car to his uncle's.

When he was finished, he stood with Jimmy and admired the car. "Excellent job," Henry remarked. "Let's go inside and square away the bill."

Once that was done, Henry thanked Jimmy and his helper for a job well done and rewarded each with a generous tip. For Jimmy, that also meant promising free horseback riding lessons in the spring.

He instructed Jimmy to leave the car in the lot and Henry took the keys.

Henry stopped next at the police station.

When he walked in the office of Sheriff Whittaker, it was like revisiting a still photo from the previous day. He still had his feet up on his desk while reading the daily newspaper, eating another banana.

But seeing Henry, he slid his feet from the desk and straightened in the chair. He stared at Henry.

"We need to talk about my uncle, sheriff," Henry said.

Whittaker pointed to a chair opposite his desk, an invitation for Henry to sit. The sheriff reached into a desk draw and pulled out a file. He opened it and studied the contents. After a few minutes, he cleared his throat and looked up at Henry.

Whittaker said, "After the fracas Thanksgiving evening, you wanted to file charges against William Cameron. I have the charges listed here." He held up a sheet of paper. "The charges were assault and battery, criminal trespass, possession of a deadly weapon, disturbing the peace, and threatening."

"That's sounds about right," responded Henry.

"Okay, we need to review these charges."

"Okay, let's do that."

The sheriff continued. "Assault involves the threat of force or harm while battery involves actually inflicting physical force or harm. Both crimes are typically punishable by jail time and fines. If deadly weapons or serious injuries were involved, then assault and battery get prosecuted as felonies carrying prison time."

The sheriff added, "This charge was leveled against Mr. Cameron's so-called bodyguard, Mr. Buford J. Lancaster."

Henry said, "Is that his name? Buford J. Lancaster? This is the first time I've heard it." Henry fumbled with his words. "All my uncle did was try reasoning with me about the inheritance. He never resorted to assault and battery. This was all Lancaster's doing."

"Okay, He's dead, so let's dismiss that charge and move on."

"How about disturbing the peace, do you wish to drop that, too?"

The sheriff looked at his scribbled notes. "Disturbing the peace is a criminal offense that occurs when a person engages in some form of unruly public behavior, such as fighting or causing unreasonable noise."

Henry just shook his head. "The noise was again coming from Lancaster, not my uncle."

"So, you want this dropped too? He paused.

Henry nodded.

"Now what about the weapons found on Lancaster's body?"

"My uncle carried no weapons. Lancaster did."

Henry nodded.

"I can't charge a dead man. So, I assume you're dropping this, too?"

"What about the threatening that took place that night?" asked the sheriff.

Henry responded. "The threatening that night came from Lancaster, not my uncle. He threatened to kill Hudson Delaney. I suggest dropping that charge, too."

"So, what are you suggesting I do with these charges?"

"Drop all of them."

Whittaker thought about this for a few moments. "Okay. I'll release him into your custody."

"I need to talk with him first," Henry said.

"I'll have my deputy open the cell. I won't be here when you finish. I've got a meeting."

The sheriff got up from his chair, put on his hat and turned to leave. But he walked over to Henry before he departed.

"I want you to know you're wearing real thin on me, Cameron. Real thin. I want you out of my hair for good. If I find out you've been spouting off about me and Maeve or anything else, I'm gonna shut your trap for good."

With that, sheriff Cormac Whittaker left the building.

It was dark and cold in his uncle's cell. He was huddled underneath blankets, but he tossed them aside and got up once he saw Henry. He was in his street clothes, and from what Henry could see, his clothes had been both mended and washed. He no longer carried an odor.

"Good morning, Uncle Bill," Henry announced.

Bill replied. "Henry," he exclaimed. "You're back. I never doubted you'd leave me in here."

"Why don't you take a seat," Henry instructed.

The two sat.

"How're you doing?" Henry asked.

"Horrible. I need to get out of here."

Henry studied his uncle's face. "Your face is looking better. Your black and blue bruises are lightening and the lacerations are healing. You still have stitches above your eye. Do you think you can drive a car with that kind of injury."

"I can. I've driven in worse conditions."

Henry didn't doubt this.

"Where is my car, anyway?"

Henry didn't answer.

Things became quiet, at least for a minute or two.

Henry piped up and asked, "When you get out of jail or prison, what are your plans?"

"What do you mean?"

"What I mean is what are your plans? Do you have any money? Do you have a place to stay? Where will you be going?"

He lifted his shoulders in a half-shrug then dropped them. "That's a lot of questions."

His uncle paused and looked down at the floor. After a while, he looked up. "I'll go back to Boston. I have a place to stay with some friends, at least for a while, but I'm broke. I have no money. I have nothing."

"You need to make a plan for yourself if and when you're released. First and foremost, you need to stop drinking and get a job. Work will enable you to find housing and put food on your table. You also need to pick better friends."

Henry sighed. "You and I also need to have a talk and create an understanding."

"What kind of understanding?" he asked.

"I need to say some things face-to-face with you, with no interruptions from you. This is personal and important."

His uncle nodded, folded his hands across his lap and became silent.

Henry reached into his shirt pocket and brought out the photograph he found in Maeve's apartment.

He handed it to his uncle, who was surprised his nephew had even found it. He studied it for several minutes.

"This is a photograph of our family before you chose to destroy it. I want you to keep it and think about our happier times together. All of us. But you ruined the marriage of my mother and father and turned against me in vicious and wicked ways. All of us deserved better." Henry stopped.

He stared at his uncle as he swiped away a tear.

"I'm sorry, Henry. I regret what I said and what I did." He sniffled. "I was wrong. I'm paying the price and will not resist the charges brought against me."

"I want you to keep this photograph and every so often look at it, think about it. I want you to study the happiness on each of our faces, the futures we could have lived, the loyalty that should have bound all of us together. Instead, recognize the pain and heartbreak that you chose to bring into our lives."

Henry waited a minute then stood in front of his uncle. "I want you to stand up," he said.

His uncle obliged. Henry reached for him and the two hugged.

When they separated, Henry let out a breath. "Once you're out of here, I want you to go home, start a new life."

Tears shone in his uncle's eyes. He nodded.

"Look at me," Henry said.

His uncle complied.

"I forgive you for all you've done. A wise woman once told me everyone deserves a second chance. I believe that. But not for the same mistakes." Henry paused. "There's a kind world out there, full of kind people. Turn yourself into one of them. It's never too late to change and turn your life around."

His uncle nodded.

Henry gently squeezed his uncle's arm. "Let's get you out of here."

"Out of here?"

"Yes, out of here. Let's go."

Henry led his uncle out of his cell, down the hallway, and into the main reception area. A receptionist produced some paperwork for Henry and his uncle to sign. She handed over an envelope filled with Bill Cameron's wallet, driver's license, and other personal belongings.

Once that was done, the two walked out of the police station and into a fairly crowded parking lot. They found Henry's car parked not too far away.

Henry drove his car to Jimmy's garage. He found his uncle's car easily enough. Henry got out of his car and started his uncle's Buick. He pulled it out of its parking spot and stopped it in front of the service station.

His uncle was already admiring his Buick. "You've changed the tires and got it up and running. The exterior is beautiful. It looks like a new car."

Henry reached over and grabbed his uncle's shoulder. "Keep it that way. You have a full tank of gas and the tires are in good shape."

They shook hands. "Why are you doing this, Henry?"

Henry started walking away, but after a few steps he stopped. "Forgiveness takes many forms. I'll say again, get yourself straightened out, search for the goodness in the world. It's out there. I left some Christmas presents for you on the back seat of your car."

With that, Henry got back in his car and drove away.

Bill Cameron looked inside his Buick. It was spotless. On the backseat was a new leather suitcase. He unzipped it and found new clothes neatly folded. New shirts, pants, underwear, socks, a few sweaters. On the seat next to the suitcase was a new winter coat, a fedora, scarf, gloves, and boots. In a separate shopping bag, he found a new razor, blades, shaving cream, a toothbrush and toothpaste, a hand mirror, bars of soap, and some cologne.

His eyes started watering again.

He also found a zippered leather satchel on the front passenger seat. When he opened it, he saw bundles of money bound together in large and small bills. He couldn't believe his eyes. He took the time to count all of it. Twice. Each time, the total was the same.

Ten thousand dollars.

Twenty-Seven

I t started snowing almost as soon as Henry left his uncle. At first, the skies became dark and revealed little else, but then the snow clouds collided with one another and before long a light snowfall began cascading down on Compton. The wind began picking up, accompanied by a drop in the mercury. The snows came.

He thought about his uncle Bill Cameron, whom he guessed was already heading back to Boston. With the roads getting worse, Henry hoped his uncle was smart enough to pull over and spend an overnight in one of the many roadside inns on the way to Boston. Any bedside location was preferably to his previous lodging, a damp and musty, cinderblock jail cell in Compton, one filled with cobwebs and leaking raindrops, along with a lumpy mattress and a musty pillow.

Henry had no regrets about giving him ten thousand dollars. He was in a position where he could afford it. When he visited his bank just a few days ago, he discovered his financial future never burned brighter. Even though one-half of his father's military benefits and investments had now been transferred to his uncle, he still stood on solid financial ground. He was the sole benefactor of his mother's inheritance as well as that of Tom Cooper, the latter including a sizeable military pension, life insurance policy, investments, and a large savings account. He inherited all of the Cooper properties, which included the entire fifty acres, the farmhouse, the apple orchards and cornfields, as well as all the farming equipment and motor vehicles. He was the sole owner of all the horses, the barn, and the training corrals. His financial advisor told him all his books were in order and that he was in outstanding financial shape. He was told not to worry about his financial withdrawal.

By the time he got home, close to a foot of snow had swallowed the driveway. He pulled in and parked his car next to his flatbed, then he hightailed it over to the barn. He shook the snow off his head and shoulders before he entered.

"How're we doing in there?" he shouted.

Hudson and Carl appeared from the darkness of the barn and greeted him. From one of the back stalls, Henry heard Abigail shout a greeting.

"So far, so good," said Hudson. Carl was dressed for combat, wearing a fully-lined green parka, a watch cap, snow boots, and bulky winter gloves. Hudson protected himself with just a shearling sheepskin vest and a watch cap for outerwear.

Henry entered the barn to gain shelter from the snowstorm. "How're the new arrivals doing?" Henry asked.

"Everyone's fine, Henry."

"I know it's early, but has there been any interaction of the herd with Ronan and Tess?"

Hudson started chuckling and shaking his head. "Oh yes, one horse was quite intent on making friends early on."

"Let me guess. It was Monte."

"You got it. The ambassador."

Henry laughed out loud and said, "If he's the barometer here, then we'll have no problems with everyone getting along."

Abigail emerged from the back, smiling as always. "I was telling Hudson that when we start gradually blending the palominos in with the rest of the herd, we should begin with

Monte and see how that goes. After that, I'd pick Norman to join the threesome."

Henry nodded in agreement. "I agree with your choices. Have you thought about a schedule for fitting saddles on them?"

"That will happen in due time," replied Abigail. "For now, we're going to keep using the lead ropes and get the horses familiar with the property and us. So far, there's been no stubbornness or lunging. These horses have been well trained."

They talked a little more before Henry said, "Listen, Julia has put a lot of time and energy into her Christmas Eve gathering. Time to close up here, get cleaned up, and greet the guests, okay? I'll meet you over at the house."

―――――――――

With that, Henry hiked his collar and left the barn. The house was warm and inviting. A fire crackled in the fireplace. Christmas carols played on the old gramophone. Decorations hung from every location.

Henry removed his coat and hung it on a coat rack at the end of the hallway. He called for Julia and within a minute she came down from the upstairs. She looked beautiful. She styled her hair in a bun and added just a touch of blush and pink lipstick. She wore a dainty black sweater, a white blouse, dark slacks, and dress shoes. Her perfume was flowery but not overpowering. At one point, Henry could see a younger Julia, a captivating woman catching the eye of many suitors.

"Wow," said Henry.

"I'm guessing that's a compliment."

"Julia, you look beautiful."

"Henry Cameron, flattery will get you everywhere with me."

"No, I mean it. You look stunning."

Julia said, "Thank you kind sir. Now tell me about your uncle. How did it go in town?"

"Well, I got him out of jail."

"How'd you manage that?"

"As you'll recall, the goon who accompanied my uncle here was later killed in an unrelated altercation. Most of the charges were leveled against him, the remaining complaints against my uncle, like disorderly conduct and disturbing the peace. Those were dropped."

"Do you think the sheriff was doing you a favor?"

"I doubt it. He said he wanted me out of his hair. Oh yeah, he threatened me again."

"Then what happened?"

"We got my uncle's car out of a nearby gas station."

Julia interrupted. "Wait, weren't his tires slashed?"

"I had them replaced, plus filled up his gas tank." Henry coughed into his hand. "I also bought him some new clothes, a winter coat, some new shoes, and some toiletries. I paid his hospital bill. We hugged and said goodbye. He thanked me profusely for everything."

"Where was he headed?"

"He said he had a place to stay in Boston."

"Do you believe him?"

Henry didn't answer, he just shrugged.

It got quiet.

Henry cleared his throat. "Julia, I want you to know that I forgave him for all his wrongdoings over the years, including the fracas up here."

"You did? Really?"

"I did, I took your advice." He hesitated. "I told him he needs to get his drinking under control and get a job. Start hanging around with good people. And then I sent him on his merry way."

"You said before that he was broke. You let him leave on a snowy night without any money in his pocket?"

His eyes drifted to the floor. "Actually, I gave him money, quite a bit of it."

"Ten thousand dollars?"

"How did you know?"

"Because that's the amount from his brother's inheritance that he thought he deserved. That's the amount he's been hounding you about."

Henry let out a deep breath. "That's correct. I gave it to him with the hope that it would bring closure to this unholy inheritance mess. I'm sick of it, Julia. Whether he piddles it away or uses it to straighten out his life is now up to him."

She looked at him and smiled. She offered her hand and he took it. The clasp was both warm and strong. "You remind me so much of the lieutenant, Henry. You're following the trail he left behind, one of kindness and compassion. It is so easy to see why he adopted you and why all of us love you so much. You give each and every one of us hope."

She changed the subject. "I've got to get the rest of our crew moving. Do you know where everyone is?"

"Last I saw, they were out in the barn. I spoke to them once before about the party. I'll get them cracking."

"Good. Oh, Henry, I meant to ask you something. We haven't gotten much mail over the past few days. Have you stopped lately at the post office and picked it up?"

Henry used the palm of his hand to softly thump himself in the forehead. The other day, he'd forgotten to bring the mail in from the front seat of the flatbed.

"I have the mail, my apologies. I'd forgotten all about it. It's in the flatbed and I'll bring it in when I round up the others."

He returned a few minutes later carrying a fairly large package and assorted envelopes. He brought everything into the kitchen. By now, the others had arrived.

Julia looked at the box and didn't recognize the return address. Henry withdrew a jackknife from his trousers, pried open the blade with his thumbnail, and handed it to her.

"It will be easier opening the package with this," Henry said.

"I don't know what it could be," she remarked as she cut the package open. Once she lifted the lid, she saw that the contents were wrapped in butcher's paper. On top of the contents was a small envelope addressed to her.

"Better open that first," suggested Henry.

She opened the envelope and removed the note. She still didn't know who it was from.

She looked at everyone gathered close. "Do you want me to read it?"

"Of course," said Henry, speaking for the group.

Julia cleared her throat and read.

Dear Julia,

I thought it best to send this package directly to you. I'm sincerely sorry for the time delay. My friend was going on vacation up north and he's the sort of guy who always takes his work along with him. I asked that he send this package directly to you when it was ready. I don't know when you'll get it but I hope it's before the holidays. When I last visited, I couldn't help but recognize (again) what a tight-knit and caring family you are. I hope you never lose the love and compassion you have for each other.

There is no charge for any of these services.

With all my blessings,
Horace Drake, MD

Julia's head was bowed. She held a white embroidered cotton handkerchief to her face. "He must've written this just before he died," she said, a lump in her throat. Carl went over to her and held her tight. She rested her head against his shoulder, shuddering slightly with each sniffle. After a while she pulled away, folded the note in half and slipped it into her pocket. She would reread it many times, tracing each word with her index finger, trying to remember the doctor's last visit to the house.

"Why don't you go ahead and see what's inside?" suggested Henry.

She unwrapped the butcher's paper and her eyed widened when she saw the contents. Inside, a brand-new prosthesis for Mickey, customized for his left residual limb, the wood polished and finished, the buckles and straps newly replaced, a tight-fitting new glove replacing the old. She unwrapped the butcher's paper for the second parcel and found a second prosthesis, once again customized for Mickey, this one made of duralumin, a lightweight metal barely weighing half as much as the wooden prosthesis. The metal prosthesis had all the straps and buckles needed and was also fitted with a new black leather glove.

Everyone was speechless, but none more than Mickey. He squeezed his eyes shut, and everyone could see that he was fighting back tears. He kept his eyes closed for a minute, then pinched the bridge of his nose to stop the flow of tears.

He reached over and touched both of the prostheses. "You don't know how much this means to me. It's been hard not having my prosthesis, and I really didn't want to go to the veteran's hospital to get another made. This will make me feel whole again. More confident, more independent, less self-conscious about missing my arm and my hand. When I'm helping Carl do chores around the yard, my prosthesis will make it easier for me to assist. Plus, when we go out, I'll feel better about inquisitive stares."

When Mickey glanced around the room, everyone was looking at him, smiling. "I can't wait to go try the fit," he said.

Julia clapped her hands together. "Great idea, Mickey. How about you do that, and the rest of you go get cleaned up and dressed so we'll be ready for our guests. They'll be arriving soon, and I could use some help setting out the food."

When the guests started arriving, Mickey hadn't come down from the upstairs bathroom. Julia summoned Henry to find him and see if he was okay. Henry found him standing in front of a mirror adjusting his metal prosthesis. He had it on but was having difficulty adjusting one of the straps.

"Need some help, mate?" asked Henry.

"I'm glad you came to find me."

"Everything okay?"

"Yeah, I just need some help tightening a strap I can't reach."

Henry tended to the strap then handed Mickey a shirt and sweater he'd picked out. When he was fully dressed, he stood again in front of the mirror.

"Well, how do I look?" he asked.

"Magnifico. How does it feel? How's the fit?"

"Perfect."

"Hey, you going to spend a little time with Ariel tonight?"

"I hope so," he replied, a big smile on his face.

"Well, we'd better get downstairs now or Julia will skin us both alive."

Twenty-Eight

The living room captured a truly magical and enchanting Christmas setting, decked to the nines in seasonal decorations. Of course, the blue spruce Christmas tree adorned with its trinkets, bells and ornaments, along with the crackling, dancing flames inside the fireplace commanded immediate attention. Julia had switched off most of the bright lights in the living room and set out a few oil lamps and candles for ambiance. In one corner, the phonograph softly played Christmas music.

All of the guests had arrived and were mingling, their happiness and laughter filling the room. As Henry looked about, he realized Julia had certainly invited a diverse mix to the party. Henry spotted a local farmer from the other side of town, the entire Winsted family, a gift shop owner, two teachers from a school where Julia once worked, the town's newspaper proprietor, the local pastor, and the family's attorney.

Throughout the room was a bounty of Christmas remembrances and keepsakes, including holly, bows and ribbons, wreaths, nativity, red stockings, snowmen, bells, Santa in his sleigh pulled by reindeer, angels, carolers, gingerbread house, mistletoe, and elves. Boughs from the Christmas tree were bundled and produced a fresh, woodsy scent. Icicles hung off the roof ledge outside the windows and the snowy winter night provided the perfect backdrop.

Plenty of refreshments were set out on long tables. Julia's homemade dishes combined with treats brought by guests included puddings and sweetcakes, pies, gingerbread cupcakes, plum cakes, muffins, pumpkin and banana bread, frosted cookies, pound cake, sponge cake and assorted candies and fruits. On a separate table were red and white wine, eggnog, punch, and hot cocoa. Snacking plates with meats and cheese were set out and bottles of rum, gin, and vodka stood at the ready. Hudson and Abigail served the guests.

Henry was busy working the room, making an effort to talk with everyone. He was sipping a glass of wine with one of

Julia's old teaching cronies when someone behind him tapped his shoulder. He turned to find Ariel Winsted.

"I'm sorry to interrupt, Mr. Cameron. But when you've got a few moments can I bend your ear about a few things? I'll be over by the refreshments."

Julia's friend touched Henry's arm. "You go right ahead and talk with this young lady. We can talk more later."

Henry caught up to Ariel on the other side of the room and they moved to the kitchen where it was quieter.

"Everything okay?" Henry asked.

She looked at him with her sparkling hazel eyes. "Everything's fine, Mr. Cameron. This is such a great party. It really puts everyone in a Christmas mood."

Henry smiled. "Thank you for coming, but Ariel you and Jacob have to stop calling me Mr. Cameron. It's Henry."

She smiled back bashfully. "I'm sorry, I'll try to put a stop to that."

Henry said, "Lest I forget, I've noticed you and Jacob coming to work these past few days even though I said you won't start punching the clock until after the holidays."

"Jacob and I just like coming to the farm. We didn't do it for the money. We just like the people, the horses, really everything about the place."

"I'll have Julia write your hours down so that you get paid properly."

"But that's not why I wanted to talk with you."

Henry arched his eyebrows.

"I just wanted to thank you for everything, from the Christmas tree to hiring Jacob and I, plus offering our father a job this spring helping with the planting of your cornfield."

She bowed her head.

"Is something wrong, Ariel?"

"No, except we're a very proud family and everything you've done for us has been very humbling. It's hard for my father, especially, to accept help from others."

"It's not charity if that's what you mean. You and you brother are good workers, and as far as your father goes, he's the one who's helping me out. I've been looking for someone with his skills to lend a hand in the spring."

"Well, he's very excited about working for you. The fact that he hasn't been working at all because of his back injury has created some dark days in our house, but your job offer has given him hope and optimism. His confidence has been restored and he just prays that his back mends in time to go back to work."

"If it doesn't, we'll gradually work him into a schedule that gives him more time to heal. We'll find a place and a pace that works best for him."

Ariel reached for Henry's hand, stood on her tiptoes, and lightly kissed him on the cheek. "Thank you, Mr. Cameron, I mean Henry. You're the best Christmas gift we've ever received."

———

From the corner of his eye Henry saw Carl approaching him. Next thing he knew, Carl was whispering in his ear. "There's a guy at the back door who wants to see you."

Henry looked at Ariel. "I'm sorry, but I have to tend to a matter. Thank you for your words. Oh, by the way, tell your family not to leave. I'd like to talk with them."

As they walked to the door Henry said, "You don't know who it is?"

"I do know, I just didn't want the people here to know. It's sheriff Whittaker and he ain't looking too happy. Maybe it's because I'm making him wait outside in the snow. His nose is bright red like Rudolph's." Carl broke out in that hyena laugh of his.

Henry saw Whittaker blowing into his hands and stamping his feet to generate some warmth.

"I'll take care of this," he told Carl.

Carl wanted to stick around in case he was needed.

Henry said, "I'll be okay. Carl, by the way, I wanted to tell you what a fine job you're doing going to the door and greeting our guests, plus taking their coats." Henry and Julia had assigned this job to Carl when they made party plans.

Henry's praise made Carl very happy. "I'll let you in on a little secret," he said. "I'm just using the greeting we worked on when we hired Jacob and Ariel. I memorized it for tonight. You know the one, 'Howdy stranger, welcome to the Cooper farm. Why not come inside and stay a while.'"

Henry interrupted, "Yeah, yeah, yeah, I know that one, Carl. Smooth, very smooth. Now you go back and enjoy the party."

Henry finally opened the door but rather than letting the sheriff inside, he joined him outside on the stoop.

"Not inviting me in?" asked Whittaker.

"Nope. Private party. You didn't make the short list."

"Jackass." He said, his fat tongue creating amusing blubbering.

Henry looked over at the sheriff's car and saw that he'd left it running, headlights on. A woman sat in the front seat.

"You got Maeve over there in the car? Christmas Eve date, sheriff? I hope you didn't forget the mistletoe."

Silence.

Whittaker said, "We've got some unfinished business to take care of, Cameron. You left the police station without clearing up your bill."

"Is that so? What bill is that?"

"You are in arrears with imprisonment fees, they haven't been paid."

Henry cocked his head to one side. "No kidding. And how much would that be?"

"Two hundred and fifty dollars, cash."

Henry just stared at him.

"I want it tonight so that I can square it away in the books first chance I get. You know, gotta keep up with the bookkeeping."

In retrospect, Henry could've easily gotten the money from a safe he kept in the house and given him the cash. Instead, a smile crept across his face.

"You think this is amusing, Cameron? Some kind of joke?"

"I'm very amused sheriff."

"And why's that?"

"Because before I left town following my uncle's release, I visited Compton's town hall and asked if there was a fee attached to the release of a jailed prisoner. I was told there was no such fee, nor was there ever one. Just to be sure, I went back to the police station and asked your receptionist the same question. Same answer, no such fee."

Whittaker just stood there, his cheeks burning. He had become the brunt of a classic 'gotcha' moment.

Henry chose to pile it on. His smile broadened. "So, here's what I'm going to do sheriff, just so you know. I intend to revisit the police station as well as town hall to inform people that you stopped by my home unannounced in the midst of a Christmas Eve party to collect two hundred and fifty dollars in cash for a fee that doesn't even exist."

Whittaker knew Henry had him right by the crankshaft. He edged closer to Henry and wrapped his arm around his shoulder. "Come on now Henry, you don't want to do that." He pulled him even closer and whispered in his ear with his whiskey breath. "I need the cash to pick up something special I bought for Maeve, and I have to pay a friend for it before we have dinner with her family. What do you say we keep this just between the two of us? We had a little misunderstanding is all, right Henry?"

Henry said nothing, but his smile got even wider when he realized Whittaker had switched to a first name basis, treating Henry like his best buddy. But his bravado and swagger had deserted him, leaving him with no other option but to beat a hasty retreat with his tail between his legs. He turned to leave, but Henry wasn't done with him.

"Wait a minute," Henry said.

The sheriff turned around.

Henry said, "You and I've got some other unfinished business."

"About what?"

"About you, your girlfriend Maeve, and your dirty little secret, the one I know about. For starters, don't ever stand on my property again and threaten me with your tough guy bluster. I'm neither afraid of you roughing me up or endangering my life should I choose to spill the beans on you and your girlfriend. You threatened me once on this very spot, again at Dr. Drake's funeral, and once again at the police station."

"And what do you intend to do about it?"

"I'll tell you exactly what I intend to do about it. I intend to go straight to the mayor and tell him how his town sheriff conducts his business. How he likes to belittle and spook townspeople. How he likes to knock back the moonshine while he's on duty. I'll throw in how you tried to scam me tonight as well as how I caught you and Maeve firsthand in a most compromising position. I'm sure your wife would be interested in finding out about these things too."

Whittaker sneered at him. "You don't have the courage to do any of that."

"Really? Pull any more stunts around me and you'll see first-hand that I'm a man of my word. Don't push your luck, chief, and don't ever underestimate me. You've got an awful lot to lose if you choose to tangle. Consider yourself warned."

Julia was waiting for him when he walked back into the house. She had her arms folded across her chest, a frown on her face. She reached for a nearby towel and handed it to Henry so that he could dry his hair and brush snow from his clothes. She turned him around and brushed the snow from his back.

"What did that lamebrain want?" she asked. Apparently, she'd watch the exchange from a nearby window.

"You're not going to believe this one. He claimed I owed him two hundred and fifty dollars in cash for a jail fee, but then retracted it when I told him there was no such fee."

"How did you know there wasn't any fee?"

"I didn't know, I just made that part up. He fell for it."

They both laughed.

"He's such a stooge," Julia smirked. "Why do you think he wanted the money?"

"I know exactly why. It was so he could buy a gift for his girlfriend Maeve, who was sitting in his car."

"Of course, I should have known." Julia hesitated and frowned. "He was going shopping for her on Christmas Eve?"

"Apparently a friend of his was holding the present for him."

Julia signed. "Well, I'm glad you didn't buckle and give him anything. Now let's get back to our guests. Some are getting restless because of the storm and may be leaving early."

They returned to the living room.

Henry asked Hudson to join him and together found the Winsteds standing near the Christmas tree. Hudson already knew Ariel and Jacob, but hadn't met the parents, Leland and Rebecca. Henry made the proper introductions.

"It's a pleasure to meet you folks," said Hudson. "You should be very proud of your children. Jacob and Ariel have impressed everyone here on the farm."

In response, Leland remarked, "Thank you, that means much to us. We're humbled."

"They love it here on the farm," added Rebecca. "They couldn't stop talking about the new palominos. Ariel said they're the most beautiful horses she's ever seen."

Hudson agreed. "They'll both get a chance to ride at some point, if that's okay with you folks. You too, if you wish. We have a great horse trainer who I'm sure would assist all when you're ready. Have you had a chance to meet Abigail Emory this evening?"

Both parents nodded. "Lovely person," Rebecca said. "She wanted to know all about the rice pudding and gingerbread cupcakes I brought along. I gave her the recipes."

Hudson talked with Leland about operating one of the Avery Bulldogs in the spring.

"You've got more than one rig?" Leland asked.

"We've got two. Henry wants you and Mickey to operate them when planting season rolls around. I'd like to invite you over whenever you're up to it physically and take a look at the Bulldogs and our other equipment. Would you like to do that?"

"I'd like that, Hudson."

"Then we'll set something up. Now you've met Mickey, right?"

Leland scanned the room and nodded. "You mean that handsome soldier sitting on the couch with my Ariel?"

"Yep, that's him. You'll like him."

Julia drifted over. "I hate to interrupt, but our guests are getting anxious about the snow piling up and having to drive home. I'll need some help getting everyone to their cars and brushing the snow away. Carl is already out there shoveling the walkway."

"We should get ready, too," said Rebecca.

Julia placed her hand on Leland's arm. "Before you do, I'd like to share with you what kind of kids you've raised. A little while ago, Ariel approached me and said she'd be over in the morning to help me with cleaning up after the party, you know, tidying up the living room and washing and putting away dishes, silverware, scrubbing pots and pans. Along similar lines, Jacob informed Carl that he'd be over early to help with the horses, shovel snow, and make sure enough firewood had been brought into the house."

Henry said, "But tomorrow's Christmas."

Which is why, of course, they wanted to do it.

After the last guest departed, everyone pitched in to clean up the living room as best they could. They were all bone-tired but knew certain tasks were unavoidable and couldn't be postponed until morning. They started by collecting all the empty glasses and bottles laying around, then going to the sink and pouring away anything unfinished.

Julia encouraged her guests upon their departure to take leftovers home, but many delectable treats were left behind. They needed to be covered and stored. Any nibbles left behind were gathered and placed in a waste basket. Crumbs were swept up and also tossed.

Many hands made light work.

The smell of cigar and cigarette smoke, blended with the odor of booze, still consumed the room. There wasn't much to remedy this, except to empty all ashtrays and crack open the windows a bit to let some fresh winter air in. It felt good to get the outside air circulating inside.

Everyone was tired, but when they were finished, Henry suggested they throw a few extra logs on the fire, pull the chairs close to the fireplace, throw on some blankets, and unwind together. He brought out two unopened bottles of rum and glasses. Once he served everyone, he sat down and enjoyed the flames with the people he cared about so much. They listened to Christmas carols and watched the snow fall, a gentle blanket from the skies above. They refilled their glasses. They were happy and most of all, at peace.

Henry stood at one point and thanked them all, especially Julia, who was in charge of the whole evening. "All of you made this party a success, and I thank you for your efforts. I want to say I chose rum on purpose now to share a toast with you tonight. When the lieutenant was stricken, we often shared a shot of rum before I tucked him in at night. Dr. Drake joined me more than once as I told our congregation." He chuckled, a sad chuckle at that.

Henry wasn't done. "Without the lieutenant, none of us would be here tonight to celebrate Christmas Eve." He hesitated and looked around the room. "Just think about it. The lieutenant brought me into the fold and I brought Mickey on board. Hudson and Abigail joined us because of the lieutenant. Julia and Carl are mainstays who kept the farm alive. Together, we've all made a difference in this community and we'll continue to do that with the lieutenant in our hearts."

They stood, they toasted, they remembered.

When Henry sat, he was drawn to the flames in the fireplace. He watched the snow fall. He was mellow but he also became introspective. In the midst of these beautiful people, he was alone. By this, Julia had Carl, Hudson had Abigail, Mickey was making inroads with Ariel. That left him as the odd man out. At one point, Henry thought Maeve would become part of his life, but that thought crashed to the ground with a resounding thud when he thought of the evil sheriff. Nonetheless, he kept thinking about what might have been with her.

All of this made him melancholy, but he shrugged it off. The rum loosened everyone and they reminisced about the evening party. How the pastor had one too many shots of brandy and started preaching the gospel to a deaf audience. How Hudson and Abigail tried to sneak a few extra kisses under a branch of mistletoe tacked above a doorway. How Hudson regaled Jacob Winsted with stories of his adventures chasing Pancho Villa, and how he and lieutenant Cooper scampered after him into Mexico, but came up empty-handed.

The rum continued to work its magic on the group and everyone except Carl and Henry dozed off. Snoring punctuated the crackling of the fire. Henry had just tossed an extra log on the fire and sat when he heard a car crunch into the driveway. He didn't know if someone had pulled in or had just turned around. Sure enough, the car backed out and drove off. He listened and not hearing much more, let his mind drift away again.

The next thing he knew, someone was knocking on the back door. Henry immediately straightened in his chair, slipped on his shoes, and headed for the door. But he was behind Carl, who hadn't relinquished his role of official greeter.

Henry thought it might be Maeve, and his heartbeat quickened. Maybe, just maybe, she'd ditched the sheriff for good and come to her senses. Perhaps she recognized this was where she belonged. Or, maybe she and the sheriff had sparred and he'd dumped her off at the farm before driving off in anger. His mind raced with possibilities.

Carl swung the door open and said in his trademark greeting, "Hello, stranger…" But that was as far as he got. That's because Henry had arrived, opened the door wider, and immediately took over. He looked at Carl. "It's okay, Carl, I'll handle this."

Carl stepped aside, totally befuddled, hands under his chin, nervously wiggling his fingers.

Henry squinted and looked at the person outside the door. It was a woman. The snow was still falling but not as heavily. Everything was tranquil and undisturbed. The feathery flakes fell upon the woman and her breath drifted upwards like puffy white plumes.

She stepped forward and stood straight on the stoop. The two took each other in, but both were taken aback and surprised. Henry was as flustered as he was speechless.

He grinned, the foolish and unhinged kind, and tried to find the right words. But he couldn't find any, in fact his mind went totally blank. The rum and slumber by the fireplace hadn't helped.

Henry knew he had to say something. He looked around and saw Carl, who was still standing to one side. Carl looked into Henry's eyes and offered a reassuring nod.

Sure enough, the words came.

Henry looked at the woman and said, "Howdy stranger, welcome to the Cooper farm. Why not come inside and stay a while. I've been waiting for you and we've got lots to talk about."

"Why, I think I'd like that very much," the woman said, stepping in from the cold.

And just like that, Lily Corwin walked back into the life of Henry Cameron.

About the Author

J eff Turner is a true dyed in the wool Connecticut Yankee. He was born and raised in Quaker Hill, Connecticut and attended public schools in Waterford before matriculating at three different Connecticut colleges and universities to earn his undergraduate and graduate degrees. He taught for over forty years at Mitchell College in New London, a stone's throw from where he was born.

Dr. Turner is the author or co-author of over twenty-five academic books released by some the world's largest publishers and widely used across the United States and abroad, including in Japan, Poland, Australia, and the United Kingdom. He has also penned five other novels: *The Way Back*, *The Hero of Willow Creek*, *Lost Boys of the River Camp*, *The Choices He Made*, and *A Rescued Soul*. In 2013 Jeff was a finalist in the Readers Favorite book award contest for *The Way Back*, and in 2022 was named a finalist in the Feathered Quill's book award contest for *A Rescued Soul*.